Candida Clark was born in 1970.
stories and journalism, and review
A House of Light is her fifth novel.

Praise for *A House of Light*:

'Entirely fluent and beautifully controlled . . . real accomplishment in a writer of great imaginative strength'   Paul Theroux, *Guardian*

'The novel segues from thriller to family saga, as long-buried secrets are gradually exposed. These develop into a mystery story of the most delicate and literary kind'   *Marie Claire*

'Her taut, meticulously structured fifth novel is charged with the romance of old-school photography'   John O'Connell, *Time Out*

'An intriguing read with a series of plots and subplots built on a family's secrets and lies'   *Ireland on Sunday*

'Deceptions are skilfully unravelled in a novel of gem-like prose that stays in the mind . . . thought-provoking and intriguing'
   Woman & Home

'A taut, poetic exploration of the need to acknowledge the past in order to stop it haunting the present'   *Sunday Times*

'Clark has honed her poetic voice to within an inch of prose, building layers of feelings, thought and images to create the world of the novel . . . She continually surprises the reader with acute observations that always hit the mark'   *Sunday Business Post*

'Exquisitely written, dreamily threatening, the prose evocative, the relationships delicately and beautifully drawn, the story seductive'
   Irish Examiner

Also by Candida Clark

The Last Look
The Constant Eye
The Mariner's Star
Ghost Music

A House
of Light

Candida
Clark

review

First published in Great Britain in 2005
by REVIEW

An imprint of Headline Book Publishing

First published in paperback in 2005

4

ISBN 0 7553 2330 0

Typeset in Perpetua by Palimpsest Book Production Limited,
Polmont, Stirlingshire

Printed and bound in Great Britain by Clays Ltd, St Ives plc

Headline's policy is to use papers that are natural, renewable
and recyclable products and made from wood grown in sustainable forests.
The logging and manufacturing processes are expected to conform to the
environmental regulations of the country of origin.

Headline Book Publishing
A division of Hodder Headline
338 Euston Road
London NW1 3BH

www.reviewbooks.co.uk
www.hodderheadline.com

For my mother

Acknowledgements

With admiration and many thanks to Charlotte Mendelson, Katy Mahood, Hazel Orme, Leah Woodburn and Ami Smithson at Headline; and, once more, to Jonny Geller.

'We photographers are dealing in things which are continually vanishing, and when they have vanished there is no contrivance on earth can make them come back again. We cannot develop and print a memory.'

Henri Cartier-Bresson

'The photographer can function as long as there is light; his work — his adventure — is a rediscovery of the world in terms of light.'

Edward Weston

part | one

1

It was the middle of August, and she had been glad to get out of London. The city was hot and emptied of everyone she knew. She had started to feel like a stranger to herself, a tourist even in places she knew well. 'Didn't recognise you, Katherine' — said by the shopkeeper from whom she had bought her newspaper almost every day for two years — had the power to unnerve her. So she said 'yes' at short notice, had her vaccinations topped up — yellow fever, typhoid — and left.

She spent a week taking pictures on the coast of West Central Africa, at Libreville, in Gabon, straightforward brochure shots for a hotel, recently constructed by an American chain. The work itself might have occupied one afternoon. The light conditions remained the same right through the week. Each day the same hot dawn, the sun's blithe progress until dusk, which was black and sudden.

It wasn't her usual line of work, which was mainly portraiture. Some landscapes, some still-lifes, but mainly people. She was best known, in the trade, for her author-portraits, which were distinctive. For the most part, her subjects liked her for them. The writer at his desk. The poet beneath the gloomy colonnade. Her images appeared on dust jackets and postcards, in catalogues, books, newspapers and magazines.

But it was a favour, and in return she had a week in a different country, one she might not have visited otherwise, and in a hotel at which she could not, personally, have afforded to stay. She spent most of her time swimming in the mosaic-bottomed pool, or practising her backhand slice against the 'AutoTennisMan' machine in the early morning, or stretched out for a massage on a soft grass mat in the shade.

'Sounds like I'll still owe you.' Katherine had laughed when the proposal was put to her. She had been surprised to receive the call. At one time Dennis James had been a close associate of her father. Now his name was seldom mentioned. He had given her a lucrative connection, back when she was starting out. It embarrassed her to realise that, while he had remembered, she had almost forgotten. She didn't do commercial jobs these days. But it seemed ungracious to refuse. 'Sounds great. What's the catch?' She had tried to appear more eager than she felt.

He laughed, but didn't answer her question. 'You're perfect for the job, don't worry. Heard they were let down, so I thought of you. You'll do fine. And now we're quits.' His voice changed slightly, as though someone had just walked into the room. 'I'll let them know you're game, have them contact you directly.'

She was glad to be there. She had been working too hard and needed the break, time to clear her head. Just under a month away, her father, Peter, would remarry after almost twenty years as a widower. The ceremony would take place at Fareham, the family's home in Kent. She would take the pictures then, too. 'Might be cathartic.' Katherine had overheard her father's American wife-to-be, Joanne, suggest this. There was symmetry to the idea: Katherine's mother had been a photographer also. It made her feel transparent, but she appreciated the kindness of the thought, and had had no trouble agreeing to the job.

The week in Gabon was undemanding. They had faxed her an itinerary: exterior shots of hotel, all angles; surrounding area, local attractions, including beaches and nature reserve; interiors of hotel, restaurant, bar, deluxe suites and standard accom.; facilities – pool, tennis courts, gym, sauna, Jacuzzi, *boules* sandpit. This part confused her at first. *Boules*? But when she arrived, there it was. She photographed it. She supposed it was a relic of French rule, along with the *hôtel de ville*, the *villages des artisans*, the Transgabonais railway.

The hotel itself appeared to have been built for a prosperity that had already come and gone, very swiftly, but had not left its mark. Spotless marble and gilt bathrooms, vigorous air-conditioning, but unreliable plumbing and even worse phone lines. There were few guests, business travellers more than holidaymakers; the staff appeared listless, as though waiting for something they knew would not arrive. Their eagerness, when it was shown – the manager, two sizes smaller than his blue silk suit, flourished open the door to her suite, hissing through his teeth at a slouching porter – seemed more like a test: hadn't she noticed the place

5

was deserted? 'Top class conference centre.' He had shown her an empty meeting room. A cleaner was sadly polishing the long table.

On her first evening, she was chaperoned to the coast to take some pictures of the sunset, a view out over the South Atlantic, and the next day, in the flat beauty of afternoon, a palm tree bending towards the water – stock shots the hotel could pick from; the rest she would hand over to her agent. They might earn her something, or come in useful at some point. She photographed what she was told to photograph, and everyone was very convivial.

She was conscious, however, at each moment, of being held clear of all discomfort, or sight of anything other than comfort, for the entire week. It was always done with laughs and a friendly hand on the shoulder. 'This way, Miss Clements! Look. We're very proud of this,' as she was turned away from the sight of rusty cargo ships at anchor for repair, directed instead to a prosaic view north along the shore at Cap Estérias, shown L'Église St Michel, the Musée des Arts et Traditions, the presidential palace. 'Humpback whales.' The guide waved at the ocean, but Katherine could see nothing, just the plume of spent fuel as a tanker approached the horizon.

She had never liked being told what she could and couldn't photograph, yet the work wasn't important to her so why should she mind? She supposed they had their reasons – a desire to be behind the camera instead of her, calling the shots. It was a job: she did as she was asked, scooped up the images they were after and handed them back to her employers, who were delighted with the results when she sent them to the hotel chain's London office.

But out of the corner of her eye, she had seen things that sparked her interest. Just out of frame, sometimes, there, she would see it: a jeep, the windows gangster black, a flash of metal in the darkness behind the driver. Ten-foot-high fencing, two layers deep, topped with razor-wire. A site that looked at first glance like an archaeological dig, where French and, unexpectedly, some English was spoken over the hum of deep drills – a pipeline was being laid.

'Oil,' her guide from the hotel confirmed, waving in the direction of the interior, then counting off on her fingers: 'Oil, manganese ore, iron ore, chrome, tropical woods, diamonds. Oil is fifty per cent GNP. A rich country. Libreville was built on the site of a fort constructed in 1843, capital of French Congo until Brazzaville took over in 1888.' The young woman recited the history, smiling as she added, 'Independence in 1960.' She said this with a note of finality, as though closing an out-of-date guide-book. Nothing more to know. She glanced at her watch. 'So many more sights.' Her shoulders lifted with impatience. She waited for Katherine to follow her. 'Next time, when you come for holidays, you can go on safari.' The guide made it sound more like an insult: 'go and get lost'. Beyond the town the undergrowth was a thick dark wedge of green. 'Gorillas,' she nodded towards it, 'biggest rainforest in Africa – Congo Basin.'

Katherine wanted to quiz her about the drilling. Why the need for such security? She was sure that the guards at the main gate were armed. The woman stepped directly in Katherine's line of view, turning back to shake her head, holding up a warning hand, her voice suddenly sharp, 'No pictures of this, Miss Clements.' A command. Not a request. It had been explained to her already at the hotel: no photographs of any 'government, military, airport, or official buildings'.

Now Katherine smiled, pretended not to care, but it irked her, and only increased her interest. There was something worth seeing here, after all. She loaded film into her Leica, slipped it into her pocket. Her eye was drawn to the half-seen figure in the margin. Being denied those shots had set her on her toes.

It had always been her chief fascination in taking pictures. Coincidence, and delay. A plate held up against a scene to see the fit, notice where it slipped. Because nothing was ever caught, and nothing coincided absolutely. The best any photograph could ever hope to be was a picture of an empty cage. Empty, but with the feral sense still hanging in the air, the breeze ruffling the straw, the shadow's glint across the bars. The endeavour was to suggest so nearly that the animal had been there that the watcher himself felt watched: you, too, just left the captivity of that moment.

Driving out beyond the town, she glimpsed familiar logos, Shell and Elf, and one other in particular, though less frequently. On the side of a silver van, a symbol that she felt she recognised from somewhere, but could not say where. She supposed she had seen the logo on the roads in Europe. Against silver, a black stamp of parallel lines, in a wave formation, with a yellow line running through it, near the top. She had noticed it at the start of the week. One of the vans had been parked half across the exit to the hotel car park. Rather than sound the horn, or jump out and complain, the driver had turned off the engine to wait. 'What's the problem?' She had leant through from the back seat to ask the guide. Both she and the driver had merely laughed. 'Can't hurry some people.' But they had seemed more nervous than amused.

On her last day, a few miles up the coast, the driver of their jeep had pulled off the highway, and they had started to walk towards the shore along a dirt track. Katherine had glanced back to see one of the silver vans slowed to a halt on the main road, turning into the gates of an industrial compound. Her guide was pointing across the estuary, 'There, Pointe-Dénis,' and she had taken a run of six shots before the young woman turned to look for her.

With the camera almost hidden in the palm of her hand Katherine had appeared simply to shield her eyes from the sun. The Leica wasn't much larger than her light-metre, and roughly the same shape. No one noticed. She used what the guide referred to admiringly as 'the big guns' for the shots that they were after: her bulky Nikon, with its wide black funnel to keep the light out of the lens; her Pentax with a 300mm zoom. In their estimation, these were the 'real cameras'. But her Leica M-3 was closest to the viewpoint of her eye. They didn't notice when she blinked and fixed her glimpse to brood on later.

She had a pleasant stay, and returned happy, and a few pounds heavier. She had been back in London, working, for just over three weeks, when she arrived home one night in September to find that her flat, darkroom and, with it, all her work and possessions, had been destroyed by fire.

2

Years of good education, frequent holidays, a career on a track she liked and was proud of, a family home she could return to, the sense that behind her, always, there would be something to cushion whatever blows the world dealt her, all this had combined to make Katherine Clements the kind of person others turned to in moments of crisis.

'I'll handle it,' had become her mantra. An only child, she was capable and confident; her life was arranged with the dexterity and neatness only possible for those who saw no obstacle to things being ordered according to their desire. No bill would ever loom too great, no hurt too damaging that it could not be settled or turned from. She was conscious each day of her good fortune, and was by no means smug. But she was secure, and her security coloured her life with a warm light that anyone might notice.

If she felt tired, she slept; if she fell ill, she treated the sickness as a hurdle that time and good medication would help her to negotiate. Her attitude to her body was a perfect reflection of her attitude to her mind, and to her life: she was at ease with it, glad to inhabit it, and when it played up, she fixed it. She belonged to a gym, and went there three times a week. Someone had once advised, 'Make your body your hobby.' She liked this idea: your body wasn't important, not the main deal, but a side-show that it was satisfying to attend to, that you might as well get right.

Limber and slim, not tall, her dark brown hair and mild manner were good for business – it was easy for her to disappear in crowds. But the more a person looked at her, the more they began to consider she might be beautiful, and wonder why they hadn't noticed this at first.

She had high cheekbones and clear skin, long hair that had an amber sheen in summer; in winter darkened almost to black. Her most familiar expression was of attention, her brown eyes alert and steady, her eyebrows raised as though in faint amuse-ment. Her clothes were well made, tending towards function-ality rather than prettiness. She did not enjoy shopping, and replaced worn pieces rather than seeking out new styles. There was no vanity in that disinterest. She had often been reprimanded by shop assistants: 'You should make more of yourself.' But she preferred to go unnoticed, and – perfectly aware of the irony – she disliked the sensation of being watched.

Her softness made men wish they had the nerve to appeal to her. But they would see her smile and remember her profession. They didn't want to be caught. That softness, surely, was a trick. She saw the thought come to them, watched their guard go up as they tried to give her their best angles. She wished they wouldn't. She wasn't in the business of trying to dupe anyone. They did it to themselves. But she would have liked to meet someone who wanted to be found, and tried not to linger on the reason why: it was just a reflection of her own desire.

She had few foibles or bad habits. She did not fuss, was seldom fretful, poor at keeping secrets, wary of pretension. Her few friends knew that they could rely on her, but that she was also a private person, and they did not often presume upon her generosity. If asked, they would have only good things to say about her, but their affection stemmed from admiration more than warmth. 'She likes to be left to her own devices,' was an observation often made of her, and it was true, up to a point. She was a little envious of people with close friends, husbands, wives and children, but she was also wary of being enveloped in that kind of life: she was anxious about how much she could give away, and still remain herself. If anything consumed her, she would rather it was work. When she gave herself to that, she found a greater part of herself seemed to return than had been expended: a good return on her investment, her father might have said. Apart from a flat-share while she was a student, she had always lived alone.

Certainly she had experienced sorrow. Her mother's death from cancer was a black monument that cast its shadow right across her childhood. She sometimes wished that she could have seen, at the time, how fragile her childish ease had been. But her devastation was sieved through her father's greater loss, which diminished it to a feeling closer to guilt: she had no right to be miserable, in comparison with him. His was the much greater suffering.

In fact, it was a point of honour with her that she did not succumb to that early grief. More even than her mother's death, this decision closed her childhood – although she did not realise it at the time. It set up a pattern of stubbornness in her character that persisted long after it had served the useful function of protection. It was a fault-line of refusal that ran deep. 'I'll handle it,' meant that for Katherine to ask for help, confess to a weakness or a need, admit to a dream unrealised – these were among the very last things she would consider. Sadness she understood to mean failure. It spelt out a lack to which she felt she had no right.

So she set aside her emotions, and focused rather on the future. She knew that the pain remained, but she saw it as a dark place that, with time, would naturally grow lighter. One day she would glance back and it would be gone. It was the healthy thing to do, and she was very good at doing it. She had a healthy soul, and did not stash unhappiness to linger over.

But her father's imminent remarriage had come as more of a surprise than she liked to admit. She was genuinely pleased for him, and she liked Joanne. Divorced, with ten-year-old twins, she was in many ways an ideal, though unexpected, complement to Peter: open, where he was reserved; decisive, where he had a tendency to brood; cheerful, where, if she was honest, her father could at times be morose – although for the most part he simply kept his emotions to himself. You had to figure out what he was feeling by guesswork. Yet with her father's decision to remarry, she had the sense that even those things that could have been relied on, in the past, to be fixed, or move most slowly, had now accelerated. But what had she been looking at while this change occurred? Suddenly even her own father seemed on the point of leaving his old life behind, stepping into a new one, complete with wife and children. It underlined her own solitude, and made her feel oddly outmanoeuvred. When she tried to figure out why this was the case, she was a little stunned by the answer: somewhere, in secret, she felt that, more than him, it was her turn now to have a family of her own.

Weeks out of college, she had worked in New York, apprenticed to a photographer she had admired for years, and written to on an impulse. 'I'm writing to you to volunteer as an unpaid dogsbody, if you'll have me. I want to be your shadow, and won't get in the way.' The photographer, a woman whose work was legendary, frequently making the covers of *Vanity Fair* and *Vogue*, told her she only agreed to it because Katherine had included a photograph of herself, along with the letter. 'The very idea,' she had laughed as they drank coffee after lunch one day at the Bowery Bar and Grill, 'of having such a youthful shadow for a time simply thrilled me to bits and I had to have you.' She laid a warm hand heavily on Katherine's sleeve.

After that – and her apprenticeship ended amicably enough – Katherine returned to London, and put the deposit on a flat not far from Liverpool Street. It was just ahead of a property boom, and the purchase was shrewd. Her financier father had been impressed. 'The best of both of us.' He had seemed proud that she took after him as well as her mother, Julia, although he had paled – very slightly, and denied it afterwards – at the then-elevator, a fetid service lift that clunked through the levels to her flat on the top floor. 'One day,' she had been arch, 'this place will be very des. res. and you'll be amazed at my foresight.'

There was a year in London, then a friend had asked her out to LA, and she spent a six-month stretch in Santa Monica, stringing pictures to magazines back home. *Ingénues* on the make; landscape studies and cowboys gawky in the Mojave desert; abandoned film lots; 'the very rooms where Scott Fitzgerald and William Faulkner worked'. When she returned to London she had made a show out of her six-month stint, and it had received sufficient attention to ensure that commissions flowed.

Now she had been in fifteen group shows, three solos. Her work had taken her sailing in the Caribbean where she caught a barracuda off an author's fishing skiff, to Mexico to do a poet who lived on the side of a volcano, to Venice to take the last picture of a photographer who had laughed as he quoted George Eastman at her: 'My work is done, why wait?' Her work had even taken her across the Atlantic on the *QE2*. That trip was for *Condé Nast Traveller*.

She was doing fine. She was proud of what she had achieved. When, seldom, she dwelt on her feelings of there being something else, some *thing* that would complete the picture of her life, she reminded herself that she was still young, and that there was plenty of time yet for her to discover that missing aspect of herself. There was no hurry. It was not urgent. Her camera was a buffer between her and the world, and she supposed that this contributed to her feelings of delay: the world developed slowly for her, in her darkroom, shaded by the red light, halted at will in the stop bath.

'You're a photographer to your core.' Her ex-boyfriend, Miles, had told her this once, admiringly, looking over her shoulder at some new work. But she had felt the chill of his remark. A photographer to her core? As though whatever happened, she'd be able to take its picture and not flinch. There seemed something unholy in the idea, a moral vacancy that bordered on malice. She didn't think she was as hard as he supposed. She was quite sure that she had her cracking-point, the same as most people.

Later, during a fight towards the end of their year-long relationship, he had turned to her: 'Your problem is you're too much in control. You live in a dream, as though nothing can touch you.' She had tried to reason with him, and to make light of what he had said, but he had pushed her away, as though she had made some physical show of strength that had threatened him. She had been knocked back against the wall; the next day her head was sore, the side of her hip bruised. It was a game too dangerous for her to wish to join in. As she half fell, regained her ground, he had stared at her for a moment in astonishment: he read her strength as a provocation, and when he spoke, he was cold, much more than angry, as though voicing an immovable conviction: 'I'd be surprised if you're even capable of suffering, or feeling anything very deeply. It'll do you good to get hurt some day – it'll wake you up.'

He had been sorry afterwards. But she couldn't forget what he had said, or done. It spelt out how little they knew each other. They had no shared history, had met by chance, had no friends in common. He worked freelance, as a journalist, insisted on his need to be able to disappear at a moment's notice. His independence was one of the things that had drawn Katherine to him: he had seemed determined to make his own way in life, which she admired. But she often wondered at what point his determination was merely stubbornness — a kind of fear, much more than courage. He hated to share bad news, and kept good news secret from her, too, until, by the time he told her — simple things that had happened in his life — his announcements felt more like confessions. It meant that she was forced to live one pace behind him, never entirely sure what he was thinking. She didn't suppose he did it deliberately, but she read it as a form of exclusion, all the same: stay off my patch.

It was in the nature of city life. Anonymity was often mistaken for privacy, a solitary life for freedom. They had been so conscious of one another's right to be an individual, that she had often found herself missing him even when he was beside her. He was reluctant to be found, she knew that perfectly well, but she would have liked him at least to want her to look for him. His defensiveness was a kind of mistrust, and also a warning. She had let him into her life when he could have been anyone.

Katherine had heard from Miles only once since they separated. He left a message on her answerphone. She had returned home late one evening, stretched out on the sofa, picked up an exhibition catalogue and started to flick through it while she listened to her messages. And there he was: his voice on her machine, very quiet, as though he were on a conference call, or somewhere very far away.

'It's me. Miles. You're not in? We should talk. Kate?' The way he said her name was full of suspicion. He clearly thought that she was screening her calls, and she had the impression of him having phoned from within sight of her flat. She imagined him looking up at the windows – she always left a light on when she knew she'd be returning after dark – and suspecting that she was trying to avoid him. She could still hear his 'You live in a dream, as though nothing can touch you. It'll do you good to get hurt some day – it'll wake you up.'

She erased the message, thought for a moment, and then decided: she wouldn't avoid him, had to face up to this, and if there was to be trouble, she would deal with it head on before it got out of hand. His voice had sounded more lost than threatening. She didn't wish to hurt him. Perhaps he needed help? She took a deep breath and dialled his numbers: both were dead.

3

On the night of the fire, Katherine stepped out of the taxi, a smile still on her lips at the driver's joke about irons left on.

She even nodded, yes, she was lucky that it wasn't where she lived. The cab moved away slowly into traffic, the engine idling as the man craned to see, one hand on the wheel, the other waving 'cheerio' to her through the open window. It was a warm evening, almost humid. She set her bags down on the pavement. It was just after ten thirty. She had been out since midday.

She waited at the far end of the street until he had left, then slung her camera bag and tote diagonally across her back so that her hands would be free. She chose a camera, loaded film, straightened her collar beneath the camera strap, and moved towards the burning building. For a few minutes, habit was one pace ahead of instinct: she had reached for that camera without thought.

A speck of ash fell on her face and she brushed it away. She trained the zoom on the top floor, the fifth storey of the building, her flat, where the fire burned brightest. Smoke funnelled out of the windows on the floor below.

Three fire engines had arrived, and a couple of police cars. The street was blocked off. Arc lights lit up the front of the building. She took the pictures: the fire, figures below, a group silhouetted against the background of a silver van, parked at the far end of the street. A cable van perhaps. Reflection from the fire had turned its near side golden. There were only a couple of other cars, left overnight in the pay slots. It was a no-through road, narrow, double-yellow lined. Few lights were on in the other buildings. There couldn't have been more than fifteen people in the street, most of them either police or firemen. Everyone was turned towards the fire. No one noticed her. She did not know her neighbours. It was not that kind of neighbourhood. She recognised the bleary guilt of the security guard from the office block next door: he was talking to two policemen, waving his arms and pointing.

The silver van edged its way forwards along the street. She hadn't realised that anyone was inside it. Two figures, indistinct behind tinted glass. It drove half on the kerb. She stepped aside. It came so close she might have touched it. It disappeared into Bishopsgate. She could smell the fire and hear its hiss. There was an obstruction in her chest but she would not let it by.

She wiped her forehead with the back of her hand. Her skin was hot and damp, her hair a dark rope against her neck. She wished that rain would fall, fast and heavy. As she took the pictures, her camera felt useless in her hands, less like an instrument than an excuse – at least she had something to cover her face. She clung to it like an amateur, slipping on the focus. But without it she knew she'd be lost. Her eyes were sore with smoke and squinting in the dark.

When she had shot a reel of film, she stashed the camera back in her bag and leant against the wall of the building opposite her flat. She felt as though she were being forced to look at something too close to make out. She shut her eyes. She saw herself leaving earlier that day, strolling to the Underground to go to Oxford Circus. Low cloud cover had made the sky over London flat white, the air very still and mild – a day like a thousand others. She had spent the afternoon at the Langham Hilton, doing a portrait of a Danish author in town for her new book. When that job was done, she had deliberated on the way to the Underground: nip back home, or go straight on to a friend's drinks party. She had stopped to buy a cup of coffee. 'In or take away?' It was five thirty. She hadn't yet read that day's newspapers. The café kept them on a rack by the till. A headline caught her eye. On a whim she decided to sit in the café for an hour until it was time.

She saw herself glancing through the *Herald Tribune* and the *Standard*, drinking a mocha, making a few notes about the day's work, ordering a Coke, watching the flow of people heading home. Had she joined them, gone back to her flat instead of staying away – what then? She might very easily have decided not to go out at all. She might still have been at home when it happened. She saw herself back inside her flat, taking a bath, or working in her darkroom, listening to the radio, sleeping.

She loosened the collar of her shirt. She felt nauseous. Smoke had made her eyes smart, and her tongue was rough and dry against the roof of her mouth. She inventoried the things she had with her at that moment. Two bags, one full of equipment: Pentax, two different lenses, flash, light-metre, small foldable tripod, her Leica, four reels of used film. The other, the contents of her tote: laptop, wallet, cash and credit cards, lightweight mac – she hadn't trusted the sky, had hoped for rain although none yet had fallen – notebook, folder of negatives and contact sheets, a few rough prints, her phone, makeup bag, the keys to her flat, the Danish author's novels, inscribed in thanks. It wasn't much. It was all she had.

Her throat was tight, as though someone's hands were upon it, pressed against her jugular. Her fingers grazed brick as she reached out, and the building seemed to tremble until she realised that of course it was she who was unsteady. She was conscious of a policewoman looking at her curiously, then walking rapidly towards her, as though Katherine had called out to her, yet she had said nothing.

For a while she could not speak. She had one thought in her mind: an impression of Miles, looking up at the flat, hating her for not picking up the phone, thinking she had betrayed him. *'You live in a dream. It'll do you good to get hurt some day – it'll wake you up.'* She thought of his expression when he said this, as though that vision of her being hurt had reassured him, and she remembered his violence: it had felt less like an ending than a threat. She could not speak for fear of saying all that. Surely it couldn't be possible. That kind of thing didn't happen. She told the policewoman that, yes, it was her place, but she felt full of guilt when the woman asked her if she had any idea how it might have started, as though she herself were to blame. She mentioned the lights she always left on, the fact of the darkroom, the photographic chemicals.

The woman was kind, asked her if she had anywhere to stay, would she like her to call someone for her? There was nothing she could do here. All questions could wait until tomorrow. She was given instructions where she should go. Ten o'clock. Everything would be dealt with then. But it was absurd that she should leave. It was her place. She felt as though she should take control in some way, give advice, do something to help, to save her flat. Of course that was ridiculous. There was nothing to be done. She had failed. She could not even dislodge her own emotion. It stood directly in front of her, a black weight that she could not budge but that at any moment she would have to pass through. It seemed impossible that she should do so. She was aware of speaking only through the changing expressions on the policewoman's face. She could not catch her own words, as though she had whispered in the face of a high wind.

A blanket was thrown around her shoulders and the woman's arm offered to her for support. She was chaperoned away from the scene as though it did not concern her. The firemen moved around unhurried and methodical beneath the flames.

At the end of the street she allowed herself to be helped into a car. Where would she like to be taken? The idea of being anywhere at all filled her with panic. She wanted to be nowhere.

Only the past was safe. The policewoman sat beside her in the back seat. 'Would you like me to call a parent, or friends?' Katherine stared at her. She knew that that would be the natural thing to do. But the idea of confession, of transferring the burden of her trouble to someone else, horrified her. 'I'll handle it,' she told herself inwardly, though now without conviction. She would stay in a hotel. She reached into her bag.

The policewoman put a hand on her arm. 'Take your time.'

That afternoon, finishing the job at the Langham, out of habit she had swiped one of the hotel's tariff cards, and the girl at the concierge desk had told her that there were vacancies, mid-week deals, if she'd like . . . ? Katherine had smiled – 'a little out of my league' – and told her that it was just through curiosity.

Now she pulled the tariff card out of her bag and handed it over to the policewoman. The expense would swallow her earnings from that day's work. But she could think of nowhere else to go. She'd put it on credit, worry about it later. They drove to the hotel, and she checked into a single room with a window that looked out over Lower Regent Street.

She woke abruptly at dawn. It had rained in the night; the curtains were open, and a cold grey light ran through the room. She turned over beneath the white cotton sheets and cried, sound-less in her grief.

4

Just past nine o'clock, Katherine's cellphone rang. She had not slept since dawn, caught in a nervous limbo of exhaustion and wakefulness, and she answered the call before she had chance to give it thought. It was the company who supplied her with photographic equipment, letting her know that an order she had placed – the materials and lights she needed for the wedding that Saturday – was ready, and should they deliver it, or would she collect? They had just tried to leave a message on the answer-machine in her flat, but there was a fault with the line. 'I'll be round some time today,' she told them, and hung up.

She reached for the hotel phone and ordered breakfast, asked them to leave it outside her door, and then she took a shower. When she stepped out, she found that the tray had arrived: toast, two boiled eggs, black coffee. The *Telegraph* and *USA Today* had been delivered with the food. She slipped into the hotel bathrobe, glanced through the papers and tried to eat, but she could feel the weight of her fear, rising up in her chest and running out along her arm. Her hands shook and the words refused to focus. She couldn't swallow, dropped food, spilt coffee.

Through the hotel window the sky showed clear and blue, and she saw herself stepping out into the daylight, walking straight into Miles. She had to get out of London. She would leave town today and drive down to Fareham, if the police would allow it. No harm would come to her there. She would sink into that safety and deal with everything at a distance. But the thought of telling her father – telling anyone – about the fire filled her with dread.

She could still see the smoke rushing from a broken window – her bedroom window. She had the smell of it still in her lungs, deep as though it might never be expelled. To confess her doubts about who might be responsible was to enter a world in which she could not bear to believe.

She pressed her forehead against the window and shut her eyes. She would go to the police, figure out the practicalities, but otherwise she would keep it to herself, at least until everything had been resolved. People had their own troubles; she did not want to involve friends in unnecessary bother, it was too much to ask of anyone; and her father's wedding would be ruined by worry over what had happened. She would tell them everything when they got back from honeymoon. It was the right thing to do. She needed to get some distance before she could think clearly and, given a few days' investigation, it would turn out to have been a simple accident, a matter of faulty wiring, insurance claims and inconvenience, nothing to do with Miles.

But the mere thought that it might be otherwise made her heart race. She was always careful, didn't leave lights in precarious positions or her TV on standby, and the wiring in her flat had been redone only last year. As she dressed, her skin felt sore and cold, and she wished she had more clothes, something to hide inside. Her neck stiffened and her forehead became suddenly damp. She stumbled to the bathroom and threw up quickly and hard in the toilet. Even her body was failing her. She cleaned her face, rinsed her mouth, retied her hair and went through to the bedroom.

The air-conditioning was turned up and the room was icy. She sat on the edge of the hotel bed and looked at her reflection in the mirror. She steadied her breath. She could be anywhere, in any number of hotels. So much of her life so far had been spent in places not her own. Her mother had been the same. She would be out of the country for weeks, sometimes months at a time, and would return home with a sharpness about her that it would take days to soften and wear down. 'Full of angles,' her father used to say. Julia was apologetic, but it was her job. 'There you are' – Katherine would catch sight of Peter welcoming Julia back two days after she had arrived home.

But now when she looked at her reflection there was something about it that she did not recognise, as though a vital aspect, a layer of skin, had been taken from her and, without it, she was not herself. Hotels had made her feel safe, before. The simplicity of the transaction, paying for a bed, had always pleased her – you paid and left, caught the running tail of time inside the definite space of a four-square room. Now she wanted only to leave, get away from the city and home to Kent. She clung to that idea. Here, she felt she was being watched.

She could not shake the fear of what might have happened had she stayed at home. What would she have seen? The start of an electrical fire, easily put out, or something else?

'You need to be messed up before you're even real.' Openly, on a number of occasions, Miles had pointed out her comfortable life, the security of her background, as a thing she might be ashamed of, were she not so 'hard', as he called it. 'It's not very feminine to be so tough, you know. It's almost like you're a guy, you're so clear-cut.' He had blushed, adding, 'You've got it all!' as though wishing he had put it differently. But she couldn't change the family she had been born into. 'You don't even think there's anything wrong with it!' He had laughed at her, talked about his own family. 'Paupers', as he called them, painting in vivid colours the extent of his disadvantages. An alcoholic mother, a violent, disappeared father. A childhood of hand-outs and humiliations. 'You've no idea.' It seemed to make him more angry than glad to have succeeded against those odds.

But the thought that he, or anyone else, might have wished her actual damage, was so painful to her, so hideous an idea, that she recoiled from it. It could not be true. She refused to think it. But she halted on the brink of it, and wondered at her confidence. She felt like a child suddenly discovering that she was despised by her schoolmates – and for a reason she had never once suspected or been aware of. Yes, she was fortunate, and knew it. Miles had only underlined this: he hadn't made her hate herself because of it. She had led a life of safety and hard work; had accepted few favours — that trip to Africa had been rare. She had never, to her knowledge, caused anyone any harm, and yet she was a target.

Her reflection in the mirror seemed very small to her, and dark, the space around her alive with menace, as though someone might step from the shadows, have been waiting for the right moment when her guard was down. She glanced at the door. The safety bolt was still across. She checked her watch and looked in her bag for the card the policewoman had handed her last night. Her name, the station she was expected at, at ten o'clock. She would be home by this evening. She told herself that if she could just fix her mind on that, the end of the day, she would make it through the intervening stretch of time.

As she gathered her things together, she thought of Miles and the last time she saw him, just over a month ago. It was at her flat, and when she shut the door after him the stairwell had been silent for a few moments before she heard his footsteps fading on the concrete. She had leant against her front door and even then considered him with regret. In those seconds before he left she had seen herself throwing that door open and taking him in her arms again, seeing if there wasn't, perhaps, some way that they could be together, some way that would not hurt so much. But now she recalled his hesitation with fear, wondering what might have been in his mind at that moment.

She had always tried to regard his attacks as self-defence, a kind of bluster. They puzzled her far more than they harmed her. She knew, also, that he had problems she couldn't guess at, motivations she couldn't understand until she knew him better. Perhaps, as he said, she was the stronger of the two, but physically she was not his equal, and his insistence on her strength was just his way of being free to punish her. She didn't wish to abandon him, but their affection had lapsed to the doggedness of loyalty: his anger had ruined the spontaneity of love. He had seemed to relax when she told him they should separate. She stared down at her two small bags and her heart turned over: everything was gone.

She looked away. She saw herself arriving home almost empty-handed. After she had been to the police, she would have to buy some clothes for the next few days, and for the wedding. Her car was parked in a residents' slot a few streets away from the flat. There was also the equipment to collect.

As she left her room her hand on the door was unsteady as she thought of all the things that had been lost. Letters, books, clothes, half-forgotten objects of negligible worth to anyone but her. An imprint of her life wiped out. Years of work, boxes full of pictures, her own, and old prints collected over most of her lifetime – her private gallery of lives. She had prized those pictures above all else that she possessed. That she *had* possessed. She made that alteration in her mind and felt no lighter, nor more free now that she had little beyond what she held in her hands.

But she had two cameras, and four reels of film. Three were work. The fourth, she trembled to remember it, contained the fire.

5

The house stood back from the road, and was largely screened from view by a line of tall Scots pines. But as one descended from the hilltop where the road bent and narrowed into the curve, Fareham's chimneystacks could easily be seen and, in winter, whenever the pines were weighted by snowfall, the slate rooftops showed dark as a rook's wing against the white.

Now September had arrived in the same breath as August, and late heat meant that harvest dust still filled the air. Darkness came more suddenly than before, but glimmers of light were still playing at around ten o'clock – or even later, when the sky was clear of clouds.

Fareham was built in 1839, a fact which had pleased first Julia Clements and then her daughter, Katherine: in the same year, the public learned of the invention of photography. Louis Jacques Mandé Daguerre announced his use of the technique whereby an iodised silver plate, exposed to light, produced a one-off image if developed with mercury fumes; and William Henry Fox Talbot revealed his salt prints – images fixed on paper. Before Talbot's discovery, photographs faded, with time, to nothing.

Daguerre's prints translated the world in a mirror: the images were reversed. Fox Talbot talked of photography being 'the pencil of nature'. His experiments with light resulted in the negative to positive process, familiar today. For both, as for everyone since, the camera was a secret room where time was halted, made to show its face from darkness.

The house had been built by an undistinguished architect, torn between the age's two vogues: Gothic, thanks to Sir Walter Scott, and Classical, after the Roman Renaissance style popularised by Charles Barry. But somehow Fareham did not suffer for this divided impulse. In fact, it benefited, although it was only in this century that it was considered to have done so. The Victorians had written it off as the fancy of impressionable industrialists — which was only partly true. The Clements family's interests did not lie in industry, but much further afield than that, in industry's raw materials.

'Clements' was at first 'Clemenceau'. From there to 'Clemence' and then a little later 'Clements' was achieved without fanfare. The once-Belgian name fell into English; the house became a half-hidden mark on the landscape; the family's origins sank into the past and were, almost, forgotten.

But in the early years after their arrival, local Kent society, such as it was, did not let the family's ambition to start anew pass entirely without notice. There was the feeling that they had arrived by stealth, and put down roots in the garden of another person's land. The family neither aspired really to belong, nor attained that privilege, but remained, subtly, on the outside. Local fêtes would be held on the lawn. Everyone came, and was pleasant. But there was the sense of wanting to see what the foreigners had done – to judge them in the manner of assessing the value of a prize vegetable, shipped from an exotic climate: would it flourish in English soil? This judging went on behind closed doors: the Clementses were never sufficiently accepted to receive the compliment of being openly criticised.

By the standards of its age Fareham was not a large house, and with the years the land around it had shrunk to just over twenty acres. But in its appearance could be discerned the desire to be something far better – finer, more venerable – than in reality was the case: the dream-house exceeding the limit of bricks and money.

At either end of the building, as signal of the architect's Gothic ambition, two low crenellated towers implied that impression of history – shots being fired from rooftops, a sense of duels and lookouts for the hunt. But this was an illusion: had someone clambered on to the roof, the battlements would have reached no higher than the knee.

In many respects the house was a folly: inside, there was a dark Jacobean-style panelled hallway. Outside, the two towers might have suggested a French château. Above the windows, the triangular pediments of the Roman Renaissance insisted on a kind of Palladian symmetry that the part-timbered extension could not bear out.

The extension, referred to as the annexe, had at first been the servants' lodging: home to butler, groom, cook, housekeeper, scullery- and parlourmaids. Today it housed Mary, Katherine's one-time nanny, now nurse to her grandmother, Edie. It also housed Julia's darkroom, used in turn by her daughter. The idea in building the annexe, it seemed, had been to suggest that the main house was an addition to a much earlier Elizabethan construction, when in fact that was not so. No building had stood on this patch of land for the simple reason that until the 1830s it would not have been possible: the land was swamp.

So a spot was chosen in a pleasant hollow at the head of an uninterrupted vista, set to parkland, and the land was drained, creating a small ornamental lake. The architect, however, was not only undistinguished but also relatively inexperienced, and his sentimental choice of view meant that the location of the building site was ill advised. The error was felt for many generations: a problem with damp on the north-facing walls; subsidence in the annexe, which was later propped up by iron supports; a coolish dankness in the rooms along the ground floor, sometimes even in high summer, and in particular after dark, or when the shadows lengthened.

For this reason, the trees close to the house had to be kept cut back, and the damp-loving rhododendrons were hacked down to keep them similarly distant. Ivy, too, was not allowed to cling – although this was a constant fight, perpetuated even into the late twentieth century. It seemed that the stuff shimmied somehow just beneath the soil, emerging with deep-grown ancient roots that had attached themselves to the foundations so tightly that, in later years, gardeners warned against ever prising the stuff off for fear of disturbing the house's swampy hold on the land.

But the overall character of Fareham was one of great charm, if not beauty. What the architect had lacked in experience, he made up for with instinct. He was clever with light, and judicious with darkness. There were rooms where breezes funnelled west to east; others where no outside sound could penetrate. As a child, growing up in Rochester, he had watched ships moored along the estuary, and had longed to go to sea. Then he fell in love with a girl from Chatham. She didn't love him. He tried in vain to impress her and, although she didn't know it, all his buildings were for her, and for his love of ships.

In drawing up his plans, his intention was always the same: to build a house where his passion, secretly, might dwell. There were turns on the back staircase where people could stand together unseen. A narrow corridor running between the main house and the annexe, cool as an open furrow. An attic with dimensions elegant as a child's dance-hall, the wide, smooth boards set tight with the skill of a well-made deck. The staircase allowed for descents in silhouette – a large high window stood directly at the top, mullioned so that scattered light fell through. The view from all the windows at the back of the house was uninterrupted until the high point of the valley, which was thick with oaks.

But Fareham was in no sense an 'ideal' house. Technically, it was irregular in appearance, and erratic in mood. It had whims and apparent foibles: doors that would swing wide open, very slowly, when no one had passed through; sash windows that stuck even in cold weather where no rain had come for weeks – one window, on the top floor, had been wedged open for as long as anyone could remember. Rain fell in; in winter, snow briefly gathered; in summer, swallows nested nearby and sheltered there. The tilt of a floorboard, a slanted ceiling, a wall, even, where no picture would quite hang to true – all these imperfections meant it was, in the end, an ill-made building, on a poor piece of land. The architect's love remained unrequited.

Even the fact that, from the road, it was invisible, seemed to indicate its insignificance. An eye-blink might destroy it. It would never be marked down as one of the great minor English country houses.

But whenever Katherine thought of it, she smiled. It housed all her memory, and all her longing for home. It was her ideal, and she loved it for that, and still more because it was where she had known her mother, as she remembered her alive and at her happiest.

6

It was less difficult than she had imagined: obviously such things were routine. Katherine was at the police station for just over two hours, and most of that time was simply waiting. They agreed with her that, yes, most likely it would turn out to be an electrical fault. She had left a light on, set another on a timer switch. Did they have access to her family's financial history? They didn't seem to consider for a moment that she had done it herself, for insurance money.

Instead they asked her about her work. She mentioned the flammable chemicals involved. 'No.' The policewoman from the previous night, Sergeant Holden, was back on duty. 'I meant have you any reason, professionally, to suppose someone might wish to destroy your work? You're a journalist?' She bent forwards expectantly. She was a young woman, her questions tentative but thorough.

Katherine had been relieved to rule this out. 'I don't take those kinds of pictures. Nothing anyone would be interested in in that way.'

'Nothing scandalous.' Sergeant Holden smiled.

'Not even remotely.'

She asked all the questions Katherine had anticipated. Had she seen anyone suspicious? Noticed anything unusual, workmen, builders, anyone she didn't recognise in her block, in the street? Anyone she knew say or do anything, 'however irrelevant it might seem now' — her eye became keen as she asked this, and Katherine frowned as though in concentration, praying the woman wouldn't notice her nerves at this question — 'anything you think might be connected in some way?'

Katherine supposed that the choice of sergeant, a junior, reflected the importance placed on the case, which evidently had not aroused particular suspicion. And why should it? She tried to see it from their perspective, and that way, it was true, it was plausible enough that it should have been a simple matter of an electrical surge, an overheating lamp left too close to some papers perhaps, sparks jumping from a loose-wired socket. Nothing at all. 'No,' she answered, 'I haven't noticed anything unusual, no strange people, no pyromaniac friends.' She tried to joke, and it was only then that the policewoman became stern, as though her easy manner had been in place solely to catch her out once she'd let down her guard. She handed Katherine a sheaf of papers. 'We'll need your signature on these,' she cleared her throat, 'and a few more details.'

With reluctance, or so it seemed, Sergeant Holden told her that she was free to go down to stay with her family in Kent. Once the police report was in, she had fourteen days in which to make a claim to her insurers. 'As long as you bear that in mind,' the woman said, 'you can take a few days' grace.' But her eyes narrowed, openly suspicious, when Katherine asked if they would not telephone her on the landline in Kent but, rather, on her cellphone. 'My father is getting married at the weekend. I'd appreciate it. I don't want to worry him unnecessarily.' She told them the full story, and was aware of her voice shaking. It sounded like a pack of lies, as though her family was the secret she had to hide. Too bad. She straightened her back and looked impatiently at her watch, although she was in no hurry.

When she was released, she stepped out of the station and saw that, in the hours she'd been inside, her father had left a message on her phone, asking her when she was thinking of coming down to Kent. 'We're all expecting you.' She could hear Joanne's children, Roy and Ellen, chattering in the background. She returned his call as she headed for the Underground, walking fast so that he would not notice the emotion snagging in her voice. 'Maybe I should come early? I could come today, even, if you like?'

'Great.' He sounded busy, as though he'd forgotten he had phoned her earlier. 'Leave it all behind. Your work will be there when you get back.'

She steadied her breath, a hand covering the mouthpiece. 'This evening, then?'

'Fine, just whenever you like.'

She went to Oxford Street to buy clothes: white T-shirts, a three-pack; black trouser-suit, duplicate of one she'd owned before; pair of Levi's; trainers, flats, heels; a dress that would do for the wedding; underwear and socks; couple of sweaters; a large holdall.

In return for money she received small pieces of a possible life. Not her own – that was gone – but one very similar. She made the choices swiftly and out of habit. There was a clear logic to them. It was what she had always done. But she dressed with her back to the mirror, turning only briefly to check the fit. The imitation of her past was too painful to her. More unnerving than had she jumped tracks to lead another life. A hollow repetition now that all the comforts of security had vanished. She was shadowing a girl who would not come again.

The entire process took no more than a couple of hours. She thought of the clothes in her flat. This was all she needed.

Then she remembered: rubber bands for her hair, and Kirbygrips. This last purchase was the moment when she faltered. The edge of herself felt suddenly grazed, heavily diminished as though scraped away or burnt by standing too close to the flames.

She stood in the aisle at Boots and stared at the hair-clips and combs, the false twists of nylon hair and the metal-toothed clamps, and a few minutes passed before she was able to make sense of what she was looking at. The hours lost preening slipped out of reach, and with them went so much that she could not bear to lose. No moment ever comes again, as the camera shows. She tried to think instead of future moments of hair-pinning and tying back, but they would not come to her either. She looked away. Instead of buying what she had come for, she picked up a pair of hairdressing scissors.

Handing over the money, she thought of the coils of her long black hair floating towards the plug-hole after she took a bath in her flat. She would often lie there, soaking and musing on the significance of her hair's fragility. It was thick, and perhaps to keep itself in check, clumps fell out whenever she washed it, as though her root to the world was growing steadily less strong. She wound her hair into a tight braid, and set the thought aside.

Now she went into a department store and, in front of a changing-room mirror, in a few swift cuts, she chopped off her hair. The sight of it swiped off and lying in her hand was a greater shock than the look of herself with short hair – which suited her, and only made her appearance lighter, and not strange. She wore it tied back most of the time anyway, and it was a surprise to her that she looked less changed than she had thought she might. But it loosened something in her chest to have done this, and it steadied her. It was an act of efficiency, not madness. The surprise of it was that, with short hair, she looked less like her mother, and this was not something she had thought she might like.

She felt clearer this way, and in sharper focus, as though since last night all certainty and colour had been ebbing from her. More herself; most safe.

She packed her purchases into the holdall she had bought. She looked at the hank of cut hair. The thought of simply throwing it away frightened her. She wrapped it in a carrier-bag and pushed it beneath the clothes. When she left the cubicle, no one registered any change in her appearance.

By the time Katherine had collected her car, it was approaching late afternoon. She stood beside it for a moment, faintly incredulous that it should be there when everything else was gone. But there were the same dents and scratches on the bodywork, the same identifying marks of rust. She drove away, avoiding the end of her street.

After collecting the equipment from her suppliers in Old Street, there was nothing more to keep her in London.

Only once, as she leant over the boot, wedging the lights between the boxes of paper and film, checking that she had the right cables and spare bulbs, did she feel any threat. She had looked up, cursing at the sound of a car horn, and – was that Miles? Someone stepped beneath the shadow of an archway on the opposite side of the road. The movement was fast enough for her to notice it against slow traffic. But then the figure was gone, and she supposed that she had been mistaken. Just someone in a hurry at the end of the day.

It was then that she noticed the piece of paper pushed beneath the windscreen wiper of her car. Her nerves tightened. Had someone put it there when she was inside, signing for the equipment? Was it Miles? Had he seen her? She looked around, and her back stiffened with the sensation of being watched. She read the note. It was nothing. A record sale – 'Vinyl Countdown'. She felt faint with relief. She glanced at her watch. It was almost six. She headed out into the traffic.

*　　*　　*

Fewer than twenty-four hours had passed since the fire. That distance was negligible: it gave her no kind of protection from what had happened. She tried to fix her mind on everything that had gone before, all the work and ordinariness, and on everything that must come after – the wedding, the continued pattern of her days. But now both times seemed implausible, and she could only see the burning centre in between.

She drove along Embankment. The river air was clear and still. Lights were already lit across the bridges, and as she sat in slow traffic she felt the loneliness, too close, a persistent presence beside her, of having lost so much that for so long had been integral to her life. Her collection of photographs had been the grain and substance of her memory, and for that reason it had been invaluable. Nothing could be done to recollect an image of someone now dead, or in any way bring those pictures back to life. There had been well over a thousand faces.

She flicked through the bands on the radio. She could not bear to think of this now. She rubbed her eyes and concentrated on the road. The traffic thinned out and she drove fast along the widening streets. But the back of her mind was making notes, running through a catalogue of those nameless people whom she longed to see again and knew she never would. The delicacy of the thread that bound those faces to her had always been uppermost in her mind.

It was entirely different from the pictures she herself had taken. Much of her own work was kept on file at Fareham, in the annexe darkroom, or had been made public and dispersed to safety in publishing houses, scanned into computer systems, logged with her agent, available in galleries, on postcards. The thought of rebuilding her archive was exhausting. It would take months. But at least it was possible, a task that with patience she might achieve. The fact that those pictures were not secret had safeguarded their existence and given them a future that her collection of old prints did not have.

Red lights gave her the chance to stretch out her arms. Her left hand reached with the instinct of habit to rest on her camera bag, lying on the passenger seat. She had those photographs: four reels of film. She could work on them later at the house. Tomorrow, not tonight. Tonight she would rest and pretend to her father and the family that all was well. She would need a stiff drink to do it, but she would manage it somehow; she would not burden them with this. The car behind her sounded its horn and she saw that the lights had changed while she was staring upwards at them through the leaves of a birch tree, silhouetted against the darkening sky.

She waved at the car behind and pulled away towards the exit for the tunnel and the motorway. Already she felt the image slip: it had coincided with the pattern on a dress which had always reminded her of leaves, and when she peered at the photograph more closely through an eyeglass, she discovered that the rough, hand-blocked fabric was indeed patterned with a birch-leaf design. The dress belonged to a farmer's wife – she supposed the woman was a farmer's wife. Her arms were strong as a baker's, or of someone used to birthing livestock, and she had exactly that steady preparedness about her posture in this photograph.

The woman looked sideways into the camera, as though not liking to take her gaze from the slighter figure of a man standing beside her. She sat. The man's hand rested on her shoulder, and her left hand reached up to touch his fingertips in a gesture accidental and unstaged – although the image was clearly a studio commission. The date, in the early 1900s.

The couple appeared to be dressed in their best clothes. The man's neck bulged with unfamiliarity in his high starched collar. The woman's dress was held together at the neck with a jet brooch, and belted with a silver buckle. The fabric billowed over the contours of her body. Both were late middle-aged, and the unretouched gelatin silver print did nothing to disguise the woman's wrinkles or her grey hair. But her eyes shone and a gentle smile was on her upturned parted lips. A wisp of hair had come loose from her bun and lay against her cheek. Her knees were slightly apart and one foot was blurred where she must have moved at the moment the shutter fell.

There were no marks around the edge of the photograph to suggest that at any time it might have been framed. It was, Katherine supposed, among the rejects of that particular sitting. But it was one of her many cherished finds – part of a job lot bought for three pounds in a junk shop in Lyme Regis – and she was quite certain that the final formal portrait had been nothing like so successful at setting down the fact of love between that couple. It was right there in the accident: in the blurred foot and the woman's off-kilter glance. Had she been looking up at her husband as the photographer lowered his hand to take the shot?

The photograph was pocket-sized and the back was brown with age and dirt, as though it had been carried right through a person's life. For this reason also, Katherine had treasured it. It witnessed a love that might otherwise never have been remembered.

Katherine pulled the car on to the hard shoulder and bent over the wheel to catch her breath. Her nose was running and her eyes had clouded with tears so that she could not see the road. Cars slowed down as they passed. Was she some kind of accident? Who did not like to gawp at such things?

7

Into the tunnel of trees on the last few miles before home. From evening to sudden night, lasting only for a mile of forest, the car headlights streaming over close-set pines, the camber of the road tending towards the ditch. There were no other cars and, without streetlights, the way ahead was pitchy as a mineshaft. Katherine slowed down as she entered this stretch, peering into the darkness — a few times in the past she had seen deer, grey and russet shadows passing close behind the bars of tree trunks. She wound down the window and the forest air was warm and clear. To turn off the car engine would be to land square inside dark silence.

She had set the miles between herself and the fire but entering the trees it seemed as though its heat had followed her down here and now lay smouldering just out of sight, where the pines and tangling briars grew closest. Directly ahead, the headlights lay on the Tarmac and the way appeared cool and blank, an icy pathway through the night. But on either side, the light caught and lingered on the rosy trunks, as though embers lay ready to crackle into life, blown to flames in the car's swift slipstream.

Summer was finished, yet the heat of the season appeared not dead but waiting. She glanced into her rear-view mirror. Nothing was behind her. A curve in the road had curled the trees more tightly around the car, snug as thick fur absorbing darkness, catching light. Further into the trees she felt the sensation of being watched begin to vanish, and only then, with no pursuing headlights, did she realise that the drive down the motorway had been a kind of nervous holding of her breath: was she being followed? She thought of home, the house shining in its nest of fields and undergrowth, and it, too, appeared remote at this moment, a place she might never reach.

She had last been at Fareham a couple of weeks ago. It seemed an impossible distance. She could hold the two pictures, before, after, up to the light and see that, in almost every detail, they were identical. Yet one image held the key, the other was redundant, already in the past — the safety of another world that, by comparison, was not real. She drove on beneath the canopy of pines. The hiss of rubber, the faint rattle of the engine: in the corner of one picture, layered over with the darkness of a too-long exposure, but hidden there all the same, the snake in the garden. She felt the chill around her ankles and wrists, and against her throat, her bare pale skin too vulnerable now.

She could see nothing, but she could sense it, the imminence of danger burning alongside her, somewhere close by. She could not outrun it. She was already exhausted.

She slowed the car, and turned off the engine, remembering the first time she had seen a deer on this forest road. She had been with her mother. She was small, four or five. It was after a few weeks spent with Edie in London, while her mother was away, one of many trips. It had been late, well after midnight. Julia's flight had been delayed, but she had insisted on driving down to Kent that night. There had been a particular reason for her wishing to get back there.

Katherine had been asleep at her grandmother's, and woke only when she was lifted into the back seat of the car, wrapped in a blanket. Now she could remember lights strung across a bridge, and along the Embankment, shining across smooth yellow and silver water, and the long emptiness of wet roads. It was later in the year, October, and it had rained all that day.

Julia had driven fast out of the city, under the tunnel, down the motorway to Kent, and into this stretch of road where the pine trees scattered raindrops on the metal roof. This might have been what woke her. She could remember being already awake when the engine stopped. A window must have been lowered that night, too, because the air was noisy with a damp breeze running about the car and through the trees. Her mother was leaning forwards over the wheel, her breath high up under hunched shoulders, as though listening out for something, a sound she could not quite catch.

Julia said her name very suddenly, but quiet, and Katherine had looked up to see a tawny stag standing dead centre in the road, a foot or so from the car. It did not move. The wind caught in the hair on its neck and flanks, and its chest quivered, its great heartbeat appearing to race beneath the surface. Katherine was aware of her mother's hand poised over her camera bag, lying beside her in the passenger seat, then drawing back and instead reaching over to prod Katherine to make sure that she was awake.

'Can you see? Isn't he beautiful?' The stag was huge, its antlers gleaming in the headlights. They could see the breath funnelling from its nostrils as its eye held steady on the car. It lowered its head briefly, then walked on across the road, unhurried, and disappeared into the trees.

Katherine was wide awake, and had seen everything. 'You didn't get a picture.'

Her mother turned to face her, shaking her head. 'Couldn't catch him. No chance.'

'But there was ages,' Katherine protested.

Her mother smiled. 'Silly, back to sleep.'

Katherine had lain down, listening as her mother started the car and they drove away. She felt her face flush with understanding of something that only years later she could properly grasp: life first, always. The moment before the image. There had been ample time for her mother to snap up that stag, commit him to film, but she had made the choice, and instead her hand had reached out to check that her daughter was awake, and seeing the moment too, before it disappeared.

Now, with the engine off, Katherine tried to see into the forest. The trunks shone dull as iron in the headlights and, between them, the warm blind space of darkness was empty, the trees noiseless, the forest floor undisturbed.

She thought of the untaken photograph of that stag, and tried to imagine exactly where that moment had happened. Somewhere very close to here. For a second, leaning into the night, seeing no life there, remembering the immense life that had seemed to snag like a bright jewel caught in the pebbles of a clear stream, Katherine wished she had a picture like a window to clamber through and, that way, step back inside a time where none of what had happened since was true. She thought of all the lost pictures, the windows of a beautiful house now shut and boarded up. She wished she had something tangible to remember that time in the forest with her mother, the jewel scooped up from the riverbed, held in her hand, stashed in her pocket to gloat over. She wished that there had been no fire.

The shadows fluttered where a breeze riffled through the high branches of the pines, and with it came the certainty that those pictures were the very least part of what she missed, and that now or in future, whatever life brought her, still she would give anything to have the moment come again: her mother's hand in the darkness, reaching, making the choice.

8

The car broke out from beneath the cover of trees into the lighter evening, starless, with no moon.

Hawthorns leant close over the road, and the verges were banked high with tall grass. Under the oaks and sycamores the unmarked road began to narrow, vanishing into familiar curves. The changing landscape reached her on the air: the cidery tang of fallen apples fermenting into meadow grass; new-turned clay soil, the chalkier high ground and a stand of pines; the bitterness of razed barley, a field turned to stubble . . . The damage was done. She was looking up once more at the burning building.

On past a stretch of land now laid to vines, as it had been during the Roman occupation − her father had pointed this out to Joanne when she had laughed at the sight. 'Hope springs eternal with you English. It's hardly the Napa valley.'

'Actually, darling . . .' He had corrected her. She merely raised her eyebrows and yawned, laying a hand on Peter's knee as though he were a fanciful child.

Katherine thought of the bright house and the family waiting, the noise and contained chaos. She supposed that they would have just finished dinner. There would be something kept aside for her, and she would eat at the kitchen table, have a drink with her father, find out how Edie had been keeping, see that all was well. She would say that she was tired, had been working hard – this always seemed to satisfy him, and would be easy to insist on.

Now the trees stood back from the verge, thinning out until only the high hedgerows lay between road and open countryside. Here and there, shining out of familiar points on the landscape, Katherine could see the faint yellow lights that meant their nearest neighbours, and, as she came up on to the high point before the road descended to the valley and the house, the clustered lights of Whealdon, blurring now around the edges as the small town grew.

In darkness the lights of the house could usually be seen flickering in and out of view, as though someone were semaphoring to the road from inside the building. But tonight Katherine could see nothing, and was puzzled. Perhaps the undergrowth really did need cutting further back, as her father had said: the briars, and worse, in his opinion, the rhododendrons, which ate up light along the east wall, their waxy leaves clattering in high winds, their rattle and hiss like the cluttered hush of a mangrove swamp. Joanne compared it to the Atchafalaya Basin in Louisiana. 'Going to have to employ a 'gator-killer next, start charging for guided tours,' she had said, whacking at the clambering root of a particularly ravenous plant.

She slowed down as she took the final curve in the road – and still no sign of the house. She remembered arriving that night with her mother, just after two in the morning. The house had been similarly unlit. Despite the hour, her mother had honked the horn to signal their arrival. Katherine had been tipped out of the back seat of the car, and it had seemed like a joke that she and her mother shared. 'Daddy, we're home!' A light had gone on inside the hallway, shining golden through the fanlight; her father had appeared at the door fully clothed, and when she ran to him he smelt, as he often did, of the outdoors – an under-trees, long-grass smell. There was a noise from behind him in the house, and Mary, at that time Katherine's young nanny, emerged beside him in the doorway.

Katherine could remember the way her mother had stayed over by the car when she herself had gone towards her father. Mary took her hand and led her upstairs to bed. Peter went outside to Julia, and Katherine could hear them talking together in low, hurried tones as she was taken upstairs. Julia had been gone for three weeks. Katherine looked back as she went upstairs, but her parents were still outside. Peter had hold of two heavy bags, and was waiting for Julia to follow him. His back was half turned to his wife, spelling out his impatience.

Mary had turned to Katherine then, and said something that stuck in her mind. She had heard a sudden noise from outside, a sharp snap and thud, and had been dragging on Mary's hand, craning to see what her parents were doing. 'Nothing for you to worry about,' Mary had told her. 'It's the wind in all those trees. Need to keep things battened down.'

The expression stuck in her mind partly for its oddness, but also because it was something her father often said. When speaking about his business in particular, he used the idiom of a ship – battened hatches, braced mainsails, a different tack, a swift clip. 'Nothing for you to worry about,' Mary repeated, which only made Katherine more wakeful. She had not thought there was cause for worry until Mary put it that way. The vision of the encroaching trees being a constant menace lodged itself in her thoughts. Now, with still no sight of lights from inside the house, she made a mental note to discuss having the undergrowth cleared with her father.

Katherine frowned as she turned into the driveway at Fareham. She noticed that the gateposts were in the process of being painted, and wondered if this was part of the pre-wedding 'arrangements'. The wrought iron had flaked to rust, patched up now with grey paint against the black. A deeper hush closed around the car as she drove beneath the cedars of Lebanon and cypresses at the gates, and then on through the avenue of poplars. No, she had not been mistaken, no lights were on. Even the annexe was in darkness.

She parked beside the front door, not liking the idea of putting the car at the side in the old coach house, behind a screen of firs, then having to walk across the unlit gravel. It was true: the rhododendrons really were a problem. They looked too thick even to push through now, and without their flowers they appeared strong and leathery as a new-tanned hide, vaguely feral, as though they were not plant but animal, flayed and left out to be cured in the night. She shuddered and turned away, checking for her latch key, just in case, before running across the short stretch from car to front door.

As she had feared, the door was locked. It opened stiffly – swollen in its frame with damp. The ground was wet as after heavy rainfall.

Inside, the panelled hallway was dark and silent. She flicked on a light and called, 'Hey, Dad, I'm home!' But it shocked her, the sound of her voice alone in the so obviously empty building.

She set down her bags and raised her right hand to her chest, rubbing at the bone there to try to quieten her heart, fluttering high and fast inside her ribcage. She stood absolutely still, with one light above her in the hallway. The stairs curved upwards into darkness, and for the first time she saw the place as it might appear through a stranger's eyes, full of menace. She heard the wood settle and give, cracking faintly in an unseen part of the house. She held her breath.

9

As a young boy, the architect of Fareham had lived on the Kent coast: this was the story Julia Clements told her daughter one night during a power cut.

It was long before Edie had come back to live at Fareham and, the previous week, Mary had returned to live in London. Katherine had not been told why. There had been au pairs before her, all for short periods, but Mary did not fit into this category. Without having heard it being discussed, still, Katherine had believed that Mary would have liked to stay for longer.

So that night she and her mother were alone in the house. Katherine was in bed and had been promised a story. The lights went dead just as her mother opened the book, and all the noises that were barely noticeable when there was light became loud with threat.

'Sorry – no light, no story.' Julia had crossed to the window, seen that the whole area was affected, and turned to go.

But Katherine insisted: 'Make one up.'

So Julia told a story about the architect of Fareham.

All that was known for certain was that he came from Rochester; Julia was obliged to embellish. She described the clippers and tall ships, the cargo boats running up the coast through the channel towards Gravesend and the Thames Reach; racing back and forth from China and India, Africa and the Americas for coffee and tea, spices, silks and Indian cottons, ivory, gold, silver, diamonds, precious stones, teak and sandalwood; on the old spice routes, catching the trade winds around the Cape of Good Hope, into the roaring forties and around Cape Horn to Australia for wool.

Julia crossed again to the window: there was still no light. 'Maybe all that standing about on the dock, watching the freight arrive and get parcelled off to be delivered to the cities, maybe it gave him ideas.' She went back to sit on the bed beside her daughter. 'The ships must've seemed magical to him, full of treasures and wonderful things, endlessly arriving. But perhaps he suffered from sea-sickness, so instead of going to sea he built houses, and made them just like the ships he so loved.'

Outside Katherine's bedroom, on the landing, a floorboard creaked so suddenly and close that, even with her mother beside her, Katherine jumped. It was impossible to believe that no one was there.

'And that is why', her mother followed, speaking more loudly, 'this house is so full of creaks on the inside, and why it is so well protected from the outside. Listen. The outer walls are like the great hull of a cargo ship.' Katherine tried to listen. It was true. Outside, all that day, there had been fierce weather and, if you watched from the window, it seemed incredible that it should be so: the trees bent steadily in a strong east wind, but there was no sound of it from inside.

'You see,' her mother explained, 'it's like a ship's hull where no water must leak through, or else it will sink. But it can't be so rigid that it does not give, slightly, in bad weather, and this is why it makes those noises, as though the walls are breathing in and out according to the temperature and weather. It's very cleverly built, and in that respect just like a great ship, only on land. You should sleep now.' Her mother kissed her and left the room.

Katherine settled down beneath the covers and Julia went to look for candles or a torch. She heard her mother swear at the head of the stairs as her heel caught on the rug. Then the light came suddenly, and Katherine heard her exclaim, 'Shit!' And then the sound of another voice, her father's, very quiet, from some way distant, close to the front door perhaps. 'Oh, it's you. Thank goodness for that.' Her mother's voice again, the sentence starting angry, but ending in amusement. Katherine heard her laugh. A door clicked shut somewhere low down in the house.

Katherine had been glad her father was back, and that the lights were on, and most of all for her mother's explanation of the house's strange noises, which had always bothered her, but which after then she tried to see as another aspect of the weather. A creak might mean a storm brewing beyond the brow of the hill, Katherine had thought, falling towards sleep. The click of a floorboard settling might be to do with a frost settling across the fields in France. Perhaps that rattling sash window on the landing was because a warm breeze had found its way here from the coast of Africa, where Mary's mother was from, and was trying to get in at the window to look for her – hushed whispering, remember me? This idea comforted her only momentarily. Mary was gone now, and that wind would not find her here. She heard her parents' voices rising up from the hallway, and longed for them to come upstairs to her. She tried to stay awake, so that if they should, she would not miss them, but no one came, and she fell asleep with that loneliness beside her.

Now, no longer a child, her mother's remembered story did nothing to dislodge her fear. Katherine stood with her back to the front door, wondering at the empty house that had been left in darkness. For the first time in her life, it did not feel like home.

10

She moved through the ground floor, flicking light switches as she went. There was no note on the kitchen table. Nor was there any food left out. But the fridge held various edible things – cheese under a glass dome, a soft slice of chocolate cake, a large ripe peach on a Crown Derby saucer, fresh salad with water still clinging to it, as though it had been washed only moments earlier. So they had not gone away. And there was no sign of disorder or struggle, only vanishing.

She filled the kettle for tea and made a sandwich: lettuce and Gruyère. The bread was fresh. She ate it and wondered. No one came. It was just after half past ten. She checked in the cupboard by the stove: cooking brandy, in its place. She poured and drank, felt a little warmer, and heard a noise in one of the rooms directly above her. This house – she cursed it under her breath, and sympathised with Joanne's feelings towards it. When there were people here it was friendly enough, but when you were alone, as now . . . What was it that made the place so unnerving? It was not the thought that it was empty. Quite the reverse. After

all, why should anyone fear an empty house? It was the sense
that it was full of people that made her nerves race, the skin at
her nape prickle with expectation of touches. Katherine shook
herself, hand rising to her neck, newly revealed. She felt blinded
by a kind of stupidity, as though she were dull-witted: why could
she not see anyone? It was as though she was too slow to catch
sight of them – as though she arrived always too late into a
suddenly empty room.

The noise came again. Katherine finished the glass of brandy
and decided to take a look. Only by looking, she knew, would
she quieten her fear. She would see with her own eyes that
nothing was wrong, and that there were no ghosts of any kind
– living spooks or echoes of the dead. She smiled to herself, and
put herself in the bracket of those photographers who try to
capture the spirit world on film: it was easy enough to doctor
negatives, a child could do it, and how many times had people
been impressed by the shadow on a loch where the monster
lurked – 'It must be true, it has a shadow!' Why was this always
considered sufficient proof? Shadows could be invented. High
fair-weather cumulus could be rendered the sign of thunder-
storms – it was just a matter of how much light was given to
the exposure. Even stone could seem to breathe, given the right
technique. She had done it often enough herself. It was partly
a matter of concealment: cover up one part of the print, expose
another, and even within a single image the truth could be turned
into something else – not a lie, not exactly, but was it still the
truth?

Her mother had been famous for this technique: 'burning in', as it was called. Her landscapes were full of drama and sensation. People complained. They visited the spot, expecting to find the picture. But there was nothing. Just a field of straggling cows, some sheep swarming towards the gate like bees: pastoral, unheroic. The trees were smaller somehow, and the sense that the sky was a weight of thunder overhead disappeared in that one glance. 'They'll ask for their money back next.' Her mother had laughed. But Katherine could see that she felt their complaints as a kind of rejection: had nothing been conveyed that they might care for? It was her mind's secret imprint she had put upon those landscapes, and was that so unclear; or if clear, unwanted?

Katherine looked up to the head of the stairs. The window-panes' silver could just be seen. She turned on the light and went up.

There was definitely noise coming from the end room. Perhaps a wind had gathered outside, and someone had left a window unlatched. She flicked the light switches as she passed along the corridor. On both sides, the doors were shut. She paused beside one, her old bedroom, but hesitated, and could not say why, and walked on rather than looking in. The sound came again, and this time, with it, a voice, so soft and weak that Katherine stood still to catch it. No, she must have imagined it — it had sounded like someone calling her mother's name.

Julia, Julia is that you?

*   *   *

They had been able to laugh about it afterwards, but not at first.

'You scared the hell out of me,' Katherine said.

'Kate, darling . . .' Edie had smiled, despite that reprimand. Mary had just come through from the annexe.

'I thought you were calling for Julia.' Katherine's voice was still trembling. 'It sounded like someone was calling her name.'

Edie looked at her curiously, wrinkled her brow and croaked, '*Is that you?* That's all I said. Thought I heard Mary coming to rescue me. Didn't hear you arrive at all, must've nodded off after I toppled.'

Mary put her arm round Edie's shoulders. 'You going to be OK now? You sure?'

Edie had fallen out of bed, and had been on the floor – 'For hours, I suppose, but it felt like longer.' The noise Katherine had heard had been her final resigned yanking of the bedclothes to join her. 'Made quite a comfortable nest for m'self. You shouldn't worry and fuss so much, Mary.' She patted Mary's hand.

Mary frowned and lifted Edie's face round so that she could assess the mark on her forehead. 'Don't like the look of that. And why won't you use that button like you're meant to?' She looked around for it. 'Where've you hidden it now?'

Edie bowed her head like a chastised child. 'I hate that thing. Makes me feel geriatric.'

Mary gave Katherine a look: see what I have to deal with?

'And you shouldn't whisper behind my back.' Edie narrowed her eyes at Katherine.

'I didn't breathe a word, but I bet you make Mary's job imposs-ible.'

'Listen to your granddaughter, see, even if you don't to me.'

Mary squeezed Edie, and Katherine turned away to look for her alarm-call button, hating to see how much frailer her grandmother appeared to have grown, even in the space of two weeks. She should have been here when that happened. It was as though she had looked away at the decisive moment, and now it would never come again. She was guilty, and sorry, and exhausted. But for all that, now that she was here, with these two women, she was more relieved than she could say: a part of her had doubted that she would see again anyone she loved.

She kept her back to them for a moment so that they would not notice her expression, or the redness around her eyes that would soon mean tears.

'Here it is – she's slipped it down the side of the bookcase.'

'*She!*' Edie grinned, triumphant in her perception of bad manners. 'It's all that *thing*'s fault anyway.' She gave the red button a resentful prod. 'If I hadn't had to hold it out of the way while I reached down for my book I wouldn't have fallen in the first place. Didn't have enough hands, that was the trouble.'

Mary shook her head. 'You use it next time you want anything you can't get, you hear me?'

Edie shrugged.

'You will, do you hear? There'll be no more accidents.'

Mary was stern, and Katherine could see that she was done with humouring.

'You gave me such a fright.' Katherine helped Mary settle Edie back into bed.

'Hospital corners'll keep you fixed in nice and tight.' Mary smiled, efficient, lean and strong-backed as she bent over the bed. Grey showed at her temples, but her movements were still those of an agile young woman.

Edie groaned, mock-furious. 'See how she tortures me?' She gave a gentle kick, and smiled. It was clear she hadn't the strength to fight her way out of one of Mary's well-made beds.

'Didn't you hear me come in?' Katherine watched Mary straighten the coverlet, put a hand on Edie's forehead, reach down into the cabinet to look for an aspirin. Aspirins, in Mary's wisdom, were the cure for all ailments, however serious. Edie swallowed it without complaint.

'There,' Mary stated, satisfied, and turned back to Katherine. 'I heard you, but I thought you were them.'

Edie looked up through lowered lashes.

'The lights were off.' Katherine was puzzled.

'I was taking a nap.' Mary looked at her, stubborn. She did not move. From downstairs, there was the sound of the front door being swung wide open so that it knocked against the pillar, and then the sound of footsteps running across the hallway, but not coming upstairs.

'TV,' Edie murmured, raising her eyebrows.

Mary held Katherine's gaze.

'She took them to the cinema in Canterbury.' Edie touched Mary's hand and looked up at Katherine.

'*She.*' Mary sighed, shaking her head as though to set aside a grief.

Footsteps could be heard downstairs, gathering, hesitant. 'Katherine?' Her father's voice. Then, more quietly, with amusement. 'Yes, of course it's her car. Who else's would it be?'

Mary clicked her tongue and Edie drew a long breath. Katherine heard the television blast overloud before it was silenced, and in the drawing room someone turned on Radio Three. She heard her father's footfall along the corridor. The entire house seemed suddenly to be full of people, moving about, making noise. Only in this room the three women looked at one another, and were quiet.

'Turn off this light, won't you?' Edie's voice was hurried and complaining. 'It's too bright. There's no need for it. It's killing my eyes.'

part | two

11

The summer had been long that year, but not so long as to spoil the lake. Willows and hazels dipped low along its banks; shade gathered beneath their branches. The herons were a menace, claiming pike. One year, after a fierce August, fish floated starved of shade to the surface and lay there belly-up and golden, rotting in the sun.

From the house, the lake was a silver plate where images of the sky emerged and lingered. Nearby, the oaks were in full sail, and all this, the ruffled motion, gave an impression that, at any moment, the house itself might move, inch by inch, towards the near horizon.

But from the outside, from any angle, that impression was reversed. Fareham appeared beached, as though long ago it had gone aground in a favourable spot from which further progress was impossible. The green sea of trees and meadows, the tilting hillsides, seemed to hold it fast.

From closer up, the mildew on the north walls looked like a high-tide mark; and from the angle of the lakeside, the building even appeared to list slightly, the surrounding trees suggesting the pits and troughs of Atlantic breakers, gathering full force mid-ocean. On this evidence, the house might be thought to have no hope, almost to be sinking, its once planned-for certainty in vain.

Katherine, waking in her old bedroom, thought only of safety. The room was virtually unchanged since her childhood. The same white wallpaper, patterned with blue cornflowers. The same relics of her teenage years: a poster of a Duane Michals print; another of a Matisse cut-out; a large cork board covered with postcards and photographs.

She had felt as she went to sleep that she might sink into the darkness, and not rise again. But now she had the sensation of finding the bedrock beneath her feet, the familiar sense of home, and she used this to lift herself back up. Perhaps she wasn't, as she had feared, a lone figure set against the greater force of another's hatred and ill-intent. 'I'll deal with it,' she told herself, and felt certain that at some point, although not yet, she would find herself again. By that she meant that she would be secure.

She thought of what had happened, and it seemed to have been removed, in the night, to a position just clear enough from the house to be no cause of immediate danger. She would deal with it at a distance, she told herself, like taking its picture through a powerful lens. If she could keep it secret for the next few days, as she had decided to do, it would be even easier once her father and Joanne had gone on honeymoon; then she would tell them about it when they returned. She pulled the blankets higher up. The bedroom was cold. A thin silver light shone through the crack in the curtains. She could hear muffled steps downstairs. She shut her eyes.

When she had arrived last night she had been shocked by more than just Fareham's appearance of emptiness. Alterations had been occurring over many months, and somehow she had not noticed. Apart from the kitchen and her bedroom, it was as though the entire place had been taken over by strangers. The changes were not major, but they were decisive. Perhaps, she thought, she should take some photographs around the house in the short time before the wedding – before her mother had left it completely. She turned over in bed and wrapped her arms round herself.

'I'm in real estate and interiors.' Joanne had adopted a serious expression the first time Katherine and she had met. 'Buy things cheap, do them up and sell them on when they're really wanted. Bit like your dad's game – speculation, gambling. Or a weather forecaster.' She had started to laugh. 'Really, though, I just like playing house.'

'She says the place needs a shake-up,' Katherine's father had warned her then, when Joanne was out of hearing. 'Hope you don't mind. She's got some quite . . .' he smiled as he searched for the word '. . . exotic ideas.'

Now furniture had been moved around into different rooms, reupholstered. Some of it had vanished, presumably sold off. There were a few new pieces: a gilt and red velvet *chaise-longue*, its purpose presumably ornamental, in the hallway. Why would anyone choose to sit there – to recline there? It looked like the showpiece of an auction, about to be removed. Certain walls had been repainted, repapered; curtains had been changed, or replaced with blinds. Leaning round the door of her father's study, Katherine had noticed that this room, at least, appeared to be little different; perhaps it was out of bounds. But she noticed that his ergonomic Aaron chair, upholstered in black leather, had been replaced by what looked like an impressive, but certainly less comfortable, Rennie Mackintosh piece. And on the desk, again with the suggestion of ornament, a quill pen, resting in a Lalique crystal holder. It was as though the house was being readied for a film crew to arrive: it had exactly that gleam of false decrepitude.

Even in the last couple of weeks, Fareham's transformation had accelerated at hothouse speed. Indeed, there were potted plants around almost every door: palms, rubber plants, rows of geraniums and orchids, even a stagy-looking aspidistra, perched like a prop on a china pedestal. The glasshouse itself was crammed with foliage pressing against the roof. Those plants inside the house, presumably, were migrants from that warmer atmosphere.

As she had walked through the ground floor last night Katherine had had the odd sensation that the garden, the long dark avenue of poplars, the running increments of rhododendrons, had followed her inside. When she sat down at the kitchen table, she had been aware of the trees rustling close to the building as though they might unhook the window catch to pursue her, one pace behind.

In a way she had been glad to see the changes to the house. It signified a kind of letting-go of the past on the part of her father, or so she hoped. It was good that he had at last handed responsibility to his wife-to-be. But although he had never paid much attention to interior decoration, preferring comfort to show, she wondered whether the changes to Fareham were more far-reaching than he might have liked. Even the use of certain rooms had been transformed. Joanne had filled with chrome and black lacquer a room that had once been used only in summer, with tall french windows opening on to the terrace. 'More elegant, Joanne thinks.' Her father had laughed as he confided this on the phone the previous month. 'Made it rather deco, I suppose it's called.'

She had peeped round the door last night. She remembered dripping on the marble tiles as a child: she'd go swimming in the lake and run in through the open window to be rubbed dry by her mother. It had been Julia's favourite room for reading. At that time it was scruffy, with garden furniture that shed basket-cane through to the hallway outside. Now, looking into the room, Katherine could not imagine ever having done this. She had turned away: she couldn't see her mother there now.

She heard someone pass along the landing. It must be late. She slipped out of bed and dressed quickly in the clothes she had bought yesterday, then pulled on an old sweater from the cupboard. She looked in her bag for her hairbrush, and remembered: there was really no need.

She cleared her throat, rubbed her breastbone, calmed her breath. Also in her bag were those four spools of film. The only ones she had left. Three meant work, the author portraits from the Langham, and with a prevision of the relief that it might bring, she saw herself shutting out the world for a few hours of concentration, conjuring up a time before the fire; the fourth, which contained all that, filled her only with dread. She had a perverse desire for the film to be blank. She thought of breaking it open, ruining it with light. She couldn't see how she might find the courage to work on it – she couldn't even bear to take it out and look at it.

She crossed to the window and raised the sash. The air was clear and cool after heavy rainfall in the night. She told herself that it was a stupid idea she had had earlier, of photographing inside the house. What was she hoping for? Her mother had gone many years ago, and now the place was changed: her ghost had been dislodged. She was too late to catch her. Almost all her photographs of her mother had been in her flat.

Katherine held tight to the window-ledge, momentarily unsteady. She felt the sharp pain of missing her mother, a profound shock after so long of being reconciled to that loss, as though her reaction had been delayed for almost half her life until now, a fuse ignited by the flames.

12

'Sure you're not sore at us for last night?' Joanne hugged Katherine as she came into the kitchen. Very blonde, a little smaller than Katherine, though less slender, more strong, Joanne held her by the forearms for a moment, before letting go. 'You sure?' She didn't seem convinced. Katherine had always felt guilty about being reserved around Joanne. More so, now that she had something to hide. But it was better than the alternative. She was relieved when Joanne turned away.

Breakfast things were on the table. Joanne reached into the fridge for more. 'Yoghurt, grapefruit, cheese slices, pancakes, muffins, juice. Sing out when you want stuff.' She shook a box of wholewheat cereal experimentally, set it aside, reached for a chocolate muffin. 'The hell with it.' She grinned at Katherine, poured a glass of soya milk. 'I'm in training.'

There were a number of new electrical appliances that Katherine hadn't noticed last night. A steamer, juice-maker, deep fryer, elaborate multi-storey toaster, cappuccino machine: objects landed from a world of speed and convenience. The kitchen appeared more antiquated because of them. Joanne threw fruit into the blender. 'Smoothie, anyone?'

These people had their own life. They were a family, with a purpose and pattern that had little to do with her. Joanne's once-airy movements had quickened; even in indecision their focus had become more deliberate. The twins ate fast, and with intent. They appeared to be in training too. Joanne was drawing the family along with her. All eyes now were on the wedding.

Only Peter seemed substantially unchanged. Perhaps more wary, Katherine considered, as though preoccupied with a conversation running only in his head. Still dark, very tall and a little hollow-chested, he had the ability to tune in and out of his immediate surroundings when it suited him. It was one of the reasons he was successful. He absorbed only what was useful, disregarded the rest. He talked of 'gutting' a book, not of reading. He would appear to have been concentrating only on that day's leader pages, when in fact he had extracted a news item from the radio along with a scrap of conversation overheard from the next room, all the while ignoring a domestic drama occurring right beside him. He had inherited his excellent hearing from his mother. But he only tuned in to what he considered relevant. Otherwise he was deaf. He recoiled from bad news as though it were a too-loud sound.

Joanne handed her a glass. 'One of my specials.'

'So what was the film last night?'

Her father grimaced. 'Some colonial fantasy.'

'Delusion, more like.' Joanne went to stand behind him,

leaning down to kiss the top of his head: a gesture of reassurance, not for him alone but for them both. Peter's hand reached up to touch her.

Katherine smiled at the children. She wasn't expected to play a part. She felt as though the family would lapse into greater intimacy if she left the room. 'You liked it?'

'Was all right.' Ellen shrugged.

'Based on a true story. Can we . . . ?' Roy slid down from his chair. Joanne nodded, and he and Ellen shuffled from the room.

'That'll be it till dinner time.' Peter straightened the *Financial Times*.

Joanne handed Katherine a plate. 'Don't mock.' She nudged him. 'They're really hard at work. They have a project.'

'The famous project no one's ever seen.' Peter folded the newspaper.

'It's the reason we had to suffer that awful movie last night.' Joanne poured coffee and smiled at Katherine. 'Sure you didn't mind being alone?'

'Edie and Mary were here. Really, I was fine.' She wished they would make light of it. She didn't want their attention on her. She had the impression that Joanne had scented a weakness in her and would not be satisfied until she had run it to earth. She tried not to care that Joanne had referred to the house as though Katherine had not spent her life growing up here. Why should she mind being here without them? But last night she had minded very much. 'It was an easy thing to forget.'

Her father set down the paper. 'Now we know you're hurt.

Come on.' He pulled out a chair so that she could sit down beside him. 'I didn't realise we'd be back so late. Heaven knows how I could be so stupid, but there it is. Your old man's getting dim. A lot on my plate at the moment.'

Joanne stood up and cocked her hip at him, a hand at her waist. 'So that's what your wedding is now – a lot on your plate.'

Peter laughed and held up his hands. 'I'm no good at this. I meant work, as you know.' He turned back to Katherine. 'She's pretending. Ignore her.'

'Everything OK?' Joanne was waiting for his answer, too, as she poured more juice, pushed the toast rack towards Peter. He shook his head. Katherine had the impression that both he and Joanne were skirting round a subject not yet discussed but touched upon.

'Sure, absolutely.' Peter leant back in his chair. 'Just been an odd week. A lot to fix. Few things came unstuck. Bad timing.' He waved his hands as though to clear away the mess in that one gesture.

Joanne went to sit on his lap. She slipped an arm round him. He leant against her. Katherine looked away, took a slice of toast.

'I don't mind being on your plate, honey.' Joanne tugged him close and smiled at Katherine over the top of his head. 'A secret, Katie.' She covered Peter's ears as though to stop him hearing. 'You know what's been keeping your father from marrying me all this time?'

Katherine hadn't been aware that it was so much time. She sipped her coffee.

'My reputation.' Joanne raised her eyebrows. 'It's true. But I had a few deals come off better than expected this year, more hot prospects on the go. Earned a mint on a place I did in Baton Rouge, and snapped something up just north-west of New Orleans on River Road, plantation country – it's a ruin but it's a mansion underneath, more or less, built around the same time as this place, and well . . .' She tilted her head as though contemplating a large stack of money. 'Your father, anyhow, had been anxious about my appearing like a gold-digger.' She smirked. 'He was worried for my reputation. Can you believe it? Spilt the beans the other day.'

She touched the corner of her mouth with the tip of her tongue, as though cleaning away a bead of saliva. 'But now I'm safe. I'm probably more loaded than he is!' She threw back her head and a hacking ex-smoker's laugh popped out.

Peter's face was grim. Joanne ruffled his hair. He pressed it, discreetly, into place. Katherine ate her toast in silence.

She could see that her father adored Joanne. It hadn't been in doubt. But it puzzled her that he minded so much for her reputation. 'Mud-slinging. Forget it' – that was his usual response to bad press, the stories in the financial columns that seemed to play up any news that harmed his company. Katherine was surprised he had not taken this attitude with Joanne. She had always supposed Joanne cared even less than Peter about other people's opinions of her. Now Katherine could see how she might have been wrong in this assumption. It really did matter to her. Those jokes about being a gold-digger were just a double bluff.

Joanne smiled broadly at Katherine. She wore a sweatshirt with a red tartan bunny appliquéd on to the front. The rabbit wore a red silk bow, which flopped and quivered. Joanne twirled it round a pink-nailed finger. She seemed happy enough with the way everything was going. It seemed to thrill her to have landed so much money on her own; not because she minded about being rich but more as though it were a trick that might earn her the approval of those she loved. Katherine was quite sure her father wasn't guilty of withholding approval for that reason. Why would he? He had suffered. Joanne had ended his penitence. He adored her for it. That he had minded about her reputation was just one way of going public with how much he cared.

'Oh, you great big—' Joanne didn't finish her sentence, but leant down to press her face against Peter's hair, clinging to him. 'I do love you.' In appearance and manner, she had never created so stark a contrast with his previous wife as she did at that moment. It was a shock for Katherine to hear Joanne say those words openly to her father. She couldn't recall her parents ever being as demonstrative as that.

Peter's face relaxed with gratitude, and when his eyes met Katherine's, she understood something about him that she had not fully realised before. The fact that Joanne was so precisely unlike Julia was, at the very least, what made her possible for him. There would be no reminders of his first wife; the less Joanne resembled her, the more Julia's ghost would stay away.

It worked for Katherine, too. Watching her father enraptured with another love removed her mother one stage further into memory. She wanted his happiness. But seeing it made her lonely: she would have liked to see her mother more. She was like a child bawling in an empty room for a presence that solved everything. She was frightened of the darkness she felt on her own.

She chewed a slice of toast, forced it down with a gulp of milk. She glanced out of the window. A wood-pigeon had made her jump, its weight sending the branch of a pine tree snapping upwards.

In her heart, wishing more than anything that she could lessen the burden of her secret, she had the intimation that, in fact, it would solve nothing to share it with these two people. It was her mother she wanted. She stared down at her plate, bit her lip hard.

'Isn't he a darling?' Joanne patted Peter's knee and stood up. 'More coffee?'

13

'I'll walk with you, if you like.' Peter leant out of his ground-floor study window. Katherine was half-way across the terrace that led out to the lawn. 'This stuff can wait.' He waved a sheaf of papers and she watched him disappear from view and re-emerge at the french windows.

It was late morning, and the sky was clear apart from a few clouds high up in the south. There seemed to be no sign of rain, but the air held the damp hush of it, and the trees hissed with sudden gusty bolts of breeze. Shadows were quick across the grass, which was soft underfoot; the crushed stems remained as prints behind her. She stopped at the balustraded limits of the terrace, and looked back at the house, shielding her eyes from the sun's white brightness.

The sash window of Edie's room was raised up high. Pale blue curtains billowed inwards. She insisted on fresh air as the key to good health. Even when there was a frost covering the park, she preferred to sit swaddled in blankets than suffer the indignity of central heating.

Last night, she and Mary had seemed complicit in their feelings about Joanne. Katherine supposed that, in part, it might be
an attitude adopted for her benefit, neither woman wanting to
be disloyal to her mother. But they had appeared guarded when,
had they so wished, they might very easily have been open in
their disapproval – if that was what it was. It was as though Peter
was the one whose behaviour they disparaged: an indulged child,
who didn't know any better than to be foolish. But Katherine
couldn't see his error, either. She wondered if he had been heavy-
handed in defending Joanne's right to fill the house with what
Mary had once referred to as 'expensive show-off *knick-knacks*'.
She had poked at a Perspex Rietveld chair as she said this. 'Sit in
that?'

She supposed it had more to do with their desire to keep the
house as it was. Edie's room, noticeably, was unchanged. She
stuck to her Irish linen sheets and coarse woollen blankets; said
the mere thought of duvets made her feel 'spineless'; and dressed
more formally for dinner whenever she had spotted Joanne and
the children 'slouching about', as she put it, in jeans and sweat-
shirts. It wasn't malice; Katherine was quite sure, that made her
behave thus. It was a combination of stubbornness and regret. A
refusal to allow that times had changed; a desire that they should
not have taken her along with them.

Her father called out, and was laughing as he came towards
her. Katherine had her camera with her; she took the picture.
'My father, pre-nuptial.' She smiled. He had been almost running
from the house.

'Don't tell Joanne this,' he spoke low and quiet, 'but I'm glad to be out, just to get away from the arrangements.'

Katherine laughed with him. 'It's not that bad, surely?'

He squeezed her arm. 'Best get out of earshot before I answer that.'

They set out across the grass towards the bottom gate. A low stone wall separated the lawn from the parkland beyond, and the cows were huddled beneath the nearest trees. He glanced back at the house before he spoke again. 'She's a wonderful woman, Katherine.' She waited for him to continue. 'She's wonderful just to be taking me on.'

'You're not such a bad catch.' She nudged against him.

'Right.' He seemed uncertain, and frowned. 'Things have been – lately things have been difficult.'

'Between you?'

'No, business. It's a sensitive time. I've had people on my case. Been some hard decisions, which I haven't liked. It hasn't been easy.'

Her father never talked to her about business. She would have hesitated to say, with any precision, what his 'business interests' amounted to. He seemed to exist above that plain of specifics: his company bought and sold other companies – often a brand was the only asset they possessed; talk of speculation and futures made his work appear to occupy the realm of theory. The very fact that he had mentioned it at all made her wonder how serious things might be. Was he in financial trouble? She had heard nothing to suggest it. Bits and pieces often filtered through to her second-hand, either from Edie, in whom he confided – at least, he had in the past – or through the news.

He shrugged, walked a little ahead of her. 'You know how it is.'

'Sure.' Katherine tried to keep her voice light. They passed beneath the canopied shadow of an oak tree; she was glad of that concealment.

Now would be the time to say something, to tell him not to worry but that she knew all about being laid low by sudden trouble. She thought of the reel of film, the pictures of the fire, hidden inside her makeup bag in her luggage, still unpacked in her old bedroom. It had been an instinct to hide that film. The first thing she had done when she got to the hotel was to empty the camera and stash the film alongside the tubs and pencils, the tubes of cream. In her mind's eye it smouldered there.

She still couldn't understand the part of herself that had needed to record something at which, in life, she had been barely able to look. It would have happened – would have been true – whether or not she was there to take its picture. It was as though she needed extra proof, yet now was too ashamed to see that the proof was all her own making: she was the one who had held the camera. Now she couldn't even bear to see the film. It felt like an invitation for disaster to follow her right down here to Kent.

By 'disaster' she meant Miles, and was horrified that, with the intervening nights, her fear had not dispelled but strengthened. That, too, was an instinct, given weight with dreams – she assured herself that she had nothing else to go on. Just impressions of suspicion and threat. Things replayed in her mind until the image built up to something more than memory: a definite sense of what might yet be possible. Taking those pictures had started something. A photograph was never the end of any story.

Now she felt the menace of what might happen next in every shadow, behind every covering tree. She had left the house to go for a walk to test herself. She would be damned if she gave in to paranoia. But when she saw her father coming out to join her, her heart had lifted. Without him, she wouldn't have got further than the bottom gate.

Last night, when she threw her luggage into the wardrobe without unpacking, she had hated to think of the unworn clothes she now possessed. Aside from a few things left at Fareham, most of them scruffy or outgrown, all her real clothes were gone now. But she badly wanted that familiar shell back, and felt deceitful as she ripped out the price tag from a pair of jeans and hoped Joanne and her father didn't notice that everything she wore was new. Of course they neither noticed nor cared, and it was then, perversely, that she wished they had at least said something. Was she really so hard, so definite, as to be unchanged? She disliked herself for being able to carry that off.

But she missed her old clothes. She had not suspected that they might have been important to her. As it turned out, she attached a sentimental significance to particular shirts – a couple had belonged to her mother; there was a pair of cowboy boots she had bought in Nevada that had always cheered her up, her 'lucky boots'; a long cashmere coat she had had for years, a man's coat, that had been given to her by an author on a cold day. 'Look at you.' She had arrived at his house in the Catskills just ahead of a blizzard, in a thin sweater, hatless. 'Borrow this,' he had insisted. 'You can post it with the prints.' By the time she arrived back in New York, that coat had become a gift. 'Keep it, it's yours. Don't take this the wrong way, but you looked like you could use a good coat.' It was true. And now the coat was gone.

She raised a hand and touched her hair. Miles had said he loved it. Cutting it off had been an attempt to keep herself clear of all that. But even cropped it felt like an extravagance, or as though it might be harmful in some way – the short dark wick of a bomb. When her father had seen it last night, he had stepped back a pace, as though surprising himself with liking it. 'Hey, you look great. Very . . .' He hesitated. 'Gamine!'

Joanne had walked round her, as though assessing the effect. 'You certainly have the head for it,' she had said, frowning as she tugged at her own hair: long and bright, the blondeness grown slightly stiff at the ends. 'Not me. I need all the help I can get.' She had giggled, pinched Peter's arm for a denial as they went off to bed.

Now Katherine glanced at her father. He had stopped, and was looking back at the house. She hated having this secret from him. It made her feel guilty. She wondered if it was ridiculous to keep it from him: perhaps he would simply take it in his stride, suggest they keep it between themselves, not tell Joanne – perhaps she was the one whom it would really upset. But his suggestion of difficulty, of having his own troubles, held her back. When he turned to her, his forehead was creased with worry. 'I can't be too easy for anyone. I get a lot of things wrong.' He stood a few feet away from Katherine and, with the sun behind him, she couldn't quite make out his expression. His shoulders drooped, and he shifted his weight from one foot to the other. If it hadn't seemed implausible to her, she might have thought that his posture was the one that most suggested the desire for confession.

He stiffened, noticing something at the house, and Katherine turned to see Mary walking slowly round the side wall from the annexe, carrying what looked like a large basket of washing. She seemed to have stepped out from another season: the sky showed signs of more rain and the air was too cool for washing to dry on the line. Peter appeared to be watching closely as Mary bent down, unfolded large pieces of red material – rugs, by the look of it, Katherine supposed that made more sense – and pegged them out on the line. Then she began to beat them steadily with a brush. At this distance, the activity looked futile: no dust could be seen. It seemed sad and pointless, as though she had run out of things to do; as though this were a last rite of some kind.

Katherine could feel the tension of her father's watching. A blackbird fussed in the fallen leaves, its eye upon them.

'She was good to take me on, honey.' He turned back to his daughter, walking past her, further away from the house towards the line of trees.

14

Mary first arrived at Fareham in 1976, when Katherine was three years old. It was high summer, towards the end of a hot day in June, and she simply walked up the driveway to the house and stayed. That, at least, was how it was remembered.

Studying a photograph of her with her father and the new nanny, taken the following week, Katherine was not sure whether it was this, in fact, that she best recalled: the image of Mary reaching down to lift her up, her dark legs slender, her lean silhouette outlined beneath a pale green cotton dress. At that time her hair was braided in cornrows close against her skull, and Katherine could remember the feel of them beneath her fingertips.

The photograph had been taken on Mary's birthday. Julia was behind the lens. The family was having a celebratory lunch outside on the front lawn. In the background, half in the shadow of a cedar of Lebanon, a trestle table could be seen, covered with a white cloth, weighted in place by a stack of china plates and a row of tumblers. A breeze caught its hem.

The way Mary explained her arrival to Katherine, much later on, was that she had been working nights as a nanny, and by day in 'a dead-end job in Tooting Bec', as secretary to a chartered surveyor, whom she did not like. He assumed too much familiarity, and recently had started to suggest she might like to have 'a nice quiet drink' with him after work. She had read the signs, and known that soon she would have to leave. It had happened before. The one thing that had made the work tolerable was that she had to spend time at Companies House, fetching details of company records for her boss. This part she found interesting. It was what had given her the idea to look up her family's history. So, on her days off, she went to the Public Records Office in Kew and set to work, and that was how she traced herself, through her maternal line, to Fareham: her great-great-grandmother had worked there in the mid-1800s.

'You found me, in a manner of speaking.'

This was how she had put it to Julia. She was twenty-four, and she had taken the train to Kent from London on her day off. She had never been into the English countryside before. She had travelled through it on a train to Portsmouth, to take a ferry; she had gone on a coach to Manchester; and she had been to Welwyn Garden City, where she had had a temporary job. But she had never before travelled into the countryside, alighted at a rural station platform. 'No one else got off at my stop.' She described the silence and the scorched grass, the stillness of the full June trees. The station was no more than a platform, a signal-box and a small, covered shelter. A few cottages stood nearby, but that was all. She set off on foot with her map. Fareham was just under two miles away.

She explained that for some reason she had supposed the house might be empty, possibly even derelict. She had discovered a photograph of Fareham that showed it during the war, when it had been used for a short time as a military hospital. She had known what to look for. She had intended simply to take a quick glance around, and then go.

'But then I saw you,' and this was the part of the story that Katherine had always loved to hear. 'You were playing with your mother on the front lawn as I arrived. Just the two of you, laughing away with things spread out over the grass. She had you balanced on her legs and you had your arms and feet stretched out like you were pretending to fly. You didn't see me at first, but when you did you jumped up and started waving as though you knew me. Your mother asked me straight in for tea, soon as I'd said hello, without even knowing what I was about.'

She had not thought that she might leave London or her job quite so soon. But when she and Julia got round to talking, and Mary mentioned that she had been thinking of moving on, it turned out that by chance the au pair had left that summer, and Julia had been meaning to find someone to help with Katherine. Mary had replied that she could do with the change, and by the time Peter arrived home, his wife was making plans for her to move into the annexe.

'She's virtually family, Peter.' When Mary left the room, Julia explained what she had told her: that her great-great-grandmother had worked in the house when it was first built. For some reason he had not seemed surprised. Her connection to the family was not discussed again.

Mary was hired, and when she mentioned that she was doubly pleased because next week was her twenty-fifth birthday, both Julia and Peter had insisted that she celebrate her quarter-century with them, and with her new charge, who was delighted with this idea. And so it was decided. She quit her job and moved to Kent. She had no other family in England. She had never known her father. Her mother had remarried, and now lived with her new husband's family in Montréal. They were not close.

She had lived at Fareham for a few years, then moved on, back to London where she had had a child, although she never married. Again, a father was not mentioned. She had returned to Fareham at Edie's request, to be her nurse, when Mary's daughter, Alice, had grown up and gone away to college.

Now, out walking with her father, Katherine had sensed him half regarding the house once Mary had disappeared from view. Her movements through the building could easily be traced, even when she could not be seen. She had an order about her days that did not shift. In this respect, as in many others, she was unlike Joanne, whose manner it was to flit, and to pounce upon ideas and novelties with the surprised hunger of a child. Mary had method, and this was evident now, as sash windows were raised on the ground floor, the french windows propped open to let the swift breeze penetrate the house.

'We're lucky she's here, you know.' Peter stopped at the low wall that separated the parkland from the lawn. He had his back to Katherine, and she could not see his expression. Joanne's Range Rover could be heard on the drive. She must be taking the children up to town.

'Is that why you're marrying her, Pa, to stop her doing a bunk?' She had supposed he was referring to Joanne. Moments before, he had mentioned her, describing the quality of independence in her that he so admired.

He turned to Katherine and stared at her, as though he had spoken his thoughts aloud: had he said too much? Katherine was puzzled.

'Sure, so she doesn't do a bunk.' He opened the gate and they went back up to the house.

15

For a number of years after her mother had died, in certain rooms and at certain times of day, the memories would come so thick and fast, and would seem to land so heavily, covering everything, that Katherine had had to blink to see the scene as it then was.

Her mother's death was a high wall separating her from her previous self. Sometimes she would feel that she might peer over it and find herself still there, or look for the gate beneath the trees, turn the handle and simply walk right through.

It rattled her to realise that she could not return to that place where she would have given anything to be. But time passed, bringing changes with it, and those had left their marks. She became a different person, a stranger to her earlier self.

Now there were few rooms left at Fareham for those memories to gather and take shape. It was not as though the process of painting and reupholstering had loosened their hold on the house; but it had forced them into ever smaller corners, caused them to gather most powerfully around the people who had been a part of them.

Katherine had anticipated, before she arrived last night at Fareham, that her secret would be impossible to conceal. Since then there had been chances for confession. Yet she felt like a person running against the flow of a crowd: the family was moving away from her, towards something that would only set her further apart. Taking pictures of the wedding was confirmation that she was, as she felt herself to be, an outsider.

Now she was standing in the unlit corridor that led to the darkroom. The decorators had not been here yet. An open door behind her, closed door ahead, meant that her shadow was cast in front of her. Her right hand touched the wall: chalky pale green impasto, unevenly plastered beneath, where the shape of the building, like a gut or artery, swelled and billowed in silken curves. She knew every kink and chip of it. She lowered her hand to thigh height where her memory dwelt strongest: her ten-year-old fingertips running along the corridor to find her mother at the other end, behind the darkroom door. At this height the paint-work was smooth, unresisting as powdered skin, cool to the touch. Although she did not move, the floorboard beneath her creaked, as though just then nudged by a hidden current, the tide gathering to turn.

She drew breath and listened to the sounds of the day stirring in the body of the house. The light was clear and green. The air smelt as it always had: the dried grass scent that reminded Katherine of hauling the dinghy through the few yards of meadow to the lake. The heads of barley would snap, catching in the rowlocks, and the slither of tall grass would gather speed where the hillside hurried the small boat towards the water. It was the scent as the boat struck the surface, with the grass broken and the insects dancing and disturbed. She breathed it in.

Through the cotton of her shirt and jeans, she could feel the cold wall press against her bones. She closed her eyes and saw the rows of grey boxes in her flat, arranged according to the years, each full of prints.

In the green corridor she slid to the floor and felt the heat running up the stairwell to her darkroom, saw the paper curling and buckling, the ignition of her life that she had unwittingly prepared for: the long muslin drapes where flames would have run; the doors propped open to let the draughts blow through and hurry up the fire. It was the tail end of summer she had hoped to catch, and she saw herself moving quickly through the flat, raising windows, and, on one day in particular, stacking old papers ready to be cleared out. Miles had been there. He had helped her clear the flat's junk into piles and boxes – into tinder. It was a few weeks before they split up, and partly for this reason she had left some of those boxes where they were. A kind of sentimentalism had touched her: she hadn't liked to erase that last joint act.

She buried her head beneath her arms and rested it on her knees. She remembered the heat of the day – it was late July – and she had been sitting on a tower of old papers when he came back from the shop: he had been buying chilled beer, and they sat together in the window to drink it, watching the City emptying for the weekend, its noises whirring down to nothing. Later, they had gone out to eat at the Italian restaurant on the corner of the next street, and she had been very happy. It was a day of truce between too many arguments.

She could see the flames running along the rugs in her sitting room and rushing the glass to break out to the night-time air. She thought of Miles going to her flat – had he had a key cut, without her knowledge? – and throwing a match that destroyed everything: love, trust, and all security. It was an old and buried feeling, that loss. She recognised it too well. Sitting on the floor at the height of her ten-year-old self, she remembered perfectly the first time, and one day in particular: running through to the annexe darkroom in disbelief, looking for her mother who, by then, could not be found.

The door to the annexe opened, and Mary stepped through to find Katherine crying in the dark. She ran unhesitating towards her, as though she had half expected to find her there. 'Is it a boy?' This had been her first question for years now, at any sign of joy or sorrow. 'Is it Miles who's made you unhappy?'

Katherine said nothing.

'I see, I see.' Mary appeared to take her silence for agreement. She held her so close that Katherine could feel the muscles of Mary's thighs pressed against her own, and her ribcage swelling with emotion. 'No man should have that power.' She stood back, drawing out a handkerchief, wiping Katherine's face dry as though she were a child again. 'No man, no one at all, do you hear?' She shook Katherine, very gently, and smiled. 'You're alive, aren't you?'

She led her away down the corridor into the annexe.

Entering the room, the first thing Katherine saw was a large brown box, labelled with her own name, on the table.

'Oh, those.' Mary waved, dismissing them. 'Photographs.' She raised her eyebrows. 'Looks like a real jumble. Your mother's. Haven't gone through them so I can't say. Baby snaps, probably, school snaps, holiday snaps, in-the-garden snaps, at-a-party snaps.' She grinned. 'Snaps! I rescued them for you – from her.'

'Joanne?'

'She says she wants to turn the coach-house into a – what did she say it was? A *dacha*, if you can believe it.' She laughed and patted the box. 'They were in the roof along with the pigeons. Heaven knows how they came to be hidden away up there. They were going to be stored but they needed sorting first – the damp was getting to them.'

Sunlight filled the room. Katherine blew her nose and pushed at the cardboard box. It was heavy. There were years of photographs inside, and there were other boxes. She would go to the attic later to check. She wiped her face, pushed aside her hair.

'See? You're back already.' Mary left the room, returned with a plate of pink-iced sponge cake, smiling. 'You want some cake now that you're better?'

16

She had the room to herself. Mary had gone into the garden, and Katherine could see her snipping green beans. 'Skinny damn crop this year, too much damp about.' She had left the room with a pair of antique silver grape scissors, twirling them on her index finger. 'Those kids have nabbed my kitchen scissors for their *project*.' She narrowed her eyes and looked at Katherine with a question, unasked, before she left, her right shoulder raised in defiance. 'Have to use these, and if anyone complains, well—' She snipped the scissors in the air.

The cardboard was sealed with packing tape, but the glue had perished and it was easy enough to pull away. She wiped her hands clean on her jeans. The box released the scent of mildew and something faintly pickled – the formaldehyde tang of fixative and dampened chemicals. It was crammed with photographs. The top layer had adhered to the brown cardboard and was ruined, although many of the scenes were identifiable. Polaroid snaps taken in the garden, a few black-and-white contact sheets, half-cropped test prints of one of her birthday parties. As Mary had said, 'snaps'. Katherine recognised the images. The final prints had been kept in an album.

Beneath were colour shots that she recognised as off-cuts of her mother's work. Rejects and duplicates, documentary stuff. A line of refugees standing close against a barbed-wire fence, seeming to hang there like black wool snared in briar. Red earth stretched away on either side of the fence. Which side had they wished to be? It was unclear. A small child perched on a tin roof, smiling and waving, a Kalashnikov slung across his back. A dried-up lake bed, with watermarks around the banks, a jetty leading nowhere. Her mother's handwriting was scribbled across some of the images, notes to herself from over twenty years ago.

Indirectly, because of images like these, Katherine had first met Miles. It was where their work had coincided. She had been at the opening of a group exhibition where some of her mother's pictures were being shown. He wrote mainly financial news, but at that point he had been working on a feature about press morality and human rights. They fell into conversation, and he blushed when she told him her name. 'In the family business.' His manner changed, as if he was studying her from a slight distance, or examining a copy for flaws. 'But she quit, didn't she?' Miles had not appeared to want to pry when he stated this.

It was a difficult subject. Katherine had been too young at the time to understand the decision; she was glad simply that her mother had started to spend more time at home. And while Julia Clements had given up documentary photography – and this was news in the trade – she still took pictures. That she had quit, as

Miles put it, was assumed to be an aspect of her femininity: the going had got too tough, after all. Her mother's reply was silence. She trained her lens on the English landscape, and critics praised her poetry. They read in it a pastoral yearning where none existed. Although few saw it, her landscapes were her most selfish work: the attempt to heal a damaged eye.

The story of her decision was half told. Katherine still puzzled at it. It was seldom spoken of.

But as she and Miles stood in front of the pictures, he had touched her arm lightly: a kind of brotherly cuff. 'I love your work, you know.' He stressed 'your' and she looked at him again.

'Oh, come on.' She smiled. It was just a line. She didn't think he knew who she was, beyond being her mother's daughter.

He reeled off a list of portraits: of writers, painters, other photographers.

'What are you, a dust-jacket junkie?' She was surprised: he really did know what she had done.

'I saw your show in Antwerp, they were all there. I was at a conference on pollution. Toxic emissions.' Miles widened his eyes and laughed. 'And that was just the lectures. It was in 1995, so an early show for you, right?'

They talked until the crowd thinned, and left, and then he gave her his card, crossing out his work numbers and scribbling his home and cellphone. She called him the following week.

As she looked down at the pictures, she remembered how he had sounded that first time she spoke to him on the telephone. She honestly hadn't recognised his voice when he answered. He had sounded different: more secretive than she remembered him, as though just at that moment he had been reading something personal about her – oddly guilty, and annoyed with himself for having revealed his interest. Later, when they met, he confessed: he had been looking her up on the Internet, and the trace had led him to her family. 'Quite the little rich girl, aren't you?' He had laughed; she had taken it as a joke. She supposed he was just being light-hearted, and hadn't seen it as something he might come to hold against her.

She shifted the box. The damp had dried and left the card-board stiff and brittle. With the top layer spread out on the table, the room had started to smell of old clothes. She supposed Mary wouldn't be happy with her going through it here, in her part of the house; she gathered up the pictures and carried the box through to the darkroom, at the far end of the annexe.

She entered the room backwards, kicking open the door, and pulled the cord for white light. It was the first time she had been in here since she had arrived last night, and she was relieved to find the room unchanged. Everything was as she had left it: she was safe.

She set the box on one of the benches and rubbed her face. She would look at her own films later today, those author portraits, and, working, she would find her equilibrium again.

It was then that she noticed, hanging on the line to dry, a number of prints she had forgotten. She filled the kettle to make coffee, unclipped the photographs and laid them out on the white Formica table top. It took her a moment to remember where the pictures had been taken. She did not recognise them immediately. Her inner eye was still on the photographs in the box.

There were nine prints. Africa, like her mother's work, but this time Gabon, Libreville — that hotel-trip favour now seeming like a lifetime away.

She spread out the photographs in a row. There was a kind of sequence. They weren't the shots for the hotel's brochure, but the other images, the ones taken by stealth with her Leica. She hadn't remembered leaving them here. She studied each in turn, trying to see what was there.

They were inconsequential images, bad pictures, nothing at all. She saw all the other photographs she had ever taken burning, their significance erased to ash. It was a kind of insult that these remained, and she gathered them together meaning to rip them up. Her hands were shaking. She felt the weight of the stack of pictures, the surface of them like skin on a hot day. They were hers, and she had so few. She hesitated, looked for a folder, and hid them out of sight.

She spooned coffee into the pot, wiped a mug clean, and tried to think about when she must have made those prints. It would have been the last time she was here, before the fire. She had driven down from London for the night at her father's request, to 'help Joanne with arrangements'. He had confessed he was worried about a lapse in taste. 'She has some rather extravagant ideas about silk swags in the gazebo.' He had laughed, but sounded anxious. 'See if you can't talk her out of it.' Katherine had agreed to try, but Joanne had seen straight through her. 'I get it, he thinks

I'm going too far.' She laughed and shook her head. 'You guys have no idea.'

Katherine had taken her father aside. 'Best if you don't get involved,' she had warned. 'You'll only make it worse.' Having driven down for nothing, she had gone to work. The hotel job itself was done, the prints delivered. But she had had this other film, the secret film, so she spent the afternoon developing that, running off a few prints. She was just messing about, seeing if there was anything of interest, and there hadn't been much. It looked as if this time her hunch had been misguided, a red herring. One glance could tell her that.

She had made nine prints, and taken the negatives back to London, where, with the many other things she had meant to look at again, later, they had been destroyed.

17

When photography began, photographs often went with words: explanatory texts divulged the secrets that the pictures held too tightly to be seen. The texts exposed the pictures' significance: 'Traktir Bridge, La Tchernaia Valley', an 1855 salt print by James Robertson, might have been no more than a picture of a heath, a pastoral study, with remote trees and a distant chalk escarpment, a head of clouds coming in across the plain. In fact it was the scene of one of the fiercest Crimean battles: French Zouaves and Sardinians against the Russian infantry.

It became fashionable, a hundred years later, to rip out such images from their bindings and put them in frames, give them only their title, or nothing, or even something new. Then Traktir Bridge might become 'Rural Scene' and all that blood and destruction, gunfire and the reek of saltpetre was lost beneath a false name.

Katherine lifted a buried handful of pictures from the top of the box, and spread them on the white Formica table in the darkroom.

One picture: Julia standing on the terrace, the house behind her. Her dark hair was in a high pony-tail, her face tanned. She was wearing a short white cotton dress, patterned with small black parasols, her beauty predating Katherine's memory of her, as though she had simply been shot in sharper focus.

Another showed Julia and Peter together. It looked like the same day, but who had taken the picture? Neither held an automatic button. It had the hurried joy of a photograph barely meant, snapped by someone inexpert with the machine. Her mother leant forwards slightly, Peter's hand around her waist, and her lips were parted as though she was giving instructions to whoever held the camera. Her father grinned, and with his teeth bared he appeared oddly guilty. He often looked this way.

Katherine smiled. The next showed her, aged around eight, perhaps, maybe younger, with her mother's slender arms looped right round her. Had she herself, as a child, taken that other picture?

She recognised the tree – a horse-chestnut in the garden behind the house. In the background were two pear trees and a rope hammock, where Katherine would lie on warm evenings and listen out for the sounds of silver on china, the thump of dishes that would mean dinner.

Her mother played the piano still, often at that time of day. She gave it up later, citing rheumatism, although her hands, as Katherine remembered them, stayed supple and straight to the end. Bach two- and three-part inventions were her favourite. She played them as though they were Schubert, which did not ruin them, but gave them a gentle, musing quality that meant Glenn Gould came as a shock, the first time Katherine heard him. Was it even the same composer?

And so she would listen to this as well, and the thrushes growing hushed in the high dry leaves, the cattle stamping in the field, and the horse-flies rising and circling, the raindrop tapping of them where they landed on the mirrored surface of the rhodo-dendrons.

Here was another photograph, taken inside the house. A table set for dinner, with little available light, and the centrepiece a low cut-glass vase of roses, overblown, as on the point of falling – Edward Steichen roses. That was Steichen's trick for still-lifes: he put them in a box, with one pinhole of light focused on them – roses, pears, apples – the exposure drawn out over hours. The final image had the quality of a pencil sketch, layer upon layer of lead and light. Steichen had tried this trick on Garbo – her hands, raised to her face, held open her eyes, unblinking until the shutter blinked first.

In that dinner-table shot, shadows filled the room with smoke; the crystal seemed wet where the last sunlight fell upon it; marmorial, the damask curtains fell in thick folds to the pale stone floor. And, by the french windows, half out of frame but clear enough, she could see the shadow of a bare leg, a child's, just leaving the picture. Hers, perhaps. She bent closer. That part of the image was indistinct, but no, she corrected her assumption, it was a black girl's leg. She supposed Mary must have brought her daughter Alice to Fareham. But if that was so, why had Katherine not known her when she was little? She studied the pictures, looking for another shot taken on that day, another clue. But there was nothing.

She set it aside from the others. If it was Alice, why hadn't other visits followed this one? She remembered what she had always thought of as the first time she met Mary's daughter: Edie had asked her to persuade Mary to return to Fareham. She had been happy to have an excuse to visit her old nanny, and when she arrived at Mary's house in Vauxhall, a girl was just leaving. Around her own age and height, late teenage, lithe and smiling, a tin-foil wrapped cake in one hand, a bag of books in the other, she had been kissing Mary goodbye at the top of the steps to her house.

'She's in a hurry,' Mary had manoeuvred the girl forwards out of the house, as though to speed her on her way, and they had barely exchanged greetings before she was gone.

'Was that your daughter?' Katherine had watched the girl half jog away along the street to catch a passing bus. She had been on her way to meet some friends: 'They're in a band,' she had waved over her shoulder. 'If I miss their set they'll kill me!' It was months later that they were reintroduced, once Mary had come back to live in Kent with Edie. Now they were on familiar terms, but that first impression had stuck with Katherine: of the younger girl always on the move away from her, inhabiting a different world with a life and friends of her own. She would have liked to know her better.

Katherine shone the light back on to the print. She would

ask her father if Mary had ever brought Alice down here for a visit after she'd left, solve the puzzle that way. The image was blurred, as though the girl had stood too long and was starting to fidget. Her shadow fell on the curtains – long since gone, even before Joanne's blitz – a light shade of violet, the colour of dried lavender. In their hems, Katherine remembered, was a row of dressmaker's lead weights. She knew this because once, intrigued by the feel of them as she lay on the floor to play, she had cut through the waxed cotton seams, hoping for hidden treasure, gold ingots: no, she discovered, only stamped lead bearing the brand of the haberdasher where they had been bought. She could remember even now how guilty it had made her feel.

But how strange to have remembered all this about a pair of curtains yet not know the identity of that girl. She wondered if there were more clues. She peered inside the box.

Beneath the top layer of off-cuts and rejects she could see a fat stack of contact sheets. She slipped her hand beneath them and felt the stiff edge of photographic paper – inches deep. The sensation was thrilling. There were so many rooms, compartments of time opening their doors, when she had believed there was nothing new to be discovered.

'Katherine?' She heard her father outside the darkroom door, his feet shuffling on the lino. 'Are you in there? Red light or white?'

She hesitated. Much later, she would wonder what instinct had convinced her, with that image in her hand – the girl's leg leaving the room, the shadow on the curtains, retreating – that he should not enter.

'Red light, Dad,' she lied. 'Just finishing up, won't be a minute.' She heard him shift his weight.

'I'm making lunch. You want some?' His voice held a plea. 'Everyone's out apart from Edie. No rush. Come through when you're ready.' He cleared his throat. 'You OK?' He still had not left.

'Fine, sure. Won't be long.' She heard him walk away.

She folded the lid back across the box, then slowly, uncertainly, unwound a piece of tape from the reel and sealed it. She put it under the table and tore off the label Mary had put there that read: 'Photographs for Katherine'. It said too much.

She turned off the white light and went to find her father.

18

Just past one o'clock and the house was cool and still. Few sounds: Peter chopping onions on a teak block; Edie upstairs in her room, rattling a Biro against her bedside table before pressing quick solutions to the crossword in the *Telegraph*.

'All the news I want to hear,' she told Katherine once, 'is right here in my crossword. Vocabulary chess!' She nodded in satisfaction. '"Brothers sensitive to plates". Eight across?' She sighed. 'You should know this, dearie. Goncourt. The Goncourt Brothers. "Sickness sensitises the soul like a photographic plate."' She settled herself more comfortably against her pillows. 'Oh, these easy ones exhaust me, they really do. Without a fight, a crossword can be very tiring.' Katherine could see that Edie was delighted with herself.

'When this goes,' she had said on another occasion, tapping the side of her head, her breath narrowing in her throat, her voice in earnest, 'when this goes, shoot me. Promise?'

Katherine had hugged her. 'No way. Forget it.'

She had had to leave the room so that Edie couldn't see her

expression. Recently Edie's health had seemed to slip from her, as though she were spooling it out idly through her hands, too tired to keep tight hold of it any more.

Katherine passed through the hallway and stopped for a moment by the back door that led out on to the terrace. She could see Mary in the bottom field, a wicker basket looped over her arm, green carrot fronds trailing. Her hat matched the sky, the washed colour of royal blue chalk.

The red hall carpet was in the process of being lifted. By the weekend, and the wedding, the black-and-white marble tiles would be revealed. It was up in just one corner, by the back door, reminding Katherine of hopscotch as a girl. Her feet were too big now to land square on the tiles.

'These would look great in my new place on River Road.' When Katherine last came down to Fareham Joanne had been crouching down to touch them when she said this, stroking the smooth Purbeck surface as though it were a mink coat. Joanne had looked up at Peter with a questioning expression. He did not return her gaze, and she straightened up and went into another room.

Peter had turned back to his daughter. 'It's a beautiful house.' His eyes followed his wife-to-be as she re-emerged and passed through to the kitchen, carrying two tie-backs in shades of gold and copper. She swung the tassels like a majorette. 'Miss Mississippi Delta!' She grinned.

'If the pictures are anything to go by, it's really something else,' Peter added. He tugged his bottom lip briefly: his inadvertent mannerism when discussing money. 'It's an interesting area.' He had been staring down at the tiles while he spoke, and then looked up suddenly, as though returning to the present moment. 'Better go and see what she wants.' He raised his eyebrows and went after Joanne, although Katherine had not been aware that Joanne had intended him to follow her.

Now Katherine could hear music from the kitchen: her father whistling along to Benny Goodman. She smiled. He had once pulled out a record of Billie Holiday singing 'Body and Soul' and Joanne had started to cry. It had been her first husband's favourite song.

'You've given it back to me, honey.' She sat down on his knee and kissed him. The twins had squealed and looked away. 'That rotten sonofabitch ruined so many good things for me, and I thought he'd ruined that song too. Sorry, darlings,' she had turned to Ellen and Roy, 'I know the book says I shouldn't say bad things about your father in front of you, but there's precious little good to say about him, so there it is.'

When the twins had left, she turned to Katherine. 'That was how I found their dad. You know that, don't you? Or has Peter been coy about it?' She hugged him more tightly. 'Between the sheets with his floozie, Pammy, listening to "our tune", "Body and Soul". He was such a dope he couldn't even be original. The tune was second-hand, she was his secretary, and she made him feel like "a real man", and like he was "young again". What an asshole!' She giggled and slipped slightly off Peter's knee. 'Oh, strike me down for speaking ill of the dead.' Her face had become mock-serious again. She sipped her drink, her hand unsteady.

Earlier that evening Joanne had insisted on mint juleps, hence the confessions. Katherine had been happy that night, too. It was last year, early summer, the week after she had first met Miles.

'The really awful pity of it,' Joanne had gone on, 'is that he was dead within the month. I hadn't even had time to file suit. As far as anyone was concerned, all was hunky-dory. Only Pammy and I knew anything was up. We were the only ones wise to what had happened. I'd intended to take him to the cleaners, really wring him dry, and had gone off to Hawaii for a few weeks to clear my head, plan a strategy, cool off, get my revenge served cold. Came back, and "You're looking a bit peaky, you rotten bastard", was the first thing I said to him, mainly to rub in the fact that I was looking gorgeous, tanned and lovely, as had been my plan. Sue him to hell on an empty stomach and spa treat-ments, I'd thought. But he really did look grey, and I remember wavering, very slightly, feeling like perhaps I was being a bit mean on the old fool, and then,' she made a swift, slicing motion across her neck, sticking out her tongue, 'goodbye, Mr Body and Soul. He was a goner!'

Peter rolled his eyes. 'Darling, I'm not sure Katherine wants to hear all the details.'

'It's a great story.' Katherine had grinned, hoping to encourage her.

Joanne patted her knee affectionately. 'Thanks, honey. Now, you be quiet,' she addressed Peter, and snuggled closer to him. 'Anyway, I just did the whole grieving widow thing, and I don't suit black so looked miserable enough anyway, real frowsy. And that was that. I was sorry he died. But then if he hadn't,' she made the shape of a gun with her right hand, 'pop!'

She sat back, eyes narrowed, considering. 'You know, I think I might've had it in me to do him in, especially when Pammy told me all about how he'd pursued her. It wasn't the other way round at all, as you might imagine. I don't think she was lying. She didn't have the brains to make things up. I even gave her a settlement. She was a good kid, and he was well insured. I thought of it as a kind of open bribe to her, so she wouldn't blabber about their little involvement. I preferred it that way. And he got to stay the hero. He was always well liked.'

Joanne had stood up, taking Peter's hands; Katherine remembered how they had stood facing one another, and she had had to look away. 'Few months later, when your dear darling father was on his Napa valley jaunt, there it was. Head over heels!' She leant against him, and told the familiar story.

'Over a barrel!' She always screeched with laughter to relate this. 'I got him over a barrel.' The barrel had been an oak cask containing '95 chardonnay. They had both been on a Wine Society tasting trip. He had taken a weekend out of a business excursion; she had been in need of a holiday, and had always wanted to 'know what they're at with all that talk of noses and bouquets'.

After a few moments, Katherine made her excuses and went up to bed. She was happy that her father had found someone who loved him as Joanne clearly loved him, and she had already heard the story of how they met. After she had gone, she could hear them talking, their voices low, laughter and long silences.

From the kitchen now came the sound of a cork being popped, and Katherine turned from her view of Mary, heading down towards the lake, perhaps, where she grew watercress alongside the wild sedge and tall reeds. Katherine had helped her clear the patch; they had had to use machetes.

'Katherine? That you?' Peter came out into the hallway. He wiped his hands on his white apron, leaving dark red stains.

At the same moment, Mary set down her basket and turned back to the house, one hand raised against the sun, the other lifted just above her shoulder as though on the point of waving. But it would have been impossible for her to see either Katherine or Peter from there. Inside the house, they were in darkness. Perhaps Edie was leaning out of her bedroom window.

'Kate?'

She turned to her father. 'Sorry, I was lost. Lunch sounds wonderful.'

19

'The secret,' Peter stood by the stove, leaning over a large cast-iron pan, 'in making a great beef bourguignon, is that it should be almost impossible to tell the ingredients from the taste. Apart from the meat and wine, they should stay hidden.' He held out a spoon.

'Not bad.' Katherine sat down at the kitchen table: his audience.

'The garlic should be fine enough to melt. The porcini should dissolve. Should be no biting on bay leaves or getting bits of thyme stuck between your teeth.'

'You're giving the game away.' She laughed. She had missed this. He handed her some bread, a long flat cob dusted with flour.

'Mary's. Can't take credit for that.' He watched her as she chewed. 'I'll take some up to Edie.' He ladled stew into a bowl and left the room.

At the corner of the house, the kitchen had windows on two sides, one looking out over the back lawn and beyond, the other into the pines. The old chimney-breast had been left in, with just space enough for one person to sit in the heat of the range. She had sat there countless times, watching her father cook.

Katherine was thinking of this when Peter came back. 'What?' He seemed surprised to see her looking cheerful, as though he had just remembered bad news. 'Edie tells me I should stop boring you to death with my culinary eulogies and just serve you your lunch. How does she do that? I swear she's getting psychic in her dotage.' He stood for a moment with his back to her, over the stove.

'Here.' He served the stew into two shallow dishes, and sat down opposite her, took some bread. A bottle of 'average claret, not bad, but definitely average', as he put it, stood opened on the table, half empty from cooking, and he poured this into two glasses. He raised his in a toast: 'Health and wisdom.'

She sipped. 'Better than average, Pa.'

She thought then of the wedding present she had bought for him and Joanne at Berry Brothers in St James's: a bottle of '85 Petrus. She had spent the earnings from an entire job on the bottle. It had been in her flat, wrapped in tissue paper, stored in her kitchen wine-rack. They would have loved it. It was a kind of joke, also. 'Not exactly Petrus,' had been one of the first lines, so the story went, that he had ever said to Joanne. 'I'd wanted to impress her,' he told Katherine, laughing as Joanne chimed in: 'But I hadn't the first clue about wine at that stage,' she said. 'I'd been a smoker all my life. Ruined my tastebuds. "Is that a good or a bad thing, honey?" I asked him – came right out with it. He thought it was hilarious!'

Katherine touched her mouth as though to press away the confession. She wanted so badly to tell her father what had happened. She felt the guilt of keeping silent, but the thought of telling him now seemed out of the question. The wedding was only days away. Later, when they were back, when the legalese had been faced and settled, when it had become a matter of insurance claims, mainly, then she would tell them both everything, once she was clear of harm. To think of it like this, feeling still the proximity of danger, made her eyes swivel involuntarily to the window. She needed time to pass, and wanted it to hurry, to set that distance between her and the fire. But she saw herself, endlessly returning to find the same fact: almost everything she owned, her safe place, her darkroom, her private gallery, destroyed.

She ate, and momentarily could taste nothing. 'This is delicious, Pa,' she said.

He set down his spoon and leant back in the chair. 'It's been an age since we've done this, hasn't it?' He studied her as she ate. She felt herself redden. She prayed that he wouldn't say anything.

She missed these lunches of theirs in a way he couldn't begin to guess at. When her mother died, they had often made lunch together in the school holidays, when Katherine was at home. They had felt like her only moments of safety when her entire world had threatened to crumble. She could remember the feeling, but she could not quite make it return: she felt safer, but not safe enough.

It was during those times that her father had taught her about cooking, and although she had a bad head for memorising exact recipes, he had instructed her in what he called 'the right attitude' towards preparing and eating food. 'And read a book while you're cooking,' her father had suggested. 'You'll always remember it more clearly than had you read it any other way.'

A few years later, she had found herself smiling in a room of hundreds of girls, marshalled into dismal rows, turning over the paper with no trepidation as, at that moment, she had remembered *Middlemarch* wreathed in the scent of chicken roasted with lemon and garlic. She missed all that. He was right: it was a long time ago.

Now her father read her mind. 'You've got me always, you know, such as I am.' He leant over his bowl, and she felt the harshness of that expression like cool air. She had been so selfish, thinking only of herself, when he was suffering still. She could see that it was hard for him, the thought of replacing Julia in any way, and that even now he did not know where to set Joanne, if not across the memory of his first wife. Where else could she go? Not alongside, like a mistress, but in a completely different chamber of his heart.

She spoke quietly. 'You and Joanne are going to be really wonderful together, Dad.'

But Peter glanced up at her, his expression suddenly distracted, as though he had been thinking something quite different. 'Damn, I just remembered. I should've mentioned – you had a phone-call earlier, when you were in the garden. It came through to my study. Sounded serious.' He frowned.

Katherine felt herself go cold. The police. She had asked them not to call her here.

'Chap said he'd call back.'

Katherine stared at her plate, cursing silently. She would have to tell him what had happened.

She looked up, 'Dad, I'm sorry—'

But his eyes were laughing. 'Sorry?' He seemed puzzled. 'It was your lovestruck Miles. Wouldn't say what it was about. Are you back together, is that it, and you left without saying where you were off to? We should get him down for the wedding.'

'Did you suggest it?' Katherine breathed out, tried to keep her voice level and light.

'No, didn't want to interfere, of course not.' He grinned. 'I like him. He's a good kid. An idiot, I'm sure, just like me when I was his age. Shouldn't let you out of his sight, that's his problem.'

'Dad, please, you've got it all wrong.' She drank a large gulp of wine. Her hands were shaking, relief that it wasn't the police mingling with fear at what Miles's phone-call had meant: was he checking to see if she had made it out of the flat? Did it mean that, now he knew where she was, he would come after her?

She looked behind her father's head at the row of black pines. She could imagine someone concealed there, waiting until she was alone. She rubbed her forehead. She must be losing her mind. This place was home. No danger could come here.

Her father was still looking at her expectantly. He seemed relieved to have this to talk about. 'Come on, spill the beans, what's the latest with you and Miles?'

The back door from the garden swung open, and a swift gust of damp air rushed in. Katherine felt her blood pound. 'My God, that gave me a fright.'

Mary was at the door, walking backwards, scraping her shoes free of mud on the step. 'I heard you, Peter.' Her voice was low. 'Leave the child alone with worrying her about her Miles. She's upset enough without your meddling. I hear all your questions.' She appeared to say this last thing to herself, turning to the sink with an armful of carrots caked in mud. 'She's got enough to be going on with, without your Miles this and that.'

But she was laughing when she turned to them at the table, her black eyes sparkling. 'Nice fresh carrot – or you'd prefer the stick?'

Peter leant over his food, and when he looked up his face was without emotion.

20

Seen from the front, the house was now almost entirely in darkness: only a faint glow showed through the fanlight over the door. But from the back the story was different: lights shone from every room along the ground floor; on the upper floor, four windows showed yellow behind drawn curtains, and a fifth, Edie's, had the sash still raised to let the air carry the unvisited garden to her. Only the attic level of the house observed the night: three small squares of black glass, rising from the slates.

Walking up the last stretch of the final field towards the house, there were sounds of neither traffic nor human habitation. The herd had gathered by the lakeside, jostling beneath hazels along the fence. The oaks rustled low to the earth. In the far field, leased to a neighbouring farmer, black-faced sheep cropped at the short grass.

Separating the long lawn from the parkland was a five-bar fence, kept in good repair, and when the gate swung open, oiled hinges made it noiseless. From here, the ground tilted more sharply upwards, and after a long walk from the far end of the valley, this last stretch made the breath come deeply in a walker's chest. The passage of many years of feet had worn steps into the earth, and pebbles had been laid to make the pathway firm, even after rainfall, which tonight, very lightly, had started to fall around seven o'clock.

Moving closer, out of the cover of trees, stepping on to the smoother grass of the back lawn, even with your eyes shut, there, you'd hear it – almost imperceptible at first, but then there would be no doubt: the house was full of life.

A radio was playing: someone reading from a novel, broadcast into a bedroom on the upper floor. Downstairs, jazz was on the stereo, and voices mingled in the kitchen, laughter sounding the brightest note, easily heard from the distance of the garden.

Approaching, certain words and then phrases could be heard: the kitchen window was open. A bell sounded on the upper floor: Edie calling. Footsteps moving at a swift jog up the wooden staircase to answer her call: she wanted to come down for dinner tonight, and the family would eat their first meal together since Katherine had come home. The radio was turned off upstairs, and the curtains were drawn in Edie's bedroom, though the sash was left open and the wind, gathering, ruffled them so that from the lawn, looking up, that sound of fabric could be heard.

The thump of someone being helped along the top landing with a walking-frame, reaching the stairs, and then the sound of them being carried down: a man's footfall, Peter's, on the oak staircase. An exclamation as Edie entered the kitchen; laughter as she made a joke; movement of feet into the dining room. She must've insisted on that formality. The pop of a cork, and then, even this audible as you approached the house – the windows of the kitchen and dining room were both wide open – the liquid decanted into crystal.

Moving closer, through the french windows, one panel propped open with a heavy iron weight – the air was still warm, though damp – and the sounds of the day now over could be heard retreating in the building's walls. The creak of wood as the heat left it, the pressure of the quickening breeze running through the fabric of the blinds: the day's residue stirred again on the brink of night.

Laughter, oblique commands, vital things not yet spoken of, secrets unimparted. Everything was to come.

Mary hesitated a few feet from the dining-room window. Earlier that day she had fixed Peter with a look: 'You haven't told her yet, have you?' she accused him. 'You do it before I'm back, or I'll tell her myself.' She put on her boots. 'Someone should check the bottom gate. Seems like the sheep have got in with the cattle again. I'll go.'

Upstairs, Edie heard this exchange, which occurred by the kitchen door. She had leant forwards to watch Mary heading out across the lawn at dusk, and decided that certainly she would take her dinner downstairs tonight.

Now Mary saw that they had broken the news but, from outside, Katherine appeared to be smiling. Peter's hand rested lightly on her arm. 'I wanted to tell you at lunch, but couldn't find the right way, or the moment.'

'We've been thinking of it for quite a while, and my latest deal clinched it.' Joanne snapped her fingers when she said this, as though relating a smart move in a game of poker.

Katherine set down her wine glass and stared at her plate. She glanced up at the sound of Mary coughing outside as she went round the house, invisible apart from her flashlight, to the kitchen door.

'We've been thinking of it for some time,' Peter continued, echoing Joanne. But he did not look at his daughter as he spoke. 'We' included everyone at the table except her. The children, even Edie, appeared to have been waiting for this moment. There was an almost audible release of tension now that she, at last, had been told. She tried to keep chewing but the food clogged her throat, and she had to gulp down a mouthful of red wine before she could swallow.

'This house isn't really viable any more.' Peter's voice was imploring.

At the word 'viable', Katherine flinched. 'I hadn't realised it was just about money, Dad.'

'It's falling down!' Joanne looked up at the ceiling with an exaggerated show of reproach as though it might collapse at any moment. 'Sinking!' She pointed her fork at Katherine, raising her eyebrows. 'And of course it comes back to money. What else?'

The window was open to the night. A breeze was stirring the leaves on the gravel path that led away towards the open countryside. Joanne leant back in her chair and smiled. 'You'll love the place in River Road. It has colonnades and a lime-tree walk, a pool and everything. Needs fixing up – but it won't eat money like this place, even then.' She laughed. 'There's a good piece of land with it, which we can sell off. It'll be our little project, won't it, honey?' She turned to Peter and took his hand. 'Your father needs to start winding down.'

Katherine stared at him. 'You're going to retire?'

He looked uncomfortable. 'Not exactly. Not just yet. Take more of a back seat, that's all.'

The children were fidgeting, angling to get down from the table.

'Not while you're chewing.' Joanne addressed Roy, who swallowed fast and opened his mouth.

'Gone, look.'

Ellen raised her eyebrows and drummed her fingers on the table, impatient to be gone.

'It won't be right away, you know.' Joanne leant forwards, as though correcting something Katherine had said.

'Have to wait till I've popped my clogs before they up sticks.' Edie spoke suddenly, her voice quiet but clear.

Katherine was glad of her 'they': it told her that she had an ally. The table fell silent. This was the hidden part of the deal: a move to America was out of the question so long as Edie was alive. Edie straightened her shoulders. 'Might be years yet,' she threatened, grinning at Katherine.

'Oh, Edie, you know we're not waiting for that.' Joanne laughed, but no one joined her.

'It's true, though, isn't it? What else is stopping you?' Edie's eyes shone in the candlelight. 'You'd be off like a shot if I fell off the twig.'

'Mother, it's nothing like that. You live as long as you can, that's what we all want — you know that perfectly well.' Peter glanced at Joanne, who had flinched at his remark.

'Yes, off you go.' Joanne addressed the children, who slid down from their chairs.

Edie began to laugh. 'It's not that simple.' She took a large gulp of red wine and turned to her son. 'Since 1839.' She tilted her head as she watched him. 'And now this.' She breathed out heavily and set down her wine glass with a thump. 'Will you take me up, darling?' She rose to her feet and Katherine went to stand alongside her. Edie's weight against her arm was that of a small child, slight but giddy with potential chaos. Katherine was glad of the excuse to leave the room.

'Sure you don't want me?' Peter half rose from his chair.

Edie did not turn round. 'Quite sure.'

In the hallway, Edie paused before they took the first stair and turned to her granddaughter. 'I'm sorry your father didn't tell you sooner.' She had lowered her voice. 'You love this place.' She hesitated, leaning heavily on Katherine's arm. 'But sometimes we love the wrong things for the wrong reasons.' She glanced up at Katherine and her face seemed very pale, her eyes anxious, one lid fluttering with a nerve beneath the skin. 'Few things warrant unconditional love, you know. People, rarely, and all the rest — well, even less.' She smiled very faintly. 'There's a good deal we've never spoken of. Things you should know.'

They started up the stairs, Edie pausing at every third step; at the top her breath was high and rasping in her chest. Katherine put her arm round her waist to support her. Edie was wearing a long pale green housecoat of quilted Chinese silk. It stood out from her body like soft armour, and beneath it she felt fragile. Her feet were ruined with arthritis, although she still insisted on 'proper shoes not geriatric carpet slippers', and now she was wearing patent evening sandals with a slight heel. She wobbled between each small step and when they reached the door to her bedroom, she let go of Katherine's arm as though her grand-daughter were a beau seeing her from her carriage to the door – with just that tentative grace.

Katherine turned on the lights in the room and helped Edie into bed.

'You do know that, don't you?' Edie looked up at her.

Katherine knew exactly what she meant: that she and Edie had never been so close as to confide any particular intimacies about Edie's past, or about what Edie might know of the Clements family's history. Katherine had been content to live within the myths handed out to her. Entire lives had been captured within a single phrase. 'Uncle Henry who fought in the Somme'; 'Auntie Hettie who was a wonderful dancer. Died of TB'; 'Your great-aunt Jennifer who married the Italian'. And there they all were, in photographs, pinned into the family album. She had written her own stories to fill in the gaps.

Now she heard the edge of urgency in Edie's voice and held her breath, waiting for her to continue. But Edie settled herself among the pillows and shut her eyes. 'There's time yet for us to talk, don't worry.' She sank further beneath the blankets. 'They'll have to wait until I'm ready.'

Katherine kissed her and turned out the lights. In the corridor moonlight ran along the walls like water and the air was cool with the scent of rain. She listened to the noises from downstairs, the familiar whisper and creak of the house settling itself into the night. Now it was to be sold and she felt heartbroken, but her heartbreak was a kind of confusion. She had seen herself endlessly returning to this place, one day perhaps with a family of her own, but she felt idiotic to have relied on this dream. Miles had been closer to the mark than he realised.

She had the sudden sense of people watching her from every room in the house – each room a point of view that she had not considered. She turned back to Edie's door to ask her, please, to tell her now: what secrets did she know that would make this loss more bearable? But when she opened the door she could see the outline of Edie's back, turned away from her in bed. She was on her own.

part | three

21

It was just past seven thirty in the morning, and the landing was silent as Katherine went downstairs: no one else was stirring. Outside, mist still hung at knee height above the lawn. The sun was low and silver.

Work was a pleasure Katherine knew she could rely on. After 'we've been thinking of it for some time now', the smiles and jokes, while she had felt as though her life was being pulled out from under her, when she woke the next morning, she headed by instinct for the darkroom. There, suspecting it was an act of childishness, when she shut the door she slipped the catch and locked herself in.

She had four films. Three were of the author, the portraits from the Langham, and she had promised them by the day after tomorrow; she would work on those now. And one was of the fire. She had intended to run off those negatives, too, if she could stomach it, but now she balked at the idea. Perhaps she would do it. Certainly she would leave making any prints until later.

She poured developer into one of the tanks, looked for the

timer, turned off the light, unspooled the first film, loaded it on to the plastic reel, screwed on the cover. It required no thought; she could set herself aside throughout these moments, yet it was only now that she felt most herself. She paused for a second in the darkness, full of gratitude, her hands on the familiar objects of her work, listening to the liquid running through the film, the privacy of silence beyond it all hers. How much could be taken away and yet still leave this untouched? She didn't want to question how such luck was possible.

She turned the lights back on as she shook the tank, and ran water for the kettle. But she had used the last of the proper coffee, yesterday, and by now the rest of the house would have started to wake: she didn't want to bump into anyone in the kitchen.

That morning when she woke her eyes had been sore, and she realised she had been crying in her sleep. Her face in the mirror showed a deep red crease on the right-hand side where the pillow had pressed damp and tight as she turned. She had dreamed that the fire ran down here from London to swallow up the house, and she had been able to do nothing to put it out. No one else had seemed to want to. The family was taking tea on the lawn, barely glancing back at the building as it burned, and in the dream Katherine knew why: the house was a boat, and it had been set alight on purpose – a captain's decision to scupper the sinking ship.

She rubbed her face, soaked her handkerchief in cold water and pressed it to her eyes. She thought of the wedding, two days away: it filled her with no happiness now. Where had she been, what other life had she been looking at, not to notice what her father's marriage might entail? Joanne's redecorating hadn't been, as she supposed, a sign of ownership: the house was simply being tarted up before it could be sold. To think of someone else living here seemed almost as bad as wishing the place destroyed. Her unconscious had half wished it, in that dream, and she felt ashamed, and bitter, to bring out that confession to the daylight.

She poured stop-bath into the tank, tipped boiling water on to some old instant coffee and waited for the dream to leave her. She shook the tank for a short while, emptied it, poured in the fixer, reset the timer. Then she thought of the box of her mother's offcuts and 'snaps', as Mary had called them.

She lifted it on to the table, then cut through the Sellotape. The box smelt of mildew, and when she ran her hand over the brown cardboard she could feel the damp. She turned on the electric fan heater and set it on the table to see if that wouldn't clear some of the moisture.

Her first film was almost done. She prised off the lid of the tank, stood it in the sink, fitted the hose for water at 20°C, took another tank down from the shelf. But the box was a distraction. She peered inside, lifting the layers carefully, and then her hand touched metal: the smooth small barrel of a reel of film. Her breath caught in her throat. She told herself it was most likely a new film, now useless and past its date, but when she drew it out, the tab was in. It appeared to have been used and left undeveloped, and she felt the sudden proximity of her mother's ghost.

She held the spool in her hand. The shock of it was like heat at the centre of her palm. It was probably ruined now and would show nothing. She told herself this as she set it down on the table. But she knew also that there was a good chance it would be fine, and she wondered how long she would be able to resist trying to develop it.

She checked that the water was running steady through the tank and picked up her mother's reel of film again. Ilford 125, black and white, thirty-six exposures. If it was blank she wouldn't be able to bear it. Work first.

She turned off the light and started on her next film, moving from red light to white to absolute darkness and back again, her hands swift and sure. When she had finished the last film of the author, she stopped work for a moment, made more coffee and sat down. The timer was whirring through the minutes until the negatives would be ready, but she still had two more films: her mother's and the fire, sitting side by side on the table.

She thought about how, only yesterday, she had fantasised about wrecking that film of the fire, ripping it open so she would never see those images. But they were impressed on her mind already, and that was the trouble. She knew she would never get rid of those scenes unless she forced herself to look at them through the distance of a photograph. The illusion of the image would overlay the reality, and she would be safe again – or at least in control. But would the same apply to her mother's film? She was nervous at the thought of dislodging what memories she had of her mother, of replacing them with anything else.

They were impressed on her mind, too, but she wanted to keep them there.

Her coffee was growing cold, barely drunk, and the timer had wound down almost to the end. The first film would soon be done. She made the decision, picked up the film of the fire, flicked the switch, and set to work. By the time she had finished, the first reel was ready to come out of the tank. There would be no way of telling whether the other film had even worked, still less what it showed, for another twenty minutes.

She had promised herself that when the film of the fire was ready she would take it out and hang it up to dry as though it were no different from the others, just a job. But she could only fool herself so far. The clock marked off the time, and even as she was bending over the enlarger, studying the author portraits, she was conscious of every second as it passed. Her palms were damp, and her eye misted like a poor lens out of focus where she looked at the images swimming through light to appear, a little out of kilter, beneath her on the square white plate. She cursed under her breath, reset the negative in place, started again, and when the timer sounded, she was so wound up with nerves that she knocked it over with her elbow, catching it just before it fell to the floor.

She wiped her hands dry on her jeans, rolled her shoulders, exhaled, and felt ridiculous, utterly unprofessional, to be so afraid of a strip of film. All the same, when she unspooled the strip and clipped it to the line, she could not look at it beyond a swift glance to see that, no, her earlier desire for it to be blank had not been fulfilled: the pictures were all there.

She moved it further away along the line, out of the circle of light cast by the enlarger, and set her back to it as she returned to work. By lunchtime the author photographs were finished and she was hungry. The strip was still dripping on to the linoleum. She wanted any reason not to look at it just yet.

While she had been working, as though she had been under deep water, she had not noticed that the house had gradually filled with noise. She heard someone walking through the annexe, just on the other side of the darkroom door. She didn't recognise the footsteps, and they did not linger. A workman, perhaps, or a delivery? There was the sound of a van or lorry on the gravel at the side of the house, the engine churning through reverse; doors closing, footsteps hurrying across stone; glasses or bottles rattling together in a crate. A couple of days away, and the wedding party was already beginning.

She straightened things on the workbench, cleared away the chemicals and paper, set the prints in order. She looked in the drawer for a padded envelope to send those portraits. She must have run out. Her father would have one she could use. With the room tidied up, her mother's reel of film presented itself to her more insistently. She had plenty of time to do it now, if she chose to. The negatives of the fire, too, would be almost dry and ready to print up. Lunch could wait. On the other side of the dark-room door, the house was momentarily still, and then, as though that silence had merely been an in-breath, she heard something crash downstairs, a muffled thud that ended in the noise of shattering china. It made the decision for her.

As she opened the darkroom door, she could hear Joanne's voice from the landing. 'If you even dream of fobbing me off with paper and not cotton *as we arranged*, then heads will roll. Do you understand?' And a little later, after a sudden high shriek and the sound of footsteps on the stairs, 'Jesus! There'll be blood!'

In the hallway a large cardboard box lay at the foot of the stairs, its sides dented where it had fallen, knocking an aspidistra off its pedestal. The china pot lay broken beside it. Appearing to ignore this, Joanne was now on her knees at the back door, peering underneath the carpet. 'Oh, it's you.' She grinned. 'Carpet gets sorted this afternoon.' Her shoulders drooped. 'But can you imagine what arrived this morning?' She flicked her head towards the cardboard box. 'A box of paper napkins.' Katherine realised: not fallen, but kicked. 'What in hell am I supposed to do with that?' Joanne shot it a vicious look. 'I just told them they could shove it. I'm trying to arrange a wedding, not a low-rent *buffet*.' She sat back on her heels and laughed. 'My God, I'll be glad when all this is over, you have no idea.'

She held out her hand to Katherine, who took it and helped her to her feet. But instead of letting go, Joanne hesitated for a second, then lowered her head and drew Katherine close into the odd, half-fumbling embrace of someone unused to receiving affection.

'I'm sorry for the way things are turning out, honey.' Joanne's voice was lower, more intent than Katherine had heard it before, bright like a girl's eager to be believed. 'I really am sorry,' Joanne said again, as though Katherine had denied it. 'This house — there wasn't a plan. I hope you'll forgive us. Everything has just happened.' Joanne drew back but her arms stayed round Katherine's waist.

'Come on, I'll fix you lunch.' Joanne half turned, then swore loudly. 'Shit, my colourist! What a dope. Sorry, hon, I clean forgot. Having my roots done at one.' She clutched at her hair and grimaced. They stood for a second, facing one another, and Joanne blushed as she turned to go, as though afraid she had revealed too much.

The door was open to the lawn, and Katherine could see that the morning mist had risen and vanished. Joanne was right, and Katherine realised that she loved her for her frankness. Everything had just happened, and the short space of days before the wedding had taken on a different character for her. It was better that she knew now. It would give her a chance to take her leave of the place. Her throat tightened. There was a courage in that thought that she did not possess; She went quickly outside, as though hurrying towards it, and took a deep breath.

22

'Edie said you'd help us with our project.' Roy appeared suddenly round the open door of the fridge. He grinned at her, and Katherine realised that Ellen also had come into the kitchen. In socked feet, the twins moved about the room in faint parallel, like friendly cats.

Ellen glanced at her sideways through her blonde hair. 'She said you'd be able to find some books for us upstairs. We can do the rest.'

'We're not allowed in the attic, unless you come with us.' Roy watched her as she found things to make a sandwich.

'Valuables.' Ellen mimicked an English accent, sucking in her cheeks.

'Sure there are none of those.' Katherine smiled. 'You want one?'

They sat down quickly beside her, nodding and tucking their hands out of sight beneath the table, watching her slice cheese, cut bread, scoop pickle for the sandwiches. 'Lots of pickle.' Roy licked his lips.

'Can we take them upstairs?' Ellen glanced at the door, as though not wishing to be found out.

'Of course. We can do what we like.'

The twins looked up at Katherine and smiled.

Never having been partitioned into separate rooms, the attic at Fareham ran the full length of the building. Although the ceilings were low and sloping, three raised windows looking out on to the front and back of the house meant that, even without electricity, the attic was often full of light. The floorboards were bare and untreated. Where the sun slanted through the angle of the roof, dust motes hung golden, suspended thick as sand in saltwater.

Along one side a number of cupboards, tall-boys, filing cabinets and tea-chests were arranged. Facing them, stacked like a liner's passenger cargo, were suitcases, trunks, an assortment of bags, taped-up cardboard boxes. At the far end, the arrangement was more haphazard: a couple of standard lamps, an old day bed, two armchairs and a small upright piano were just visible beneath dust-sheets. Also at this end lay bundled papers tied with string, rolls of maps and posters, willow-cane washing baskets full of what looked to be old toys, a stack of paintings, empty frames, a pair of mirrors dark with time and, along the far wall, the thing Katherine supposed the twins were after: a shelf of books.

When she was small, Katherine had often come up to the attic to play shop, and stayed for hours. Her uniform was a white butcher's apron, and her grandfather's Irish Guards beret. She imagined herself manager of a general store that sold everything from brass tacks to strings of Arab racehorses. Apart from a footstool that she used as her shop counter, those books were her main props.

There were about twenty, bound in identical dark red morocco, each slightly larger than A4-size, filled with columns and figures, numerical codes, followed by single letters. There were no words. They appeared to have been written in one hand but, spanning as they did twenty years, she supposed now that that might not have been the case. It was the disguise of regulation copperplate that gave them their appearance of unity.

Now the black ink was faded to a light caramel brown, although the writing was still perfectly legible. More legible yet were her occasional interpolations in ballpoint pen: 'Carrots. Ten pounds in weight, 50 pence. Mrs Baker. Paid in full.' Or, 'Rubies. Ten thousand in number. Three million pounds sterling. Mr Graham. Paid in full.' She had added notes like this at the top of a number of pages, which otherwise meant nothing to her. Pages of columns, books full of numbers. She knew that it was connected to the Clementses' shipping operations in some way, and supposed that it was a record of trade deliveries. But where to? India, she supposed, and had a recollection of cotton and tea having been mentioned at one point.

She flicked through the first volume. 'I'm not sure you'll get much from this. Do you know what you're after?'

Ellen and Roy were side by side on the floor, chewing the last of their sandwiches as they took down the books. Against the silence, the sound of a wood-pigeon landing clumsily on the roof tiles made all three jump. 'Did Edie give you some idea of what you should be looking for?' asked Katherine.

'She said you'd show us the log books, that's all. Something to do with imports or exports – something nineteenth century, Africa, she said, useful for our project . . .' Roy trailed off. He had lost interest already and was lifting the corner of a dust-sheet, peering underneath. Ellen wandered over to the stack of paintings and frames. 'Cool! Roy-boy, look at this.'

Her brother skipped over to see what she had found.

Katherine took down another book and flicked through the pages. Why had Edie said they should look at these? She couldn't see much sense to it. The figures were indecipherable, unless you knew what you were trying to find. The columns were arranged rather like a game-book, recording the spoils of each season's shoots: first, a date, written out in Roman numerals, starting in the 1870s; then a long number, ending in a letter; a column for delivery, another for payment, received or awaited. The books were arranged in twelve sections, according to the months, although the months, as with everything else, were not specifically named. The long numbers, she supposed, might indicate the type of cargo to be shipped. It was hard to decipher, but she guessed that it might indicate a tally of quantity and type. She looked at the letters at the end of the long numbers – I, G, H, F, C: the combinations were unclear, and followed no pattern that she could discern.

The books' main interest, now, was personal: the clearest

writing, her own, was a catalogue of childish wants and, apart from the rubies and Arab racehorses, for the most part they were quite modest. She had invented families and seen that they were well fed and clothed. There was a kind of pattern, running through the years. The Bakers liked carrots, evidently, and Mr Graham appeared to be a lone jewel-hoarder. About a dozen family names kept recurring. Armitage liked lamb chops in great quantity, and drawing materials. Perhaps she had imagined this family as artists? The O'Neills preferred fish, and placed orders for a variety of fabrics – silks, duchesse satin and yards of Paisley cotton, specifically, she had written, 'in peacock blue', along with a variety of trimmings, tassels, hooks and eyes, mother-of-pearl buttons.

Sometimes, she could see herself reaching for an idea – the descriptions would become elaborate. 'A black velvet jacket lined with silk, with carved ebony buttons and slashed sleeves. Special order for the Duke of Hellebore.' What on earth had made her think of such a thing? Had she read something, or been told a story? Running through the years there was a kind of child's logic of fantasy and fulfilment – a limitless procedure of supply and demand. Everyone paid up, in the end. Whatever orders her families placed, eventually they were delivered. Even 'Mrs Maxwell, fifty gazelles, one birdcage, large' must have been produced to her satisfaction. The box was run through, 'paid on delivery', with a large red tick.

She turned at the sound of someone playing the upright piano. Ellen had clambered beneath the dust-sheets and her outline could be seen moving about over the keys. 'La Mer', performed with a certain elegance and gusto. Katherine was surprised. The concealed figure swayed in time to the music, and Roy, on the outside, made little elfin skips and leaps, twirling so that the dust rose, whitening his black-socked feet.

He laughed as he danced. It was their house now, as much as hers. The great difference was that they could leave it when they wished: it was the first time they had been up here, and might well be the last; but even had she wanted to, she would never be able to extract herself from the place entirely. And soon another family, and other children, would come to live here. Katherine started to put the log books back on the shelf. She would ask Edie about them.

Last night, when Edie had said there were things Katherine did not know, her voice had held a kind of promise. Now Katherine felt more nervous than curious, as though a parcel were being passed around, the paper torn off, and in the end what might be revealed was nothing at all, beyond the other players' desire to know what lay inside. She wasn't sure she wanted to find out; wasn't sure if she could bear it, if the news was bad. Everyone assumed her strength because she had acquired the habit of conveying it; now it felt like a false impression, as though with one word she might reveal her weakness.

She wiped one of the volumes free of dust before she replaced it. She had the strange intimation that her movements were being observed, or as though Edie was propped up in bed downstairs, listening out for her, urging her on.

The piano playing stopped, and Ellen slipped out from beneath the sheet, giving a small bow as she emerged. 'Just tinkling the ivories,' she flourished with a grin.

It had been Katherine's mother's expression, 'Come on, let's go tinkle the ivories', as she tried, unsuccessfully, to persuade her to practise.

Ellen shot her a look: was it all right for her to have played? Katherine realised that Joanne must have told them more than she had imagined about Peter's previous wife. Ellen slipped her hand into Katherine's. 'Spooky upstairs, let's go down.'

Katherine hesitated. The ivories. Was that it? Might that account for 'I' in the log books? She frowned. Edie would know. The light was failing; it looked as though later there would be rain. She turned to go.

'Can we take this?'

Roy was crouching beside one of the paintings, a small portrait in oils, covered with dust, in a gilt ormolu frame.

'Why that one?' Katherine leant down. It looked like a portrait from the thirties.

'It's little.' Roy was indignant. 'Please, I want to clean it up.' He shifted it out of the stack, and Katherine brushed the surface clear with her handkerchief. She did not recognise the subject, a young woman, but when she turned the portrait round, the initials 'E.B.H.' – Howard was Edie's maiden name – were on the back. Could it be her? She smiled. 'I think it's my gran. We'll take it down, see if it really is.'

She shepherded the twins out of the attic ahead of her, and turned back to look at the room one last time before she left.

23

'Oh!' Edie's hand flew to her lips, 'That picture.' She leant forwards in bed, her narrow shoulders lifting in shock.

It showed a young woman posed for a formal portrait in jade satin and a high pearl necklace. Her gaze rested on something to one side of the artist's eye.

'I sent you looking for one thing and you found another.' Edie glanced quickly at Katherine.

Now Edie wore her white hair tied back in a small knot, secured with pins, but at the time the portrait was made, her hair had been reddish blonde, and in the painting she wore it loose, arranged in a lustrous twist over her left shoulder. 'It was done just after my eighteenth birthday.' She touched the surface of the canvas with her fingertips. 'My parents commissioned it as an engagement present for Hugh.'

Whenever Edie said her husband's name, she tilted her head to one side as though in sympathy. Katherine had often seen pictures of her grandparents when they were first married, but it seemed implausible to her that they were ever teenagers, with all that that word had come to imply. Even at nineteen, Hugh had had an old man's moustache.

'They left it a bit late, though, and it took rather longer than expected, too.' Edie's expression became guarded, as though she was looking inwards towards an image she wasn't quite sure whether to describe. 'By the time the paint was dry, it was more of a wedding present.' She had had her son, Peter, and then the war came and three years later Hugh was killed. She had not remarried. 'It's not very good, is it?' Edie smiled. 'Very dated. The young man who painted it was only just out of art school.' She paused, buttoning her cardigan, tugging at the sleeves, fussing slightly, Katherine noticed, and wondered why.

Edie cleared her throat and glanced quickly at Katherine before she spoke. 'Lewis Briars. That was what he was called. He'd been at Winchester with Hugh, though they were in different houses. They were in the same regiment later on.'

Katherine watched her as she examined the picture. 'It's been stashed up there for years. I didn't like to have it around.'

Katherine supposed that by this she meant that she hadn't liked to be reminded of the girl she was, happy, in love, but Edie turned to her, signalling that she should shut the bedroom door. 'Hugh thought the whole business was ridiculous. And I was very vain. It was painful to me that he didn't like it.'

Katherine shut the door quietly and sat on the edge of the bed. She was amazed at this admission. She had always thought of her father's parents as existing in a sphere of curtailed bliss: the reason Edie had not remarried.

'I remember what he said when he first saw it. "My God, Edith, you look" – he could barely speak he was so shocked – "fallen." He went bright red as I remember, and left the room muttering to himself that it was "hardly moral".' She grimaced. 'I suppose it might've been hilarious. But I really was in love with him, then.'

She straightened the blanket over her legs and looked down at her hands on the coverlet. Katherine had heard perfectly clearly that qualification, 'then'. Was she supposed to have heard? She looked at the painting. 'It made things very difficult with my parents, actually.' Edie laughed. 'He didn't want to appear ungrateful in their eyes, so the wretched thing had to be brought out whenever they were around.'

'And the rest of the time it was hidden?'

Edie nodded. 'He wasn't very – emancipated, I suppose it is. He was astonished when I had Peter. I'm not sure he—' Edie turned back to the picture. 'The amazing thing is that it's hardly very *naughty*, is it?' She raised her eyebrows and became serious. 'But, do you know, the oddest part of it is that years later, a long time after he'd died, I discovered – someone told me – that the photograph he kept of me in his wallet, during the war, wasn't of me but of this painting.' Edie looked at Katherine. 'So who do you suppose he was in love with?'

Edie glanced at the window where the sky was framed by blue curtains, dead still, as rainclouds gathered over the trees. 'It doesn't matter, I'll never know, and I'm sure I remember a good deal of what happened all wrong now anyway. Do you think this is even me?' She raised her chin in the manner of the portrait. 'I'm surprised you thought to bring it down. I can't even recognise myself.'

Katherine did not mention that it had been Roy who insisted, and that it had been his liking for small ornate objects that he could tuck under his arm, more than anything else, that had made him pick out this painting over the others. Earlier, he had crouched beside her on the kitchen floor, old newspapers spread out around them as they cleaned the surface, very carefully, with a dampened duster. 'Is it really her?' He was sceptical about the sitter's identity, and had appeared to lose interest when her face was properly revealed.

'Shall I tell you what happened next?' Edie bowed her head, her voice lowered as though she were addressing the painting. 'And this is between us.' She looked up at Katherine, and for the first time Katherine could see the girl in the painting as she might have looked were she alive at this moment. It had nothing to do with age, or ageing's marks. Age was not about white hair or wrinkles, nor was it a loss of innocence, or a quality of naïvety. Katherine saw it in her eyes: it was an expectation of passion.

Suddenly she felt embarrassed to look at Edie, and almost shocked: she had seen what Hugh must have noticed, and been terrified by; he had detected in his new wife's gaze a desire for something he was not personally able to provide. It was as though she had just stumbled upon some scene of intimacy – the painter suggesting that Edie take off her clothes, Edie calmly agreeing. Perhaps it had happened like that. Edie appeared to follow the path of her thoughts. She took quick hold of Katherine's hand, forcing her to look at her. Her eyes were bright with confirmation.

'These days, of course, it might have all turned out quite differently. But I met Lewis just as I was about to be married. There was nothing we could do, he knew that.' Edie glanced at the door, as though anxious not to be discovered. 'Afterwards I put him from my mind.' She described it as a time-bound infatuation, but Katherine watched her smile as she said the word 'infatuation' and she could see that it had certainly been much more than that.

In fact, Edie met Lewis again, many years later, in 1954. She had been in London with Peter, who was then fifteen and down from school on the Christmas break. She was thirty-five. It was January, just into the new year, and a heavy frost had fallen on London. They were buying stationery from Smythson, Peter had wandered off, and she held two calf-skin notebooks in her hand, one red and one navy-blue. She couldn't decide. She had always had blue, but the red was beautiful, and she was momentarily torn. A man standing on the opposite side of the display leant across, took one of the red books and smiled at her as he turned aside to pay. Of course she recognised him immediately. He wouldn't remember her, she was quite sure. She blushed, and decided that blue would be best after all. Outside, the street was thick with fog, cars idling with headlights on, even at three in the afternoon.

Then she overheard the man address the salesman: 'Hang on a minute, excuse me.' Then he turned round and walked back towards her. 'Edie?' The man, who introduced himself as though she might have forgotten his name – she hadn't – quickly explained that during the war her husband had shown him a photograph. 'Not of you, but of my painting,' he had said. That was how she found out. She had been astonished. 'You haven't changed a bit. I'd have known you anywhere.' He had spoken to her so suddenly, handing her his card, inviting her to 'look him up, come for a drink, or tea', that she had felt caught up in the speed of the encounter, as though she were eighteen again, and it was perfectly natural to be asked to a man's house for a drink.

'Or tea' had saddened her, later. Had he looked at her and felt only pity? A widow. His friend's old wife. Someone with whom, recklessly, he had once had an entanglement. A person from his past whom it might be amusing to re-encounter – out of curiosity more than anything else, an exercise in comparison: would she be as he remembered her?

She had worried about all of that. In the intervening two decades she had done her best to shut out all thoughts of him; she had been too ashamed to remember their relation; meeting him again came with the force of those suspended years. His image had stuck in her mind and lodged there. She had simply refused to look at it, that was all; it had not faded. Now, with perfect clarity, that impression seemed to fall down on her. She found herself thinking about him constantly, and she would wake up happy and then realise that the happiness was because she had dreamt about him. She felt ridiculous. She was quite certain that her mind was playing tricks on her. 'A time-bound infatuation.'

A month later, she had been in London, staying with an aunt. Peter was away at school. She telephoned Lewis's number, and he was breathless as he answered, as though he had been waiting. 'Today,' he insisted, and she had remembered her feeling of alarm then – what was she thinking of? 'Tea would be lovely,' she told him, and heard him pause, when she could see him smiling.

She had put down the phone and burst into tears. She had convinced herself that her impression of him had had the vagueness of fantasy about it, and was more an illusion that she had conjured up than anything based in fact. But at the sound of his voice, she realised in what precise detail she could in fact recall him; might have recalled him at any point since they first met. It was as though, for the intervening time, he had been looking out at her from her mirror, and she had had only to turn round to find him, and set her hands on more than just his image. Sandy hair, over-long on top, very short at the back. A tanned face, even in January, and dark circles under his eyes, as though he had just returned from a sleepless trip. Too tall, she criticised him in her mind, and too thin. Although his shoulders and arms were broad, the rest of him appeared to have been starved, and she had poked fun at him when she arrived at the café where they had arranged to meet, just off the Strand.

'I'm a camel.' He had laughed with her, and mentioned a trip across India he had just taken that had suffered from 'organisational problems'. He had raised his eyebrows. 'No water, bad water. It wasn't a success, not for me. Smythson is my first stop when I'm back in the country. Stock up on notebooks, set it all down.' He had a way of waving his right hand in a quick circular motion just under his heart, as though urging himself on or trying to speed up time to keep step with him.

Edie closed her eyes and reached for Katherine's hand. 'Years of listening out for him have given me the hearing of a bat,' she whispered. 'Do you hear now? Joanne is by the back door. Do you hear her footfalls on the Purbeck, and then across the carpet as though she's testing ice? She has a very light footfall, and I know she's anxious to have that carpet taken up by Saturday. It's to be done this afternoon, I gather. Peter is the easiest to hear. You hear him now? Racketing in his study.' Katherine could hear only the very faintest noises from downstairs, and would not have been able to decipher them.

'But, do you know . . .' Katherine leant closer towards her. Her voice seemed to have been whittled away with too much talking. '. . . now I'm not sure if I *have* been waiting for him, after all.' Her face clouded over, almost imperceptibly at first, returning to the expression that Katherine had grown familiar with: an expectant but unwilling look, as though she could not allow herself to be abandoned to the present moment.

Her face was pale, as though she had caught sight of someone she was frightened of. 'A great calamity is what I tried to hold off,' she glanced about the room, as though expecting to see it, 'but it might have been a wonderful calamity. Who can say? And now there's just this unravelling, and the calamity will occur whether or not I hold it off any longer.'

Her eyes were watering, although Katherine could not tell whether it was through emotion or tiredness. 'I have held back,' she whispered, 'and that was the thing that was hardly moral. I kept back the part of myself that was most myself, for the day when I'd really need it, and now—'She looked up at Katherine, then glanced quickly out of the window as the first rain scattered on the glass. 'I'm not sure what it's good for, do you understand?' She tried to smile. 'It's like keeping back good underwear.' Her shoulders trembled as she laughed. 'Ridiculous.'

Edie leant forwards and Katherine straightened the pillows to support her back. A quick breeze passed into the room. There was the scent of something wild-woods and garlicky on the air. Edie squeezed her hand. 'He came here once,' her face shone, 'in April, and we walked down there through the garlic woods. It was where I told him that the painting was wrong – I didn't have the nerve to be that girl any more.' Her hand was cool and dry, as though she had kept her whole life beyond the reach of her heart: even her fingertips were without heat because of that decision. She breathed out very deeply and settled back against the pillows, turning her head to the window. A dismissal.

Katherine stood up. 'Should I take this away?' She picked up the portrait.

'No, why not leave it now?' Edie turned back to her. 'You know the real secret? I had a quota for this wedding.' She smiled, touched the frame as though for reassurance. 'And I put him on my list. He accepted. He'll be here on Saturday. Might as well leave that portrait where it is. He might find it amusing.' Her brow wrinkled. 'Perhaps not amusing.' She touched her cheek, her hand falling to her chest, as though she could feel a sudden quickening of her spirit.

24

The first of the prints came to life beneath her hands: her flat, the top of the building aflame like a matchstick against the black night sky. Edie's words had returned her straightaway to the dark-room: 'I have held back.' She had thought of that strip of nega-tives left hanging from the line: an accusation of her weakness. It had never been in her nature to be afraid, to shy away from things she might not like to face. Now she moved the first image about in the developing tray with the plastic tongs, and thought about what Edie had told her.

For a moment this afternoon she had felt as though she had stepped back through that window of the painting into a past that otherwise she might never have known, or in any way suspected. Had she found that painting after Edie's death, what would she have made of it? She might have stared at it for ever and seen nothing but brushstrokes – the scant likeness of a young woman she had never met.

Now the burning building materialised in the tray. She watched it sharpen and grow dark; she lifted it into the stop-bath, covered it, transferred it to the fixer, then to the sink, turned on the tap. It would be ready in five minutes. She returned to the light-box, studied the negatives. In some, the focus had slipped, and she supposed now that her hands – which she had felt were steady – must have been shaking after all. She chose the next picture: the silhouette of a fireman standing against a pale background. It was the silver van she now remembered turning slowly in the road and lingering. She made the print, looked for another, pressed the water from the first and hung it up to dry.

She made seven prints, before pulling the cord for white light. Then she filled the kettle with fresh water, and leaned back against the Formica table-top, rubbing her eyes.

Looking along the row of pictures hanging from the line, she felt her blood seem to snag as it ran through her. Few of the prints held any kind of visual interest, beyond a scrappy record of what had occurred that night. But it was her place. The images did nothing to distance her from what had happened. She had been naïve in supposing that they might. Instead, they sent her right back to the moments when she had taken them: she could smell the smoke, hear the sirens, the rushing hiss of the fire hydrants and the fall of glass. What had she been doing, where had she even been looking, until now? She had just been taking snaps. It was as though she had never attempted to take a photograph before that night.

She held a print in her hands and her thoughts returned to Miles. She remembered an argument, swiftly over, but fierce, when she had been exhausted, working too hard, and he suggested she give it up, abandon the client. 'How can I?' She had been astonished. 'I can't let people down, and anyway I need the money.'

'You need the money?' He appeared to find this absurd. 'I'm sure your dad will cough up if you really get into difficulties.'

Perhaps this was true, but she had never asked him for money, and he had never offered it. She didn't want to fight; but Miles persisted.

'You don't get it, do you? You don't see the difference between us.' It was late, and she had had work to deliver for the morning. He had arrived unannounced, but she had been glad to see him. Now his hand was on the door handle, and he shook his head in disgust as he looked at her. 'The difference is everything. Even if you don't exploit your background, you know it's there. You have that security. If everything in your life went to hell, you know you'd fall only so far before your family picked you up.'

She turned from him, and he must have noticed that she was on the point of tears because he came back to her, said he was sorry and didn't know what had made him say that. 'You're right, though.' She had looked at him, seen how distant from one another they were, wondered if they might ever draw any closer.

'It's just sour grapes.' He took her into his arms. 'If I fall, I fall for good. I've got nothing and nowhere to turn to. No hidden family gold, no grand forebears. Just undistinguished nobodies. No one remembers anyone because none of them did anything of consequence. However far back you dig, it's all just a blur.'

She knew that he was wrong, but he let go of her again and took a pace back as though she had said something insulting.

'You're so clear-cut, so hard.' He had half shaded his eyes as though she had shone a light into his face. 'It'd take something major to unbend you.' He smiled as he said this, as though he were offering advice. 'I'm only sorry it wasn't me. You don't love me.' He started to leave, not listening for her reply, his departure an accusation. 'I'm not sure you're capable of loving anyone, but certainly not me.'

She took down a couple of the prints and laid them out flat on the table, remembering Edie's words: that it had been a kind of immorality to keep the truest part of herself held back, fearing a calamity of some kind, either good or bad. And here it is, she thought, looking down at the pictures: all the calamity I'll ever need.

She straightened up at the sound of the kettle flicking itself off, and remembered her mother's advice: 'Where you place the camera is the first, maybe the most important decision.' It had seemed too obvious to be valuable at the time but, looking at the pictures now, she felt her mother's remark like a kind of armour given to protect her. She was only one part of the story, and perhaps no more than an observing eye.

She picked up a blue Chinagraph pencil and sat back, looking critically at the first print. Studying it in the clear light, she hesitated over a detail on the van in the background. A kind of logo or insignia that seemed familiar.

She made coffee, took down the folder of prints she had made a few weeks ago, after her trip to Gabon. The secret prints, as she thought of them: the personal pictures stolen with her Leica.

Although this wasn't the case, some of the pictures gave the impression that they had been taken with a zoom – the main subjects appeared entirely unaware that they were being photographed. Only a few glances were caught in her camera's eye: the peripheral faces: and these were wary, and conveyed a kind of warning.

She frowned, sat back down at the table. She hadn't given these prints much thought, and might not have remembered them at all had she not left them here by accident. Her motivation had been fairly whimsical and careless at the time. She had felt almost superfluous, and the work was so straightforward that it had seemed rather like cheating to accept a fee: the shots she was asked to take might almost have been done by anyone. But they were the least part of the story. Had it not been expressly forbidden, she might not have been so interested in shooting off the record: being told what to do always gave her an appetite for independence.

She riffled through the prints now, trying to find what she was looking for. There was a small industrial compound, temporary buildings covered in white dust, earth-movers standing idle and, suspended from a crane, a massive spherical segment of concrete, men standing beneath in blue boiler-suits and hard hats, pointing upwards, others swarming towards the point where it would be set down; mountains of displaced red earth. A tanker half tipped over as it was repaired, the water around it gleaming pink: even pollution looked pretty to an innocent eye. A metallic gold Lexus parked next to an open sewer on the edge of a tin-roof village.

A drilling operation of some kind, a pipeline being laid. It was no surprise: most of the people she had seen staying at the hotel were American or European businessmen, talking oil, stopped there for a few days after a stretch 'inside', as she overheard one man describe it at the bar. He was leaving the next day for Kinshasa, to take a flight across Congo to an operation outside Mbandaka.

On her return to England, she had telephoned Dennis James, meaning to thank him for putting the job her way. But he couldn't be reached. 'Oh, he's very rarely actually *here*.' Katherine asked for the address, and his secretary gave her a PO box number. She sent him a postcard but didn't hear from him. She had not expected to: the favour was a one-off. She remembered him telling her, 'Heard they were let down', and supposed his company had an arrangement with the hotel chain.

She studied one of the prints more closely through the eyeglass. She didn't see it at first, but then there it was. It had caught her eye a number of times during that week; she remembered the first occasion, the silver van parked across the hotel driveway. In this print, it was semi-obscured by the compound's high double fence, topped with razor-wire. It wasn't the same kind of van: a Ford Transit in London, by the look of it, and a Mercedes in Libreville, the windows blacked out against the heat, perhaps. But she had the print from London right in front of her; it was definitely the same logo.

The window of the van was lowered. Through the magnifying-glass she could just see the driver's mirrored Wayfarers angled towards her. She remembered the threat in the way the van's engine had idled alongside her. She had been on the other side of the fence, on foot, and had just taken a picture, when the van moved to block her view and had kept pace with her for a hundred yards or so.

She had fallen back from the group. Her guide was the deputy manager from the hotel, a young woman who also seemed to be in charge of 'public affairs', as she had put it with a smile when they first shook hands. Two men accompanied them. One middle aged, watchful, well dressed. The other a young man in a silk shirt and gilt-embossed Versace sunglasses whom Katherine had seen cleaning the pool – she was sure it was the same man – the previous afternoon. She couldn't remember their names. Their presence had been explained by someone who said that they 'knew the area', and she had expected them to point out particular sights, or things of historical interest. They said next to nothing throughout the week, by which time she had realised, more amused than alarmed, that they had been her minders.

Perhaps it was usual, a sign of hospitality rather than danger. She had quizzed the guide, asked if the men were security personnel. The woman looked startled at the suggestion but, instead of denying it, had replied that there were 'bad characters everywhere'. She smiled as she said this, and Katherine wasn't entirely certain if the woman was referring to other men, mercenaries, or the two men from the hotel. Then she had changed the subject: 'Now, Miss Clements . . .'

When the group turned back to collect her, the van had driven off, spraying dust as the driver shifted through low gears. But she had caught the moment on film and, through the lowered window, the gleam of metal was visible on the dashboard: the driver had been armed. She leant close over the image now. It was impossible from this print to say that it was a gun, but she remembered the suggestion of studied menace in the driver's appearance. She had supposed then that it was a tough act, no more. A security guard over-zealous at his job, perhaps. But, looking at the print now, she was not so sure. The anxious expression on the guide's face, half turning back to the group – 'What has she seen?' – was caught by accident within the frame. She had been given firm instructions, at the start, not to take pictures of any 'official' buildings – it was illegal. They had had to secure her a permit even for the brochure shots. Now she wished she still had the negatives so that she could make a better enlargement. But these nine forgotten prints were all she had.

One thing was certain: the logo on the two vans. A utilities company of some kind, she supposed, recalling the French tricolour. It was quite likely that a European company should have operations in Gabon: a coincidence.

She stared at the two prints on the table and was brought up short by the sudden sensation of her mother standing close beside her in the room.

'What should I be looking for, Ma?' She shocked herself with the sound of her voice: she had not meant to speak aloud. Her face felt hot with foolishness.

She felt in her jeans pocket: her mother's film. She took it out as though it might give her some clue or reassurance. She set it on the table alongside the two prints. Julia would have known what to do: instinct and fearlessness would have led her to the right place. At this moment she felt she possessed neither. She strained to hear the sounds of the house but could hear nothing beyond the irregular drip of water into the darkroom sink. She would develop her mother's film now. She shouldn't be afraid to do it: it would help to have her alongside her. It was what she most needed at this moment.

She sat back in the plastic chair, setting aside the prints. Edie's revelations had affected her more than she liked to admit. Now she felt blind and childish, as though she had been returned to the small girl she was, the first time her mother ever showed her how to develop pictures. She had got everything wrong. The principle of the process had entirely escaped her. She had had no patience. Was her mother disappointed? She had not shown it. But she herself had been in a fury of frustration, as though it meant she was not her mother's daughter. Why could she not see how it was done? The second time, one ruined film later, she had understood and, understanding, she had found herself at home. Waiting and patience: that was all it took.

With an effort of will, Katherine picked up her mother's film, went to rinse a developing tank. She had thought that the fire had ended so much of herself; it had seemed to cut short her innocence. Now, after just two days, it felt as though the fire was a spark at the end of a taper – not the end of things at all, merely a prelude to something far greater than she had first imagined. She was frightened to think of what might happen next.

The sound of fingertips came pattering on the darkroom door. She jumped, the hair rising on the back of her neck. And again, fingertips like rain on a metal drum. The prints were spread out over the table, some still hanging from the line. Katherine cleared them all away into an unmarked filing box and put it out of sight on a high shelf. Her mother's film would have to wait. She slipped it inside her shirt pocket.

'Hey, are you in there?' A little girl's voice: Ellen. 'Got something to show you. Can I come in?'

25

Ellen entered the darkroom empty-handed, laughing. 'I'm in!' She performed a quick circuit of the room, touching everything within reach. 'What's this?' She flicked the switch of the light-box. 'And this?' Her hands reached for the enlarger. Katherine explained, and Ellen listened, narrow-eyed and attentive.

'We think you must get gloomy doing this all day. Working in the dark.' Ellen picked up the eyeglass and looked through it, her mouth falling open. 'Like a miner,' she qualified. She often included her twin in such pronouncements, but Katherine was surprised to think that she had been the subject of their conversation.

She handed Ellen a strip of negatives, the author portraits, and showed her how to look at the images over the light-box. Ellen leant forwards and peered through the eyeglass, then turned back to her, disappointed. 'Edie's given us pictures like this.'

'Really?' Katherine was puzzled. 'Negatives?'

Ellen shook her head and bit her lip, as though realising she had uttered a secret. Katherine went to the shelf to look for something else. She took down some more portraits from a file, laid them on the light-box.

Ellen frowned as she looked at them. 'They're the same.' She wriggled down from the chair. 'Edie's given us them for our project. Pictures of people.' She went to the sink, peered over the edge into the water. 'Portraits.' She turned back as she pronounced the word, remembering. 'We'll show you later, if you promise not to tell.'

Edie had a few albums in her room, but nothing more than that, as far as Katherine knew. She remembered her father over breakfast: 'the famous project no one's ever seen', and was curious to see what the twins – and Edie – were up to. She cleared away some of the negatives, straightened the files, pulled the plug in the sink.

'Bit damp in here.' Ellen's voice was very quiet, and when Katherine turned to her she had perched back on the chair and was examining the strip of negatives again, long hair screening her face from view.

'Not so bad with the heating on.' Katherine waited for her to respond.

Ellen stood up. 'It's not home,' she whispered, still not meeting Katherine's eye.

'There she is.' Joanne waved at Katherine as they came out of the house from the kitchen door, and round on to the terrace. Ellen ran across the grass to look for Roy.

Now it was late afternoon, and in the few hours Katherine

had been inside, the garden had been transformed. A large white marquee, half pitched, stood at the far side of the lawn, and a number of men in overalls were constructing a dais. Others were shifting flat sections of wood to make the sprung dance floor. The overall appearance was of a stage-set, the curtain lowered mid scene-change, the action momentarily suspended.

She took a picture with her Leica. Joanne froze. 'Of this mess? Oh, God!' But it was her father she had been after, lying stretched out in a deck-chair, as though waiting for the performance to begin.

'I'm not sure this isn't a bit like seeing the bride in her wedding dress.' Peter waved a hand to take in the preparations, the men running from the front to the back of the house, sweating over lengths of scaffolding and planks of wood.

Joanne trotted across to him, carrying a clipboard. She stood over him, pen raised, 'Do we have enough—' she began, then burst out laughing. 'Oh, you poor thing, having to suffer all my fantasies.' She sat down beside him on the grass, leaning against the chair. 'It's not very romantic, is it, all this fuss?' They both seemed to wait for a reply, as though Katherine might have the answer. 'When did we decide we'd need all this stuff anyhow?' Joanne took hold of Peter's hand. He stroked her hair; she brightened, and shook herself. 'It'll be memorable, though, won't it?'

Katherine took their picture, and they both glanced up at her as the shutter fell.

It seemed that, after last night's rain, the weather would hold. Joanne had been scanning the minutely different reports on television, radio, and in the newspapers and the forecast was good. Where the breeze caught the marquee's canvas, it rippled, the loose guy-ropes flying like the jib-sheets of a sailboat snaking through the wind.

'Should send them home soon,' Joanne said, watching the workers. 'Getting dark. Way past time for drinks.' She pinched Peter lightly on the thigh: his job. He raised himself out of the deck-chair, and as he straightened, the telephone rang inside the house. Peter glanced at his watch. Joanne sighed. 'Tell them to go away.' Katherine noticed that her face clouded with anxiety. She remembered the difficulties her father had alluded to. 'Nothing to worry about,' Joanne addressed Katherine, as though she had spoken her thoughts aloud. 'Let Katherine get it, darling.' Joanne reached to take Peter's hand.

'Sure, I'll get it.' Katherine started across the lawn.

'Thanks, hon, take a message,' Joanne waved as she left, and Katherine heard her say, 'Forget about it. You can fix the G-and-Ts, and I'll round up the kids, what do you say?'

She took the call in Peter's study, reaching for a pen to write down the message. But the voice at the other end of the line was asking to speak to her. It took her a moment to realise that her own name was being asked for. She heard her father crossing the hallway – a sound of her earliest memories – heading from the kitchen towards the dining room where they kept the drinks tray. She heard the clink of crystal as the ice-cubes fell, and the faint glug of liquid as he poured gin into three glasses. He cursed softly, no tonic, perhaps, and recrossed the hallway, heading back through to the kitchen.

'Yes?' Katherine's breath caught as she answered. The voice at the end of the line was unfamiliar, with an East London twang. He introduced himself as a detective sergeant, and his voice shifted down a notch to a more sympathetic timbre as he told her that he was glad to have 'tracked her down', but that the news wasn't good.

'Couldn't you have called me on my mobile?' She didn't want to be overheard.

'I tried to reach you on it earlier, but . . .' His voice trailed off.

She couldn't believe she had been so stupid as not to check her phone: she had asked to be called only on that number. But her greater, unconscious desire was to speak to no one at all: she had left her phone switched off upstairs.

She listened for the sound of her father in the hallway. What could 'not good' mean, beyond what had already happened? Her palms were sweating and she held the receiver away from her mouth so that he wouldn't hear her breath, running high and hard in her chest.

'Nothing for you to worry about. I just thought I'd see if there's anything you might've missed out in your statement. I didn't want to bother you in person just yet.'

He paused, and her thoughts raced over what he might be suggesting. Was she under suspicion? 'I thought you said you had bad news?'

He cleared his throat, and she had the impression that she was being tested in some way. 'It's early days, obviously,' his voice had become brisk, 'but it seems likely we might be dealing with a case of arson, you see, which is why we wanted to know if you had anything to add to your statement.'

She couldn't trust herself to speak. What could she say?

Mention her suspicions about Miles, and then what? You couldn't shop someone to the police on a hunch, but was that what they were after — a clue that amounted to no more than a few threats, and her own fear at what he might be capable of?

She leant against the desk, and told him that, no, she couldn't think of anything, but even to her own ears her tone lacked conviction.

The man's voice grew slightly distant, as though he was writing something down. 'Can you think of anything you had in your flat, for example, that someone might have been after?'

She tried to think clearly: perhaps there were one or two objects of value — a few prints by well-known photographers; a few bits and pieces of jewellery. But not much. The prints would only have been of interest to art thieves, and desperate ones at that. It was very unlikely. Her TV and hi-fi certainly hadn't been worth stealing, that was for sure. She racked her brains for a logical answer, but all she could see was her ruined flat being walked around by strangers, its contents already referred to in the past tense.

'I'm going to leave it with you, anyway. If you think of anything at all . . .' He told her his number. 'And enjoy your dad's wedding.

Take your mind off things if you can, quite right. We'll talk again after all that's over. Day after tomorrow, I understand.'

She mumbled that it was, and wondered how much they knew about her. Had they checked up on her family? She could hear other telephones ringing, keyboards being tapped in the background down the phone.

'Someone will be in touch to have you back in, get it all cleared up. This number all right?'

'No.' Katherine tried to make her voice sound casual. 'Best not. I really don't want to worry my father before his wedding. Use my mobile – I'll make sure it's turned on.' The receiver was silent. 'That's best, don't you think?'

'If you can keep a secret,' he said, and Katherine imagined him having recorded their conversation to replay it later. 'Listen to this – when she says that line about not wanting to tell her dad. Telling the truth? Sounds odd to me. How d'you keep quiet about a thing like that?'

When she put down the phone, her hands were trembling. Her voice had sounded full of deceit; she was sure he must have noticed. She rubbed her forehead.

Yesterday she had passed Joanne on the landing. 'You OK?' She had put a hand on Katherine's arm. 'Feeling a bit peaky?' Before she had been able to speak, or invent excuses, Joanne had laughed and hurried off down the corridor: 'Don't tell me! Your secret won't be safe! Shouldn't even guess at the things you get up to.'

Now that she'd withheld the truth, it was as though she was

having to live inside a lie, and already she could see it becoming more elaborate as it was handed between each new person. Soon it would become so complicated, so murky, that she wouldn't be able to keep track of it. It would run out of control with a force and life all of its own, until even she would no longer have a clear view of the truth. She felt the shadows gathering already.

She heard her father's footsteps crossing the marble tiles. She glanced up and, in shock, saw him appear at the study door. She could have sworn he had been in the kitchen.

'Look like you've seen a ghost.' Her father held a black lacquer tray bearing three drinks, the ice knocking in the glasses. How long had he been in the dining room? From there you could hear perfectly what was said in the study. He held out his hand. 'Phone wasn't for me, then?' He looked at the unwritten-on notepad – no words, but a black box, heavily overscored until it had become a hard dark square of ink.

She tore out the page. 'No, for me.'

He took a step towards the desk as though to see if anything else had been written on the notepad. 'Miles checking up on you?'

She grinned, and he seemed to take this as her answer.

They went outside together on to the terrace. The workmen were packing up for the evening and Joanne was sitting on one of the wrought-iron garden chairs, her feet on a planter, the clipboard on the table beside her. 'Drinks!' She licked her lips. 'This place isn't anywhere near so bad when it has a bit of life in it.'

She waved at a young man on the lawn who had just finished nailing down the dais.

Where the sun had fallen beneath the hill the sky was turning rosy, and at its height the first stars were lit with yellow sunlight. The land itself was entirely black, and only the house was bright behind them. Stretching down through shadows to the fields, the lawn appeared to be obscured by smoke.

Joanne raised her glass. 'The future.'

26

The three of them were having dinner when the telephone interrupted the main course. It was just after nine thirty.

'You say there are no others?'

They could clearly hear Peter's half of the conversation. His tone was amiable, as though he might be discussing a round of golf with an old friend. But Katherine thought she heard the strain in it, too, and wondered if he was being sincere. She had seldom suspected her father of duplicity, but to hear him talking on the telephone now, she couldn't help but sense that his remarks were guarding something.

Joanne glanced at the door. 'Would you mind? Can't be so important that he has to take that call now. Business can wait.'

'Sure.' Katherine left the room, but stopped outside her father's study. His back was turned and he leant forwards over his desk.

'Look, pal,' he spoke fast, his voice lowered almost to a whisper, 'I don't want to know. Don't give me details I don't want to hear. I'm not listening. Do you understand what I'm saying? I can't spell it out. I don't want the details. I just want to hear yes or no. Am I going to hear that there's still a problem?'

He was silent for a moment, and Katherine heard him sigh. She knocked on the half-open door and he spun round. Then he smiled, holding out his hand to her. His tone changed. 'OK, I'm glad to hear it. Fine. Yes.' He sounded as though he was keen to get off the phone and raised his eyebrows at Katherine as though to say, 'Some people, how they chatter on.' She stepped into the circle of his arm. She could hear the voice at the other end of the line, no more than a tinny buzz, indecipherable.

Her father put down the receiver and turned to her. He pretended to laugh but his eyes were worried. 'She'll kill me.' He nodded towards the door.

Katherine wasn't sure how to answer. 'You overdoing it, Pa?'

He turned to the desk, waving at the stacked papers, then glanced at her, tugging his lip. 'You heard what I have to deal with?' He leant forwards for her answer, as though a great deal depended on it.

She faltered. She could see that he didn't wish actually to discuss his business worries with her – if that was what they were. She supposed, anyway, that he couldn't: that something approximating to insider-trading rules prevented him telling her the details of his work. But was there something he was afraid she might have overheard? It had happened in the past, and she had always insisted on her deafness – 'Didn't hear a thing!' And it was almost true: she found financial gossip easy enough to forget.

'You've always worked too hard.' She did not want to pry; she only hoped that he was all right. Her father seemed to relax when she said this, and she was reminded of a time when she had lain as a child beneath the table while he and his business partners held an afternoon-long meeting. Afraid to emerge until it was over, she had fallen asleep and only been discovered by her snores. They had all laughed about it, but they had asked her what they were discussing, as though it were some kind of test. She genuinely couldn't remember a thing. They had appeared to find this hilarious.

He picked up a sheaf of papers from the desk, as though in proof of the extent of his workload. 'I'm supposed to be getting married,' he grimaced, 'but this stuff doesn't stop.' He looked at his watch. 'Can you believe I get bothered at this hour?' He started to re-order the papers on the desk, shuffling them to one side. Katherine noticed that among them was a large scroll of plans, unbound, so that she caught a glimpse of part of a drawing, a developers' proposal. Peter glanced at her as he tightened the scroll, snapped a rubber band round it, and put it underneath the desk. As he leant to do this, a folder of letters slipped to the floor at Katherine's feet. She bent to retrieve it. 'Thanks, Katie.' Her father held out his hands.

Joanne could be heard walking across the hall towards the study. She came into the room, mock-furious. 'Now you're both at it! You're as bad as each other.' She held aloft her refilled glass of wine and took an exaggeratedly restrained sip. 'Helping him clear his desk at this hour? Shouldn't bother if I were you. It'll be a tip by tomorrow.' Peter went to her side. She kissed him.

'You must've got through a few forests in your time, darling. Come on. Pudding.' She led Peter from the room.

Katherine put the correspondence file back on the desk. She was glad that they had left: they wouldn't see that her hands were shaking. At the top of the letterhead, above her father's name and the business address of one of his company's subsidiaries, was a logo. It was unmistakable, and she had seen it elsewhere: in Africa, three weeks ago, and in London, on the night of the fire.

Katherine delayed going back to the dining room. She could hear Joanne talking, but not her father, and she had the impression that he was listening out for her: he had not seemed to want to leave her alone in his study, but Joanne's arm through his had been insistent.

She stared down at the letterhead and felt her heart racing. She had her back to the open door, shielding what she might be looking at on the desk, should anyone glance through. She lifted the top corner of the file, glanced across the page: nothing she recognised; an inventory of some kind; or perhaps the break-down of a bill, just a list of figures, not the whole part of the letter but supporting material, perhaps. She couldn't decode what the figures might mean. But there was no mistaking the logo. A noise from the dining room made her jump. Quickly she crossed the hallway to the downstairs lavatory.

She sat with her head in her hands, and told herself that there would be a simple explanation for that logo, one utterly meaningless, without any significance to her. But the phone conversation, the way her father had cleared that scroll of papers and held out his hand for the file – something about his manner had concealed a warning.

She stood up and looked at her face in the mirror, leaning close to the glass, noticing the deep frown line between her brows. She pressed it away. Two more days, and then they would be gone. By the time they returned from honeymoon, everything would have been cleared up. All that had happened would be revealed as no more than a series of coincidences. The fire had shocked her into paranoia: she was seeing patterns where none existed. With time she would forget, or maybe even mention to her father one day how she had felt. 'You poor thing, you must've been under so much stress.' He would look at her in admiration, seeing that she had kept quiet out of affection and concern for him, not wishing to burden him – more so, now that he had confessed to worries of his own.

She tried to convince herself of all this, but she did not quite believe it. Even her own expression in the mirror told her she was clinging to a scrap of trustfulness that would no longer hold her weight. The logos matched, and now all the threat she had sensed in Libreville, the horror of the fire, seemed to wait for her, very quiet but real, potentially lethal, on the other side of the door. Just a part of the paperwork; the fabric of her father's life.

But it couldn't be true. Greater than her fear was her conviction of her father's goodness: it was unthinkable to her that he should be aware of such connections. If they existed at all, they would be nothing to do with him. His look of anxiety was owed simply to the hazards of his profession, and if there were difficulties, he would see them through, come out unscathed on the other side. He had always done so in the past. And yet it puzzled her to see him behaving – she could not say, precisely, how; she hesitated before describing his manner as 'afraid'. But it was more than nerves, and had none of the anger of panic. He appeared to have an ear cocked for a sound that would not come, listening out for it with something close to dread, as though half wishing that it might. Katherine had noticed, more than at any previous time, the way his gaze rested on Joanne: not just with love or desire, but with a half-wary, half-astonished look of dependence, as though he had only recently been made aware of her strength of character, and how much he might soon need it.

This was nothing like her father's old self. Since Julia, he had never given the impression of needing anyone. It had been his independence from Katherine, and hers from him, which had made her feel so much as though she owed him her strength, and would not crumble. If he could do it, she could certainly pull it off. To see him look at Joanne that way, so hungrily, was to feel that she had to relearn him: had his strength, for all those years, been closer to a need for secrecy? Was it simply that he hadn't wanted to burden her, openly, with his sadness, just as she felt she could not risk opening up to him now? She splashed cold water on her face. She felt as though each movement forwards was on to ever more uncertain ground: she was walking towards a point of diminishing certainty that, in fact, she would never reach.

When she went back to the dining room, she was surprised to see that Joanne was no longer there. Her father was leaning back in his chair, looking at the blackened window when Katherine appeared. 'She's gone to get her beauty sleep.' He looked at his watch and shrugged. 'Only just past ten.

'What do you think of this?' He held up his glass of Margaux.

She had meant to mention it earlier that night. She sat down at the table opposite her father. She took a drink, but could say nothing now. He reached for the bottle, turned the label towards her. 'Joanne can't taste a thing.' He didn't sound as though he minded. 'Might as well be drinking Coke. She's great. Thinks I don't know.' He leant forwards, as though expecting Katherine might disagree.

He paused, looking into his glass. 'Don't think she'll ever be able to replace your mother. You don't think that that's what it's all about?' He rubbed his face. 'I love your mother still, you know that, don't you?' His eyes were urgent. Katherine had the sense that he was speaking not to her but to Julia, as though he had just heard her approaching across the hall, a jealous ghost.

Katherine couldn't stop herself glancing up. The doorway was empty, the hall silent. The only sound was the faint thump of footsteps overhead.

'And I miss her still.'

'Dad, you have to set it all aside, let it go.' Katherine spoke carefully, watching him. She felt as though they had been coming towards this place for years, ever since Julia's death. Now they were here, on the brink of a drop too dangerous even to look beyond: they were standing there with their backs turned to the fall. She wanted to say some word of warning, tell him to look out, but the words wouldn't come to her, and that fact felt less like speechlessness than like a kind of parting: she couldn't go any further with him.

He seemed very old. His chest was bowed, his arms loose on the table. She went to sit beside him and he leant heavily forwards, the back of his head showing slight baldness that she had not noticed before. She looked away. His shoulders trembled, and she could not bear to think that he was crying. She put her arm round him.

'I see her sometimes.' His voice was muffled, and Katherine shivered.

'So do I, Dad, often, as clear as ever.'

But he turned to her and his cheeks were wet. 'No. Not in a good way.' His voice was full of anguish. He looked at the empty window, as though he couldn't bear to meet her eye. This grief was all his; she had thought she knew the extent of it, but the man who had felt these things was her mother's husband, and she felt suddenly like the child she used to be, spying on an adult love, uncomprehending. She took away her arm. He poured more wine.

'Sometimes, at night, I see her. In the bedroom sometimes, when I'm alone, or when Joanne is there. It makes her jump. She can tell. You know she wanted me to visit her shrink?' Katherine tried to smile: she hadn't known that Joanne was in therapy. Peter waved her attempt away. 'Or I'll see her in the top corridor, along the landing. Nothing special. She'll just be walking along the corridor towards me. It looks like she's covered in light – I can't say how but as though she's wearing light somehow, and is bringing it towards me because I'm too much in darkness.' He looked around the room, then appeared to realise that his daughter was still beside him. 'This place!' He pretended to laugh off his confession.

But Katherine heard his wife-to-be's expression in that remark. 'This place!' That was how she voiced her impatience with it, as though she couldn't wait for it to be sold. Had she learnt it from him? There was too much she did not know.

He sighed deeply and drained his glass. 'Come on, big days ahead of us all. Shut-eye.'

They walked together through the hall. The back door was still open to the night, and they went across to it, stepping out on to the terrace. The wind had risen, rattling the thick leaves of the rhododendrons, but the air was warm, and bore the wet scent of lakewater towards the house, the bitterness of water-cress, and something faintly rotten and malodorous, the rich scent of compost, or decaying flowers.

Peter turned to go back inside. 'We all need sleep.' He walked behind her into the house, locking the door.

27

'Edie gave them to us.'

Ellen held the project close against her chest. She closed the door softly behind her.

Roy followed, and the twins sat down on either side of Katherine on the sofa.

'"The famous project no one has ever seen,"' Roy quoted Peter, and grinned. 'We don't want to tell anyone about it till it's done.'

They were in the drawing room. It was mid-morning, the day before the wedding. Ellen opened the blue scrapbook. 'See? Pictures like yours. People.' She looked up at Katherine for confirmation, riffling through the pages.

The majority were indeed portraits, mainly of Victorians; some actual prints, most photocopies. But in addition there were also pictures cut from magazines, or hand-drawn and felt-tip-coloured drawings copied from books. Images of gold, ivory, rubber, coffee, copper, tin, diamonds and, on the next page, the things that they became: a copper kettle, a steam engine, a pair of wellington boots, a diamond engagement ring, a cup of coffee. There was a picture of a bar of Rowntree's chocolate, and a list of other Quaker names, Fry and Cadbury. There was a caricature of the abolitionist, Thomas Clarkson, waving a Bible; and on the facing page they had copied out Wordsworth's poem – 'Clarkson! It was an obstinate hill to climb.' The title of the project was 'Trading with Africa'.

The images were carefully laid out, with captions written beneath each one above pencilled-in lines, the handwriting clear and deliberate. 'This is great! Aren't you clever?' The twins jostled closer, clearly pleased.

Roy leant against her, looking over her arm as he turned the pages. 'Start here.'

The first photograph showed a woman in her forties standing against tall trees, the broad leaves of banana and rubber plant forming a dark backdrop to her long white muslin dress. It might have been taken in an English botanical garden, at Kew or Oxford. But the woman's chin was raised in an attitude of poised defiance that suggested fear – or perhaps exhaustion. In her right hand, which was gloved, she held a large white hat against her thigh. Looking closely, the hat appeared to be heavily netted – to ward off mosquitoes, Katherine supposed. She read the caption: 'Amelia Briars, 1885'. 'Was this one from Edie?'

The twins exchanged glances.

'Not sure.' Ellen shrugged. 'Probably.'

'How did you know the name?' Katherine lifted the edge. 'Can I take it out?'

Ellen squealed. 'Roy's useless at sticking! It's on the back.'

The headline on the page read, 'Victorian lady travellers'. Underneath, the twins had pasted a photocopied paragraph from a book. In rather antiquated language, it mentioned Amelia Briars, describing her as an abolitionist pioneer, a woman 'of immense courage', who had carried on her husband's work after his death. She had only travelled to the Congo once, but had taken a small number of photographs of what she had seen there. 'Edie lent us the book too. Mum did the photocopies.'

Katherine lingered on the name 'Briars'. It might be a coincidence. But perhaps that was how Edie had come to give them the photograph – because Amelia was related to Lewis Briars. She would ask her later.

'And this one is *by* her.' Roy turned to a photocopied photograph on the next page. It showed a group of approximately thirty people. They were arranged in the manner of a formal Victorian wedding portrait: an extended family, grouped around a couple, the impression of a house in the background. But the house was a cluster of straw-roofed adobe huts, and the guests' ankles were manacled together along a chain curling into the dust.

On the facing page was a drawing of King Leopold II; beneath it, a muddy photograph that might have been a battle scene, with humps of bodies stacked up like industrial slag-heaps. The caption simply read, 'Congo: first genocide within the age of the telegraph and photograph'.

Roy flicked through the scrapbook. 'Amelia Briars wrote letters to *The Times*. We got one from Edie's book. Here.' He turned the page, and there was a photocopy of a letter. Katherine read: 'Dear Sirs, I would like to draw your attention to . . .' She turned the pages, the rest of the scrapbook was blank.

'We haven't finished it yet.' Ellen closed the book and sat back on the sofa, hissing, 'Roy!' She had spotted her mother crossing the lawn towards the house.

Joanne appeared at the french windows, red-faced, waving her clipboard and a marker-pen. 'Thank heavens you're all together.' She wagged the pen at them when she saw them. 'We need you in the garden. Rehearsal time.'

Roy slipped the scrapbook under the sofa cushions and groaned. Ellen jumped up and ran outside. 'No complaints and no excuses.' Joanne held out her hand to her son. Katherine followed and Joanne smiled at her in gratitude. 'You all done in there? Everything set? I've got a salt scrub after the vicar's been.'

Katherine brought her Polaroid. 'I'll take some snaps. See how it's going to look.'

'You're wonderful.' Joanne put an arm round her waist. 'You OK with my little monsters? They weren't bothering you?'

Katherine was about to mention the project but Roy over-heard his mother's question. 'Top secret!' he said. 'Don't say.' Joanne rolled her eyes and watched as he ran off to join his sister.

'They've had a rough time without their father.' She looked directly at Katherine. 'Everyone should have one around. I didn't, did you know that? Died when I was so high.' She gestured. 'Toddling. Mother didn't believe in remarriage, which I can't say I understood. "Once you've done it, you've done it," she used to say. The hell with that!' She threw back her head and waved across the lawn towards Peter. 'I hoped all you kids would get along.' She turned back to Katherine.

'I'm not quite a kid.' Katherine smiled.

'Spring chicken, at least.' Joanne brought her face close to Katherine's. 'What do you use? Don't tell me you're one of those Nivea-and-nothing girls, please! I'll die!' She looked back across the lawn to where the twins were walking in procession along a narrow line – an imaginary aisle towards the dais. 'I can't think how you guys coped for so long. No wife, no mother. I'm glad you did, don't get me wrong,' she winked, 'glad no one got to him before I did, pipped me at the post. If I didn't have those two I'd wish I'd met him years ago, when I was young. But they make up for it – make up for all that lost time.'

Katherine began to speak but Joanne cut across her. 'OK, not lost, but wasted.' Her mouth narrowed as she spoke. 'To think I lived all that time with a lie. That was the really shitty part of it. He was banging Pammy and I'd no idea.' She slipped her arm through Katherine's and they started across the lawn.

'I shouldn't tell you this, but I found a pair of her panties once – in his briefcase, for crying out loud. He told me they were a gift for me and I believed him. "Where's the wrapper?" I wanted to know. They looked second-hand. But it was like I was so set against facing up to the thought of him being a shithead that I couldn't see the obvious chink in his lies. A mile wide. Does that make sense? He seemed squeaky clean to me. Dull, but clean.' She shook her head.

Peter called to them from the far side of the lawn: 'Hey, I think I can hear a car.'

Joanne waved at him, but put a hand on Katherine's arm and turned to face her, speaking in an undertone. 'You know, that's what I can't stand. A lie. Give me the truth and I'll see if I can live with it and, believe me, I can live with an awful lot of grey areas. Jesus, I should tell you some time. I have quite a few stories.' Joanne raised her eyebrows. There was the sound of a car on the gravel of the driveway at the front of the house. 'Vicar's due at eleven. That'll be him now. I'd better see to him.'

But she hesitated. 'I've learnt to let all this stuff go. It's my vanity, I guess, that reminds me. I look at myself in the mirror and I curse that man. He had me when I was young like you. He had all that and he crapped on it. He didn't respect the fact that, more than love, I was giving him *time*. When he cheated, it was like he took an eraser and rubbed out all those years. And now I'd give my eye-teeth to have that time back again. Not for myself, but because I wish I could give it all to your father. If I could do that—' She shut her eyes. 'I love him very much, you do know that, don't you, hon?'

Joanne started to walk away. 'Don't tell the vicar what I just said,' she shrieked. 'He'll pee his pants!'

28

Seen from a window on an upper floor, the wedding rehearsal might easily have been mistaken for a plain-clothes run-through of a theatrical performance. With their backs to the house, Joanne and Peter stood shoulder to shoulder, as though confronting the vicar with an argument that he was at pains to refute. A thin, small man of around fifty, with thick white hair worn short, a brown cord jacket over his dog-collared shirt, he listed towards them, indicating something in a large black hard-backed notebook, pointing with one hand, gesturing with the notebook for emphasis. The twins had been obliged to separate and sat at either side of the small dais, very still, as though waiting for their cue.

Katherine was part of the audience. She made notes with the Polaroid. She wondered how much her father knew about Joanne's previous marriage; how much she really knew about his. Rather than making Joanne appear merely wounded, Katherine thought that that story of infidelity had made her seem almost indestruct-ible: having the ability to laugh even at her own hurts had redoubled her strength; she had simply left it all behind, chucked in even her mistrust, and now could stand alongside her husband-to-be with the frank eagerness of someone expecting only good things to come.

The first wave of workmen had all left. Later that day the lighting crew would arrive and line the green square of lawn with hundreds of tiny lights on metal stalks. Joanne had wanted flares – 'But what if someone wears nylon?' She had conceded that electricity might be safest. 'Don't want my guests going up in flames!'

Caterers and florists were due the following morning. The ceremony was at four.

Edie watched the rehearsal from her bedroom window. Mary had just given her her medication and turned to go. 'Keep me company,' Edie called her back. 'Might be rain.' She bent forwards and smiled up at the darkening sky.

'They'll be under cover.' Mary straightened the bedclothes.

'We'll all be under cover,' Edie corrected her. 'Might be rather nice if it does pour.'

Mary rested her arms on the window-sill, watching the figures move about below.

Joanne and Peter turned, Joanne improvising with a regal wave at the absent crowd, and progressed back down an imaginary line, the twins following in stately tandem. At the end of the procession, Joanne turned back to the children, crouching down to their height. 'You got that, kiddos?' She hugged them and they ran back into the garden, ducking under the guy-ropes, heading towards the cover of trees.

The sky was dark now above the house, and the lawn was lit with the purple light of possible thunder. 'What do you think, Vicar?' Joanne pointed heavenwards.

The vicar blushed. 'I'm no meteorologist I'm afraid.' He shuffled his feet in embarrassment.

'Thought you might be thick with Him upstairs.' Undeterred, Joanne linked her arm through his. 'Now, I've been dying to say this for so long you can't imagine. May we offer you tea?' She smiled, glancing up at the house as though expecting the reprimand of watchful generations of English tea-takers, the reluctant progress of countless vicars.

They arranged themselves on the terrace. 'The hell with rain – sorry. Let's defy it, don't you think?' Joanne brought out the tea things. Katherine made her excuses and went inside. As she left, her father stepped towards her as though he wanted to say something, but Joanne handed him a plate of biscuits and he stood still: those biscuits were a command. 'Vicar?' When he turned back his daughter had gone.

Stepping into the house, Katherine could just hear Edie and Mary talking upstairs, the thump of a chair being set down, Edie's quick, high laugh. A radio played in the kitchen. She went through to the drawing room and sat at the baby grand, listening to the sounds of the house. Happy sounds were easy to take for granted, to barely notice, but once they were gone they seemed most precious for being so easily overlooked. In the last few days she had grown attuned to too much that was painful, full of sadness; things it had been impossible not to hear. Now she wondered how much of the past had been simply misheard, or lost through inattention.

She straightened the music on the stand. The piano had been covered with a cream lace mantilla, and on top of this, a number of silver-framed photographs, a small collection of Georgian enamel boxes, a cedarwood cigarette box inlaid with mother-of-pearl. She tried to imagine Joanne's position, in love with a man who was still half living with the impression of his first wife, her image reappearing between them when she had supposed they were alone. It would take more than any amount of redecorating to banish that ghost, and Katherine felt worried for Joanne. Strength was pointless in the face of such a private vision: she would find herself trying to wrestle Peter's entire history to the ground.

From here, Katherine was invisible to the three people on the terrace although she could hear clearly enough what was being said. Would the vicar give the pair a pre-nuptial pep-talk? She was curious to know how they might respond. But he was tentatively broaching the subject of roofs.

'Thieves are a menace in Kent.' His voice was full of anguish: why pick on his church?

Joanne's tone was sympathetic. 'I'm surprised, I really am. You don't expect it in the countryside.'

'I caught one once, red-handed,' the vicar went on gloomily. 'Pockets stuffed with lead.'

'What's it for?' Joanne sounded puzzled.

'Quite. It's beyond my comprehension.' Katherine heard the vicar take a noisy sip of tea as though for emphasis.

Katherine had the impression that Joanne must be fixing Peter with a significant look by now: can't you spare the poor man some dough? She could hear her father clear his throat – one of his preludes to talking cash.

'Well,' the vicar elaborated, 'during the war I'm told it was in high demand, but now I'm not so sure. They trade it, I suppose, profit by it in some way. Sell it to buy drugs – I assume that's what they're after. Or alcohol. Things for their cars. They possess an awful lot of cars, for young people. I can't see where exactly they're hoping to go.' His tone was momentarily wistful. Katherine heard him set down his tea-cup.

Joanne gave a light laugh and the wicker chair creaked when she settled back. 'I was crazy about my car when I was young.' With this, she seemed to have forgiven the lead-thieves.

The vicar's tone became abrupt: 'Not at the expense of your church roof, I'm sure.' His chair scraped back on stone as he rose. 'Well, everything's settled.' Katherine imagined him straightening his lapels, fastening the middle button of his cord jacket, checking his watch, looking out across the garden. 'You'll be sorry to leave, I bet.'

There was a moment's silence, and Katherine held her breath. Even the vicar, apparently, had known before she did that they would be leaving Fareham. Couldn't they even say that they would be sorry to go?

Katherine heard her father clear his throat again. Nothing further was said outside. She remembered another occasion on which the vicar had visited the house, when she was ten. It was after her mother's funeral, on Peter's wishes a small ceremony, with few flowers. The vicar was newly arrived then from a wealthy parish in Surrey, and had seemed less discouraged. But he had not been fond of children: she remembered his odd manner with her, almost of reprimand, when he said that he hoped to see her in future in church. He had waited in vain for her to agree. But what could she say? She had no intention of becoming a church-goer; did not follow his logic of suffering begetting devotion. Her father had perhaps been generous on that occasion, too, and the subject of her attendance was never again mentioned; obviously the man had tact.

'Please, go right ahead, I need to run through my check-list.' As Joanne spoke, Katherine could hear her snap her clipboard, and she supposed that her father and the vicar were on their way to his study to talk figures. The roof might not be saved, but its decline might be momentarily halted.

'It's not good business.' Peter had spoken about it with exasperation in the past. 'Set the amount that gets spent saving that roof on the number of people who sit under it. It just doesn't balance.'

'Your thinking is scandalous.' Edie had silenced him. 'It's Saxon, and there's an end to the matter. What would you have him do? Put his congregation in a Barratt home with bells on?'

'A beautiful modern building, with good heating. Why not get shot of the past when it's no longer viable?'

'That word should be struck from the vocabulary. It is without humanity.' She had reached for her cheque-book. 'See if that'll shut you up. Do it my rotten self.'

'You gave them how much?' asked Peter, when he learnt of the amount.

'It'll teach you a lesson.'

'What lesson?' He wondered aloud if the vicar might return his mother's cheque. 'It was clearly excessive. I'm amazed that he accepted it.'

'Don't even think about it, buster.' Edie had wagged her walking-cane at him.

It had been one of the few times that Katherine had ever seen Edie in open disagreement with her son, whom she seldom criticised. That episode had coincided with the arrival of Joanne at Fareham. It wasn't Peter's attitude to the church that she objected to. 'There'll be no slacking.' She had been firm. But when Peter was out of earshot, Edie had turned to Katherine with a smile of satisfaction. 'Checkmate! That's money well spent. He thinks I have no business acumen. But you must spend money to save it in the long run – you should remember that. It's my hot tip, my legacy.'

She had seemed to find the business over the roof amusing, a smart ploy that she had pulled off. 'He's always been jealous of big spenders, has to outdo them, go one up. Thought this'd be the best way of helping out our poor glum vicar with his leaky roof. Keep Peter's cheques coming.' Edie's family were buried in that church; she intended to join them one day. 'I'm just looking after my future.' She had grinned.

Now Katherine could hear the vicar and her father cross the hall towards his study.

'You're terribly kind,' the vicar said, sounding relieved. 'As always.'

Perhaps he had feared the cheques might stop now that the Clementses were moving away from his parish. Katherine waited until she heard the study door click shut. From outside there was the sudden grate and fizz of a match being struck, then the faint whiff of tobacco carried into the room: pre-nuptial nerves.

She hoped to avoid talking to her father. She had sensed that he wanted to tell her something, and she wondered if in the night he had turned over in his mind the moment when she had appeared at the study door, and saw that it might be politic for him to give an explanation. He had not looked guilty, but suave – too relaxed, and her father was seldom relaxed, not by nature a smooth-mannered man. He was guarded, reluctant; his movements gave him the suggestion of the penitent, or of someone who had lost a thing of great value – not necessarily personal. From his usual appearance, he might have been divined as a man who had lost a fortune in a market crash, although this was not the case. He had a habit of raising his shoulders when he was nervous.

But last night he had been almost languid as he stretched out an arm to his daughter, raising his eyebrows in boredom with the voice at the far end of the telephone. Yet he had quickly replaced the receiver, and it was clear to Katherine that he had not wanted her to overhear his conversation. 'You say there are no others?'

She had never seen him behave like that, and she reminded herself that of course she knew nothing of his business self, although this was not enough to lift her disquiet. She could still see the logos, matched up in her mind, a trail that seemed to run half-way round the world to end up in this house.

Now she waited until the hallway was clear, then went through to the annexe and the darkroom. She stood for a moment in the white light, listening for anyone approaching. The room was silent. She slipped the catch.

She took her mother's film from her shirt pocket and weighed it in her hand. Perhaps it would yield nothing, all the frames turned by time to darkness. She steadied her breath. It felt like a very definite goodbye. She filled the kettle, switched the light to red, and set to work.

The cool of the unused stable-block, too damp for some of her mother's prints, had proved a tolerable culture for the reel of film, which was almost entirely unharmed. Only a few frames showed signs of damage. Katherine looked along the strip in amazement. They were family snaps: a gift from the past, entirely unexpected.

Her mother, with Katherine standing just in front of her. How old was she? Five, or thereabouts, she supposed. Her father, a similar pose, with his back to the house, the light full on his face so that he squinted against the sun. Another, taken just at the edge of shadows cast by a low-branched tree, where all three of them sat on a rug laid out on the grass somewhere beyond the lawn; the tree looked like an oak. She had few photographs of herself as a child with both her parents in the frame. Here, her father's expression, caught mid-laugh, suggested that Julia had arranged the shot, then rushed to sit beside him on the rug and taken the picture with a timer switch. It was impossible to say. One of her legs stuck out at an angle too uncomfortable-looking to sit for very long.

The next frame implied a different story. There was Mary, as Katherine remembered her when she was young, turning away as Peter took a photograph of Julia and Katherine, standing now, but on the same rug. Perhaps Mary had taken that other picture.

She looked along the strip, and lingered on one picture in particular, unlike all the rest. It had none of the appearance of a hurried family snap. Rather, it looked like a stage-managed formal portrait of a couple, proudly displaying their two children.

The couple was Peter and Mary. They stood on the terrace, and in front of them was Katherine, her weight on one foot, as though she had been about to run off. Behind her, in Peter's arms, lay the second child, hidden in blankets. From the way Mary leant towards the baby, Katherine supposed that it was her own: Alice.

She bent over the negative with her eyeglass. The back of her neck prickled. It was as though her mother was giving her clues from the dead.

She put the thing out of sight in a file, but could see it still, and felt heartsick at the thought of what it might mean. Her father's expression in the photograph was exactly as it had been last night when she had walked in on his phone conversation, and in both cases there was a kind of request in his eyes: if you can see me as I am, forgive me. In both, he had been a picture of guilt.

29

It was Edie's habit — often when the rest of the house had gone to bed and she could not sleep — to watch movies with the sound turned down. If someone entered, she zapped the screen to black: 'It's like someone craning over my shoulder to read. Makes me feel spied on.' She had a television and a VCR in her bedroom, and when it wasn't being used, the television was covered with a cloak of chintz, like a large tea-cosy. 'Can't stand the sight of that thing,' she would say, whenever the screen fell dark.

Now, on the night before the wedding, she had pronounced herself 'whacked' and decided to take her dinner upstairs in bed. It was early evening. Katherine had agreed to join her; anyway, dinner downstairs wouldn't be much of an event that night. Joanne had grown anxious, fearing the upset of her 'arrangements'. Bad weather, late guests, poisoned canapés, energetic children. She stood in the hallway counting off all the possible disasters on her fingers. 'I need a pill!' She had gone upstairs around six and not come down.

Tonight it was *Casablanca*. 'Can't help myself.' Edie grinned.

'It's my great weakness.' She had watched it too many times to number. When Katherine was perched on the edge of her bed, Edie leant close towards her, as though fearing she might be overheard. 'One of the few films from around that time that I *didn't* see with him, not quite.' She leant back heavily in the duckdown pillows. 'I think that that's why it makes me think of him so much. We'd arranged to see it together, and never did.'

With the lights off, the ceiling was alive with shadows. 'Shut the door, that's best.' Edie glanced up at Katherine. She chewed a piece of chicken in silence, then set down her knife and fork, pushing away the plate. 'Can't eat. Nerves.'

'Him?'

'Him and everything else.' Edie covered Katherine's hand with hers. 'Everything comes home in the end.'

Edie shut her eyes and Katherine watched her face, the fine pinkish skin of her cheekbones flushed with emotion. She turned to her suddenly. 'Secrets have their place, and purpose. But you must be careful that they don't make you too lonely.' She smiled at her granddaughter. 'Now . . .' With the film playing, and the sound turned almost to mute, she told Katherine about the time she had almost seen it with him.

They had arranged to meet at the Empire cinema in Leicester Square. She had arrived fifteen minutes late, and he was inside, peering into the darkness to find her. She had spotted him, wreathed in silver light, on the far side of the cinema, searching for her. She watched him bend down towards the rows of faces to see if she was there, and she had fallen in love with him all over again: she had loved him for wishing to find her. It wasn't simply manners or embarrassment that prevented her calling out to him: she opened her mouth to say his name and, before she could speak, he looked up and waved at her through the shadows.

They had missed too much of the start of the film, so they left the cinema together and met in the afternoon light outside, blinking and laughing with apologies. He slipped his arm round her shoulders and kissed her beneath the dusty plane trees in the square.

Edie settled further back in her pillows and sighed. 'Waiting is hard, and not right, you know. Men don't wait, they change themselves by doing. Women wait, it's what changes them, and not in a good way. That's about the sum of it.' She shook her shoulders and looked for the remote control in the folds of the heavy blanket. 'It's no good. If only we could all swap round for a time, the world might—'

'Why did it end, though, Gran? You weren't married any more. You were free.'

Edie frowned and pressed a hand quickly to her forehead, as though she had caught a chill and felt feverish. She pulled the covers higher and looked away. 'He was Catholic.'

'But that's not enough.' Katherine was puzzled.

Edie stared at the moving figures on the screen. She hesitated before speaking, and Katherine had the impression she was weighing up the merits of a lie. Her voice was very quiet and low, as though uttering not a secret but an oath, shameful for her to speak. 'It wasn't only then, you know, that anything happened.'

She said the words with a tightening of her lips. 'It was before, do you see?' She did not look nostalgic, but shaken; she glanced at Katherine.

Katherine remembered her intimation of that painter's suggestion: take off your clothes. She had been right. It was all there, revealed in the look Edie had given to whoever happened to glance at the canvas. No wonder Hugh had loved that picture in secret, detested it in public. It wasn't the kind of thing one admitted to being beguiled by; not when the look of desire had been inspired by another man. No one could love with that degree of freedom. Edie had been right, the other evening: few things are worthy of unconditional love; she must have included herself secretly in that remark.

'I didn't think it could happen twice.' Edie laid a hand on Katherine's arm to silence her. 'I thought it was more to do with it being forbidden, and part of being young. I had thought that to see him again, when both of us were free, would be too much. The thing would dissolve. It would be shown up to have been nothing at all, like trying to raise the dead. I couldn't risk that. I thought it was better to parcel him away in the past. But when I saw him again, I realised that that denial was only a form of waiting. I had been waiting for the moment I might see him again, and when I did it was all still there. There was no doubt.' She shook her head, cleared her throat.

She described a time, once, when they were in his flat in town. It was in Pimlico, not far from the river. London could be heard as a distant hollow drum, the sound running down the river to the mudflats of the Thames estuary. It had been September, still mild, and the windows were open that day, too. They were listening to Haydn, and he sat across the low table with their coffee cooling between them, his feet in navy blue socks, one darned with lighter blue wool, up on the edge of the table. Big soft feet, slightly flat in the arches, as though he was used to understanding the world through the impression it made upon his soles. 'His legs were bare.' She blushed, looked down at her hands, her voice lowered almost to a whisper so that Katherine had to lean towards her to hear. 'The heart is made of pictures, not things and not words either.'

With the window open, they could hear the wind gathering in the treetops outside, the first faint patter of rain on canvas. 'And music, too.' Edie smiled. 'The heart is pictures and music.'

Every detail of the room could return to her 'like that' – she clicked her fingers and smiled. Dust on the mantelpiece where there was a Chinese candlestick-holder, painted with imperial yellow mandarins, red-cloaked with umber earth beneath them; a vase in the fireplace, the glass crackled with a silver-pearl glaze, just as she had seen it being blown one time in Venice, in Murano; the painting on the wall above his head – a lengthways portrait of a strip of coastline that had turned out to be Kent, when he looked on the back, and painted perhaps not more than fifteen miles from Fareham in 1903, by an artist whose signature neither could decipher, although Edie thought she recognised the line of the cliffs. She had stood beside him while he took down the picture, and her naked arm had pressed the length of his. He had

had toothache, and smelt of cloves. He set the picture on the floor, and it was evening before she left his flat.

Pictures and music. And with the sound down, Edie told her, she had had the full summer trees of Leicester Square above her, his hand pressed to her back and his lips on hers. Edie shut her eyes. The film still played in silence in the corner of the room. There was no other light.

'You loved taking pictures from the start, I know.' Edie breathed out deeply and turned back to Katherine. 'I remember watching you learn all about it. Your mother teaching you when you were very small. I was there the first time, on the back lawn. You won't remember. She used an old Kodak Brownie – I approved of that a great deal. Thought it quite brilliant actually. "See," your mother said to you, "it's like a little room." I remember the way you had a good look inside, and must've decided then that it was magic. "But it's empty!" You seemed quite upset at first, until Julia explained that that was the place where the past came back to life. You liked this notion. "It takes darkness," Julia explained, "to make any sense out of the light." I recall that expression clearly. But I remember the picture better.'

The shadows ran like poured water across the ceiling and down the far wall. Katherine nudged Edie's arm gently. 'But why on earth did it end? You've changed the subject.'

Edie breathed out heavily and turned her face away, running a finger over her collarbone, loosening the neck of her dressing-gown. 'Yes, I have.' She glanced across at the door as though expecting someone to appear there to silence her. Then she nodded in the direction of the attic. 'This family.' She said the words as though they were a curse, taking Katherine's hands and trying to smile at her, but her eyes were nervous.

Katherine felt the weakness in Edie's touch, as though a great pressure weighed upon her, urging her against further disclosure. Her hands seemed to cling to Katherine's more for her own support than anything else. Katherine had the impression that everything Edie had said so far had been by way of introduction: the romantic picture had been built up, and all her attention had been on that, when in fact it was not the main story. Involuntarily she drew back. Edie's expression frightened her, and when she spoke again, her voice was strained: 'You helped the twins with their project?'

Katherine was puzzled: this was not what she had expected, but Edie's hands gripped hers more insistently, and she went on, not waiting for Katherine's answer: 'I have never been sure how much you knew. I thought it might make it easier for you to let go of this house, do you understand? Seeing all the ghosts that are here. Because it made it easier for him,' her voice grew faint, and Katherine had to lean closer to catch her words, 'to let go of me.'

She felt the nerves prickle along her spine. Edie appeared to sink further away from her as she spoke, as though, before, she had been composed so much of secrets that confession had now diminished her. Katherine saw the question she had meant to ask Edie – whether Amelia Briars was related to Lewis – now appear to sit directly ahead of them both; the most pressing question;

an overlooked link that completed the chain. 'There was a kind of history between our families.' Edie's voice was barely a whisper.

Katherine saw the pattern emerging and she shrank from it. She remembered how she had complimented the children for their cleverness, not for a second seeing what they had actually done – and, in part, with Edie's help. She had seen the pictures but only half of their meaning: blind as she had been as a child, playing shop with those log books, which only yesterday she had held and flicked through. The house seemed to move more closely around her.

'He could hardly look at me.' Edie's voice was a whisper. 'He came down here unexpectedly. He behaved as though I'd cheated him, played a trick on him in some way. "Were either of you ever going to tell me who you were?" He felt let down first by my husband, his friend, and then by me – as though we'd joined forces to betray him. He had always been very proud of his family. Great philanthropists, abolitionists. I knew what both families had been, but not that they had ever overlapped. It wasn't public knowledge. A biographer dug it up, and it turned out there had been a scandal. His grandmother, Amelia, who died in the 1880s, in a fire in Africa, in such a way that aroused suspicion that perhaps her death wasn't entirely . . .' Edie faltered. Wind shuffled the curtains. 'She had gone to the Congo, after her husband died, and taken photographs of some of the Clementses' – I don't know – operations. They were relayed back to England by her companions, after the fire.'

Katherine's heart contracted, tightening to a point of pain

inside her chest. Her mind recoiled from everything with which it had been presented, but she could not move away from it: it held her fast, forced her to look at what it meant; and it was most terrible for seeming to be most true. Her past did not come apart with the knowledge, quite the reverse: it started to fall into place – but how could she not have known?

'After that, he simply saw the Clements family as all bad, and that meant me too, in his eyes. I hadn't the conviction to insist to him that there were shades of grey also. For him, it was personal.'

There was a sound of someone crossing the hall downstairs. Edie waited until the house was silent. 'He pointed to Peter, as though he were proof of his argument, and told me, "That's why you'll always be a Clements. They're still there."' She gripped the edge of the blanket. 'But he was so blind.' She turned to Katherine, her eyes wide as she went on: 'He missed the very thing he should have seen.' She reached up to her lips, touched them briefly with the back of her hand as though to stop a sob. 'But at what moment do you say, "Enough, that story's over"? Turning from it didn't make it go away. Someone had to tear it all down, build some-thing new, and for a moment I had thought it might've been us.' Katherine moved towards her, taking her hands again. Edie was trembling. 'Because I did believe that picture. I thought that if I waited, there'd come a day when I could step back into it and everything that had happened, all the mistakes and waiting, would somehow disappear.'

Edie's voice had grown thin with exertion, and her pale face was flushed at the high point of her cheekbones, her eyes shining with effort. 'Instead it was for nothing. I have waited and paid and we lost a love that might—' She leant back heavily against the pillows and stared at the television screen.

'Was that how it ended?'

Edie turned slowly to her, taking her hand again. Her face was calmer, her voice steadier. 'Yes. I let him go. I wanted him to be free of me.' Her tone was guarded now, and she watched Katherine's face as though trying to read something there. 'I was worried about you when you arrived. You reminded me of myself, as I was then. Secretive – as though you'd convinced yourself that you were carrying something around in you that was too black to shed any light on, an unmanageable sadness. Nothing's so dark as that. No secret is so impenetrable that it can't be forgiven, or dismissed.' She squeezed Katherine's hand. 'I wish someone had told me that, then. I would've frogmarched him right round all the dark places in my heart and insisted that he see some sense. I'm sure he would've. But I didn't possess the courage, and instead I took the weak person's way out, and played the tragic heroine, the penitent. I sacrificed myself to a secret – and you can see that it hasn't suited me too well.'

She smiled and straightened the blanket, shuffled a little higher up the bed, pushed away a strand of hair that had fallen loose. 'One of my favourite bits coming up.' Her voice had become lighter. Katherine watched her familiar expression settle back in place, and she had the momentary sense, quickly put aside, that the secret to which Edie referred had not absolutely been revealed.

The screen showed evening, a darkened room, a woman waiting in hiding by a window; and this room, too, grew dark. Edie reached for the remote control and turned the volume so that they could just hear the dialogue. 'He doodles now, you know. Cartoons, sketches and whatnot. Things for newspapers. Probably retired.'

Katherine leant back beside her grandmother on the pillows. She felt as though a door had been flung open on to a scene of ruin, just when she had most expected, and most prayed for, the reassurance of green lawns and remembered romance. But the door had not been locked: anyone might have nudged it open; she might have done so herself. She could feel the weakness of Edie's body beside her own. 'You're looking forward to seeing him?'

Edie turned to Katherine, her eyes full of wonder, as though seeing how, very easily, that might not be true; glimpsing again all the dread and sadness of the past that had kept them separate. 'Yes. I am looking forward to seeing him.' She glanced across at the portrait, propped against the wall. The face was hidden by shadows. 'But I wish I was that girl again.' Edie's voice was quiet, as though she had spoken a private thought aloud, not expecting to be heard.

The house settled into the cooling evening, its timbers creaking; upstairs, a breeze caught the loose window catch, rattling metal against wood.

'That will be her now.' Edie seemed to speak to herself. 'It made no difference what we did. Everything comes home.' She straightened up a little, glancing at her watch. 'Mary expected her a few hours ago. Hope they've kept something for her dinner.'

30

By the time Mary's daughter, Alice, arrived at Fareham that night, there was no light left for pictures. The evening had come on quickly with a darkening head of clouds, and rain was falling fast by ten o'clock.

No picture had been taken, either, to mark the arrival of the first of Mary's family at Fareham. In fact, only by a series of inferences might her existence there be supposed: she had left no imprint of her life on film, on glass or paper. But she had been there all the same: a favoured young woman, beautiful, and good with children, transplanted from Africa to England.

The year before the Clements family had arrived in Kent, in 1838, slavery had been officially abolished throughout the British Empire. When they moved from Belgium to England, they moved with purpose, a sense of starting the family's fortunes anew, a hope that time would darken into inconsequence much that they wished to forget.

But the year was only a date: of itself it made nothing happen. The company had subsidiaries, not absolutely accountable to the holding company, dissolved when it became no longer profitable, around the turn of the century. By which time it had procured considerable wealth, dispersed with the years into ever more distant relationships of production and finance.

A connection of names and dates; a house's location confirmed in a parish record; the activities and properties of a shipping company, traced back through the tenuous lineage of holding companies and companies operating under new identities; ships sailing from different ports, carrying different cargo, mercantile, human – passengers travelling for commerce, not always to their own commercial advantage. Time had exiled both families from themselves but, with enough scrutiny, both could still be found. The lost souls revealed themselves in a gesture or a look, an angling of the eye or shape of a brow, a particular shape of skull or length of bone hidden beneath the surface, and suddenly there they would be: the same two families inside the same house.

Now, an attentive ear might detect the echoes of these decisions, taken at long distance. Katherine's mother had heard them, quite late in life, and when her career was in the pink of health it had shocked everyone that she should decide to turn her camera to a different landscape: 'local colour', as she had mockingly described one project – the vanishing countryside of south-east England, slipping rapidly beneath concrete and fat-bellied asphalt roads. She had never given adequate – to anyone else – explanation of her change of focus. She had called it her 'retirement'. But she was only forty.

Katherine had rarely given much thought to this – she had had no cause to, until recently. But in the few days since she had arrived at Fareham, almost as a reflex, hearing it was to be sold, she had taken pictures inside the house, and certain scenes had been returned to her; silent images, to which, bit by bit, the words were being supplied.

She had done it furtively. She had pretended it was for the purposes of the wedding, 'preparations', she had said, when Joanne asked, 'setting up shots, seeing what works best'.

'I know, you're going to miss this place, I won't tell.' Joanne had lingered one time, watching her arrange a tripod on the landing. 'This is its best time of year.' She had been leaning out of the window, shielding her eyes from the sun as she looked across the treetops. But she sighed as she hurried away, as though she might have added, 'Well, too bad.'

Katherine had smiled, embarrassed. She did not like whatever characteristic it was that made her feel angry, and more hurt than she would ever have confessed, that the house was to be sold. To be so upset seemed to her a form of selfishness: her father and Joanne's life did not revolve around her, and why on earth should it? They had not taken the decision to leave in order to wound her.

But as she went about the house with her camera, she felt as though she was claiming back a part of herself that had not willingly been given up: early memories, future hopes. She saw the images through the viewfinder just as they were; but, after everything Edie had revealed, and all that she had understood, she could see other things too.

Her mother standing beside the upright piano, now stored in the attic. She had been bending swiftly to lock it, placing the key inside a small silver box on the mantelpiece, out of her daughter's reach.

Katherine had been sitting outside on the terrace, half turned from them, flicking through a book and pretending not to listen. She had turned a page, unseeing. She had had a sense of some awfulness occurring between her parents, although she had no idea at the time what it meant. But she could visualise them side by side, even now, their shoulders hunched in sadness – together, though, still, at this stage. Later it would be different.

'I just can't maintain this position, as though I'm so far removed, so uninvolved,' Julia turned to Peter and her face was pale, 'when in fact how close have I been, really, all this time?' She was at pains to explain something that her husband resisted understanding. 'I'm implicated in all that.' She waved her arm in a demi-circle and her eyes rested on the small silver box where the key to the piano lid was now hidden. 'I can't bear to touch that stuff.' She glanced away from the upright piano. The keys were ivory, the black lacquer of the music stand inlaid with mother-of-pearl.

Her reaction had been triggered by a footnote: a book about the Congo had mentioned the names of various shipping companies, and one of them had been 'Clements', the date 1890. 'But of Belgium, not England.' She had mentioned it to Peter, whose face drained of colour. 'It was a very long time ago,' he began to explain to her, watching her expression change and his wife become a woman ever after removed from him – not deliberately, but as though her heart had shifted into a different chamber, and a wall had been set between them.

'They've done a great deal of good since then, Julia.' He was horrified, and had tried to reason with her: he thought she was behaving like a child, but he understood, and part of him had always known it would be thus. They were not complicit. She did not know the full extent, because he had not wished her to, and had kept it from her, given her to believe that beneath the last hundred years lay nothing at all. He had lied to himself. He had lied to her. Because of the lies he had lost her, and although at the time he did not know it, he would never have her back.

For so long just pictures in the mind, these and other impressions now returned to Katherine with the force of a physical presence: the arrival of a girl. And even now, she could perfectly remember the look on her father's face at that moment of Julia's revelation: she had seen its duplicate only recently.

She hesitated on the landing. Her own hearing was improving, just like Edie's.

It had been raining hard. Alice was glistening, scattering raindrops from her coat when she stepped into the hallway, saying, 'Coo,' at the black and white tiles, which she had never seen. 'Aren't they lovely?' She hugged her mother, who rushed forwards in her eagerness to see her daughter, whom she hadn't set eyes on in 'over a month, you wicked child'. She hugged her tightly and stood back a pace only when Alice tried to give her a present. 'It's not my birthday!'

It looked as if the two women were wrestling with something when Katherine appeared at the head of the stairs. They glanced up to see her just as Peter emerged from his study. Alice half skipped towards him and cuffed his shoulder. 'Look at you!' He had had a haircut that afternoon, and she stood back, her arm round Mary's waist, as though they were both admiring him.

Mary looked down at the package in her hands.

'Open it.' Alice pushed it towards her. Mary untied the ribbon and a long stretch of gold silk fell out across her arms. 'Like it?' Alice grinned up at Katherine, who came downstairs to join them in the hallway.

'It's beautiful.' Mary held the present against her chest. 'But what is it?'

Alice rolled her eyes and held up the dress against her mother. 'For tomorrow, silly. A proper frock. Can't have you in that frowsy number you always bring out. Don't you like it? Pulled strings, friend works at Selfridges.'

Peter stood slightly apart from the three women, shifting his weight from foot to foot as he watched them. 'It's a wonderful dress, Ali, well done.' To an objective eye, it might have looked as though the dress was a gift from a daughter on the instructions of her father.

Peter smiled as he turned back to his study. 'Better finish up before we go away,' he muttered, as he left.

'On the night before your wedding? Are you crazy?' Alice laughed at him and slipped her arm through Katherine's.

Peter turned back and — was this much her imagination? — his face seemed to brighten and cloud, as though he had seen something that he very quickly set aside. He raised his hand in an oddly formal gesture of farewell as he went into his study.

part | four

31

One evening in 1835 Louis Daguerre was tidying his studio after an unsuccessful day's work. He had a headache, and when he rubbed his forehead he wondered if perhaps he wasn't also running a temperature. He looked about for his thermometer but couldn't find it. He cleared away the materials he had been working with that day – including an exposed iodised silver plate that had, to his earlier irritation, refused to show even the faintest trace of an image – stashed them in a cupboard, and left the studio.

That night he slept badly. His body swung between heat and cold. One moment he shivered, drawing the woollen blanket closer round him; at the next he was drenched in sweat. He was by nature a hypochondriac: his bodily processes had always fascinated him. By morning he told himself that he really must find that thermometer. He rose late and tentatively, dressing in a heavy coat and silk muffler, and didn't enter his studio until just past midday.

Stepping into the room – as often happens when an old scene

is presented freshly to a person's eye – he remembered: of course, the thermometer was in the cupboard by the window, where he had put his materials last night. But when he opened the cupboard, he noticed two things: first, a piece of the thermometer's broken glass, the mercury now disappeared; and second, that the exposed silver plate was no longer blank, but bore a detailed image. He must have broken the thermometer, putting away those plates. The mercury vapour had proved a powerful developing agent. And so the first daguerreotype was made.

Without the moment and material, the coincidence and delay, what would count as evidence to say that a particular time had even passed? You cannot develop and print a memory.

Early morning in Fareham, the day of the wedding, Peter Clements was sitting alone on the sofa in the drawing room, the windows opened to a September day that had started clear and fine.

Last night in bed his wife-to-be had suddenly turned to him. 'Thank God.' Her slender body had relaxed in his arms, moved close so that he could hold her more tightly. He had thought she was asleep, and supposed she must have had a bad dream; but no, it was the English weather she referred to. 'Thank God,' she murmured. 'All the forecasts say it's going to be good.' Before he had come up, she had run through her inventory of sources: the newspapers, TV, radio, Internet, the Met Office. She paid attention to Thames, Dover, Wight, even kept her eye on what might cross the country from Lundy, Fastnet, Sole and Irish Sea. All were clear. She fell asleep, contented, in his arms.

He marvelled at her ability to find quietness. It was what he most disliked about himself: he made noise wherever he went and in its wake – as now – he was left with a feeling of unease. 'You take on too many things.' Joanne had appeared to consider the matter closed with this early diagnosis. He wondered if there was some truth in it. Was it her way of saying that he was greedy, or simply that he thrived in a state of controlled activity, his hand on the helm? He wasn't sure. But he was certain, now, that things were becoming unstuck.

He could sense it, even without the little gusts of bad news that had blown his way over recent months. Approaching sixty, he could easily retire, hand over to someone who had the appetite he had lost. But Joanne was right: he didn't like to let go. It meant that he would have had to admit to things he'd rather not look at square in the eye. Stupid things, inconveniences. He frowned to himself as he thought of them.

He had made a pot of coffee, and now he poured a cup, shifting his weight on the sofa. Something was digging into his back. He punched the cushion, settled himself more comfortably.

Only the other day he had received a phone call that had stirred in him a feeling almost of revulsion: not so much that such things went on, but that he should have to acknowledge them. It was nothing at all, he hoped, but it had unnerved him all the same. The London manager of one of his operations run out of Libreville, in Gabon, had mentioned to him – but why had he bothered him with this detail, if it had been effectively dealt with? – that they had taken a short-cut where, perhaps on balance, it had been unwise. The man had tried to make light of it, even cracked a joke about it being 'standard malpractice, out there'. Peter had not found it funny. Something to do with drilling starting a year ahead of plans; and for 'plans', he had read 'permission'.

'We're not really there yet, on paper,' the man had told him. 'SEC regulations are a bit grey there, you see, which means it can get quite expensive on the ground.' Peter could imagine well enough what he meant: the company haemorrhaging money into a stream of unthinkable causes, each smoothed-over permission the spark to any number of skirmishes and attempts on power. It happened: it was folly to suppose you could avoid it.

'Well, what of it?' He had been curt. He could hear Joanne's voice raised in the other room, and he knew how much she disliked him to receive business calls at dinner time. He disliked it, too. 'And if that's all?'

There had been a moment's silence then, and he had felt the portent of that delayed reply. 'Well . . .' The man's voice had been thin with nerves. Was it really so bad? 'It seems there were photographs.'

'Photographs?'

'A journalist sniffing around maybe, got wind of something. Eco-nut perhaps. But it's not a problem. They're gone now. I've been given the all-clear. It's been dealt with.' His assurance had sounded hollow, or as though there was something more that he couldn't bring himself to say.

'It's been dealt with,' Peter repeated. He did not wish to know any more than that. But his thoughts lingered for a second on that sentence 'I've been given the all-clear.' By whom? Were there people who handled such things on his pay-roll? He pushed the thought aside. 'You say there are no others?' He could hear his daughter walking from the dining room towards his study. 'So everything's fine.'

With an effort, he tried to make his voice sound relaxed, although he felt anything but that. Katherine stood in the doorway. He smiled at her. What had she heard?

He felt tired now just to think of that conversation. There had been too much of this kind of thing lately. Too much scrutiny and bother. He was supposed to be getting married, for God's sake. He settled back against the cushions of the sofa, looking out at the blue sky, the ruffled trees, all seen through the silver light of early morning, and he wondered, would he miss all this? It was a big move.

He thought of Joanne's dealings in Louisiana and smiled. That ruin on River Road was a more interesting project than even she knew. He had always known she had money, but now it seemed she had oil – a discovery made a few months ago, when Peter had had some tests run, just in case. He had been economical with his descriptions of the extent of the findings and had agreed to marry Joanne shortly afterwards. Had those findings hastened his proposal? He held the question clear for a second, as though it were a piece of litigation brought against him: would his defence stand up? Yes, he thought it would. He had been meaning to ask her anyway. She knew that she came with a good dowry, and had realised that this meant she wouldn't be perceived as having mercenary motives. But even Joanne wasn't aware of quite how good that dowry was. Peter would tell her the full story in good time.

Anyway, he reasoned, she had been the one to describe her new money as 'the icing on the cake'. It had been a joke, but like all jokes there was some truth behind it: having money meant her value had increased, on anyone's estimation.

He leant back against the cushions and shut his eyes. He loved Joanne most for her ability to step aside from the past. She lived her life facing forwards, walking out of the mess of history like a person stepping out of a cinema. The show's over, so move on. It astonished him, and cheered him, too. It was the best way to go about things, he was certain. But personally he found it hard. He corrected this thought. He found it impossible. He wished that some of Joanne would rub off on him and change him. He supposed that that was at the root of all emotional alliances: the vampire's desire for the soul of someone other than yourself.

He looked about the room. It had been one of Julia's favourite places to sit, with its view out across the back lawn towards the trees. He saw her beside him, as he so often did in the quietest times of day, or when he was alone. Was it love, to remember someone so vividly? He wasn't sure. He loved Joanne. He was certain there wasn't much space left round his heart to fit anyone else in there alongside her. He felt pure on that count: it wasn't a lie. His love had come as a shock, and with a shock's spontaneity, too — 'a bolt out of the blue', as she liked to describe it to him.

But he saw Julia all about this house, often, and although for years he had been glad of her continued presence, recently he had felt her ghost as the pricking of his conscience. But what had he done wrong? 'It's all the little things,' Joanne liked to describe her love for him in such terms. 'Not one thing, but all the little things are what I love about you.' She didn't specify beyond that. He thought she was simply being foolish — sweet, too, but certainly foolish.

Now the phrase was stuck in his mind as a possible reason why he couldn't step out of the past in the way Joanne was able to, why it lingered in every shadow and around every door of this house. Even the sofa he sat on now was the same, just reupholstered.

He had tried to tell Katherine something of this the other night, but he could see that she hadn't quite grasped the extent of his confession. He had talked in riddles. He had painted a picture of himself, and of his continued suffering. He had spoken of ghosts, of being haunted, and all the while he had hoped she might see the solid picture of who he was and still not mind — just see him, as he was, for a moment. He had wanted to absolve himself somehow of all the things that he couldn't speak of. Could anyone? He had done certain things wrong. He had made mistakes. He was human. Would he be forgiven? He rubbed his forehead. Scrub that. He lowered his expectations. Would he be let off?

When Alice arrived last night, and stood there dripping on

the hall tiles, he had felt the jolt of landing back in the past: her gestures and manner were an exact print of Mary's when she was young. It wasn't something that could be seen in a mirror, it could only be known from memory, and for a second he was inside a passage of time that he thought had been sealed off: the tall grass rushing where their legs caught it, the evening and the sudden rain. He had been left alone with her in an empty house, he reminded himself. But his hands were trembling; he set down his coffee cup.

To leave Fareham now was to place a line right through all that. The landscape would be erased by housing estates, the lake drained, the oaks felled to make way for roads and concrete. He had received proposals from a developer, offering an extremely good price. The house, if it wasn't pulled down, which he considered a definite possibility, would be divided into flats. He was sorry for the trees and the hills, but when he turned his thoughts to the house, his mind ran forwards with a kind of malice. He wanted rid of his wrong-doings, and of his sadness, too, and this house contained them both.

He touched his chin. He would shave later: the ceremony was at four, and there was plenty of time for his beard to grow between now and then. He watched a few high white clouds run fast across the top part of the view from the window and hoped, for Joanne's sake, that the clear weather would hold.

He drained the last of the coffee, and straightened out his copy of the *FT* on the table in front of him. As he sat up to read the op-ed page, he felt something under the cushion. He reached beneath it, and pulled out a dark blue scrapbook: the secret project. He cursed aloud when he saw what it was. Such things shouldn't be in the hands of children. It was the last thing he needed now. He would put a stop to their curiosity when the honeymoon was over. He looked up at the sound of someone crossing the hallway and slid the scrapbook back where he had found it, under the sofa cushions.

Katherine didn't enter but remained in the doorway. She seemed shocked to see that someone was in the room, and furtive, as though she had hoped it would be empty. He had never seen her looking so much like her mother.

32

The family was sitting around the breakfast table. They had been discussing whether or not Joanne and Peter should have spent the previous night together. 'And now again,' Edie shook her head in mock reprimand, 'together in broad daylight, on the morning of their wedding.'

The twins sniggered, their eyes alert as they watched their mother.

'Oh, touch wood and all that.' Joanne gripped the edge of the table as she laughed. 'What could possibly happen? The vicar's on my side. I've even had the weather fixed.'

It was true: the day had been handed to them from another season — early autumn's willingness to reprieve. Even the decline of the house had been suspended. What work was needed had been done. The front gates had been repainted, the borders weeded, the drive cleared, the hall carpet raised, the tiles polished. Although the ceremony would take place in the garden, the previous day Joanne had announced, 'I'll spit if those Persian rugs get singed,' and ashtrays had been arranged promiscuously in the downstairs rooms. The twins had received instructions on vigilance over burning stubs and coasters. 'You'll be my eyes, won't you?' They had stood to attention in the hallway.

Mary had laid a hand on Joanne's arm: 'Your wedding manager wants a word.' She handed her the telephone: at eleven the next day, Joanne would relinquish, reluctantly, her clipboard and with it all responsibility to a sharp-eyed young woman from Clapham. Her company, Weddings Inc., had been handling 'the arrangements' all along.

'But someone's got to manage the managers, or all hell might break loose.' Joanne insisted on this point now over breakfast, checking her watch. 'Should be here soon, then I'm going to think about something else.' She leant back happily in her chair. She was sitting at the head of the table, dressed in a cream velour tracksuit, her bare feet half an hour away from being soaked and pedicured. She had the satisfaction of feeling that the mood around the breakfast table was her creation, a scene expertly accomplished. Everyone was so relaxed – *positively glowing*, as she thought of it, with good spirits.

Although she had kept this to herself, Joanne had feared for tension and unrest to emerge from a hundred different fissures. Her children were a perpetual worry: they were modern kids, and she had suspected that England might quickly drown them. But no. The place had given them a quality of attentiveness that previously they had lacked. Now they rarely spoke of home. They loved Katherine, which helped, although Joanne wasn't so sure what they really felt about Peter, whom they skirted round like a topic too adult for them to mention.

Even Edie appeared happier than she had at first. Joanne glanced at her, and saw that she was being watched. When Joanne had gone to bring her down to breakfast, Edie had pressed something into her palm. 'Been waiting for a private moment when I could give you this.'

Joanne opened her hand to find a small diamond brooch. 'Something old.' She hadn't expected it. When they left the room, Edie spoke again, so quietly Joanne thought she might have misheard: 'I'm very proud of what you're doing with him.'

She had made her son sound like a difficult project, and Joanne had poked fun at Edie's way of putting it. Edie didn't respond.

It had never been Joanne's intention to find favour with Peter's family. Frankly she hadn't cared if they liked her or not. She had always been clear on this point with him. 'It wouldn't matter to us if we were still young, so let's not have it matter now.' However, she had known that that was asking too much of him. She was aware of how much he liked to arrange the various elements of his life so that they did not overlap and, where they did, he wanted the combination to be harmonious. He had tried so hard to see that Katherine took to her, Joanne had noticed, but wished he hadn't bothered. She could speak for herself. It wasn't easy with Katherine at first, but she hadn't expected it would be. Even now, she found her distant, not cold, perhaps, but certainly unbending, or as though she was doing a fantastic job at controlling potential disasters, and secretly wished that someone might notice and compliment her. Joanne had tried, but Katherine wouldn't let her in. With time she hoped she might. Joanne guessed, from Peter's descriptions of her, that Katherine must take after her mother.

Joanne understood Katherine's desire to control — if that was what it was. She, too, liked to manage things: hence her present satisfaction. But she had the feeling that, even more than this, it was the house itself that was overdue for the present moment's lightness, as though it also had been held in check in some way. There had been no cause for celebration between its four walls for far too long.

Peter had wanted a quiet registry office affair. She had refused, and outlined a plan involving orchid-filled tents, the gazebo to become a temporary silk-swagged chapel, and the guests all scattering petals when they passed. But those swags were only a diversionary tactic. It had always been her secret aim to win the middle ground.

She had wanted the wedding day to be a kind of final shake-up for the house before they left. Although they didn't discuss this, it was clear to her that Edie didn't have long to go. Lately Edie's gaze — usually so alert to what went on around her — had turned inwards, as though she was looking out for a change inside herself. The worst part was that, whatever it was, she appeared to have glimpsed it already. All her energies were now directed towards not letting on that this change had occurred.

Had no one else noticed this about her? It was one of the many things this family was reluctant to discuss. Joanne didn't blame them, although she was sorry that it was so. She had been happy to play the villain, if that helped, talking in mercenary terms about the need to quit Fareham. By pointing out the house's terminal decrepitude, the sagging walls, the rising damp, the creeping progress of the undergrowth, she had intended to spur the family on, make them rise up against her, elicit some kind of outcry in defence of the place – and perhaps, in the process, make them notice how little time Edie might have left.

It had not worked out that way. She had imagined visits from indignant Clements relatives: so you're the harpy who wants to rub out one and three-quarter centuries of family history. No one came. She had been amazed. Lately she had come to realise that she was caught in a state of vague expectation for something that would not arrive. There were no indignant relatives. It was the end of the line.

She had tried – but how was it possible to be tactful about such a thing? – to broach the subject with Peter. In bed one night – an after-dark approach had seemed appropriate – she had quizzed him about the family. It appeared to strike him for the first time. 'There are a lot of only children.' He had shrugged. 'Maybe that's why we're dying out.' She considered the tone of his voice. It wasn't the way Peter usually sounded, but it was familiar to her all the same. Where had she heard it before? She settled back against the pillow in surprise. It was just the English, from whatever class or region. They all took that tone, when pushed. As though someone had just mentioned something they were too ashamed of to admit – too many missed trains and botched connections, too much standing on an empty platform in the rain, defeated by the mechanics of a system of which even the passengers were reluctant to complain. She drew him into her arms, and he hid his face in her hair.

It was, for all that, one of the things she most loved about him: the fact that, however much she pressed, she was quite sure she would never fathom the motives and remoteness of his soul. She would never understand him; he was definitely foreign. She knew he thought that she was joking when she talked with a smile about his 'old-world charm'. But she was in earnest. He was at the dog-eared end of an ancient story, and she couldn't understand his unwillingness to throw the entire book in the can and simply write a new one.

He was caught. Reluctant and stubborn, just like his mother. Joanne had started to speculate whether, in fact, she herself didn't feel more for the house than he did. He didn't even appear to hate it. Apart from the clarity of his love for her, of which she was confident, it was as though he felt everything through a fug of shadow. If he didn't turn a light on pretty quick he'd find himself stuck there in the shade for ever, even if he went to America.

She watched him now, laughing in a faintly scandalised way at something Alice had just said, and wondered if Edie hadn't been bang on the money about what Joanne was doing with Peter. One of her first instincts towards him when they met on that Society wine tour had been to help him out, to save him. He had appeared half blind, fumbling about in that cellar, surrounded by but not fitting in with the bland and leisured rich. She had put this down to his being widowed, but suspected now that it was more than that. He didn't even seem at ease with having money, as though it wasn't something to be glad of, but a failing – a painful secret, unmentionable.

Joanne went to make more toast, partly to hide her expression of delight. Yes, she certainly did thrive on managing things and, failing that, on seeing that those who did have secret designs were given free rein to pull them off. She did not mind that she couldn't guess at Peter's own motives, but she was still amazed at his readiness to up sticks and go with her to America, and she supposed that his reasons must run deep. She took it on trust that they were both sound and good.

When she returned to the table, she noticed that, in fact, of everyone there, Peter was the only one with any look of strain. Perhaps Katherine was a little chillier than usual, and appeared to be concentrating hard on something she could see with her mind's eye in another room; a secretive girl, Joanne thought, and reprimanded herself for thinking of her future stepdaughter in those terms. But it was Peter she minded about. He seemed faintly stunned, leaning forwards over a bowl of cereal, not saying much, his eyes wearing a dulled expression of repressed astonishment. She went over to him. 'Budge up,' she said, and sat in his lap, swinging her legs like a girl.

'Touch wood!' Ellen and Roy called out in unison.

Joanne ignored them, and kissed her almost-husband. 'See, no disaster yet.'

Alice grimaced, looking at her mother. 'So trusting, can you believe it?'

Joanne glanced at Alice, who didn't meet her eye. Her half-joking remark – Joanne supposed it had been humorously meant – had struck the first discordant note of the day. Joanne overlooked it but, for a second, she was obliged to consider one of the things that most troubled her: that however much someone might manage a situation to their satisfaction and desire, everything can be undone in a moment by things far beyond one person's sole control.

Joanne didn't like to be reminded of her own deeply suspicious nature. Fate, the weather, acts of God, the terrible darkness of the past where she had not often been very happy – she felt the pull of them all. Peter was right when he thought of her, with envy, as having the ability to step out of the past. What he didn't see, however, was that with one remark, at the sound of one wrong note, Joanne felt herself cast right back in there, into the darkness. How could he know it? He saw only half of the impression she gave of her life – the lighter half.

Peter was unaware, for example, that as Joanne kissed his ear now to show that Alice's remark hadn't bothered her in the slightest – 'See if I care!' – she was wondering if the girl was right, that she was foolish to be so trusting, and that disaster was just round the corner. Otherwise content, and so in love as she was, might she have been too lucky now for too long?

33

Last night, after Alice arrived, Katherine had not slept. Climbing exhausted out of bed around eight thirty that morning she registered that for the last few days she had barely slept at all. She had been suspended in Miles's description of her: 'You're a photographer to your core.' The image had once strengthened her but now she felt as though, without her consent, she had been cast in the role of hired hand, brought in to take pictures of an unknown family.

As she dressed she had briefly caught sight of herself in the mirror, and been shocked at her appearance: stepping hurriedly into her clothes as though afraid of being caught out. She felt full of guilt, but for what? She had always tried to do the right thing, make her own life. But it had not been enough. More powerful was the fact that she had been born into a particular family, at a particular time and place; and that she had seen things. But she was not complicit. She had been duped. She felt sure of that. It made her feel sullied and ridiculous, as though the moment she left the room everyone would burst out laughing. Poor Katherine, so sure of herself, with so little reason, what does she know? But she had relied on that dream of a good family, her own safety, and of a mother and father at the very least in love.

Now it seemed that she had had none of this. As she left her bedroom, hearing the muted sounds of people stirring around the house, she had the sensation that even now she did not know just how far the line of family guilt might run.

She had always adored Mary, and was fond of Alice, but that morning she found it hard to look at them, or meet the eye of her father, and in a flash of understanding she saw herself as others might: the egocentricity of an only child, her belief that things had been arranged entirely for her convenience. Her whole life had been founded on a false premise. She saw her blithe progress, confident and secure, spooling out her mantra that the surface of things, accurately recorded, reveals the truth, when she had been blind even to what the surface told her.

Now she walked quickly through the passageway to the annexe, glad to be out of sight. She felt that she was engaged in a stand-off that had its foundations in a sham: everyone, it seemed, had agreed to act, except her.

She had kept up a convincing act of her own over breakfast, or so she hoped. But she was conscious of her father's attention snagging as it passed over her. She wished she were better at disguises. She dreaded the thought of any kind of confrontation.

By accident, she had come across him earlier that morning, sitting alone in the drawing room. She had mumbled something about the weather, said she was looking for an extension cable, and left. He had seemed dejected, not exactly the jubilant groom on his wedding day. But she no longer believed in his dejection, and saw that she had relied on his self-portrayal as the suffering, damaged father with much too little proof. Alice was five years younger than she. Her imagination was lost in calculation of what this entailed, the new light that that one fact now shed across her life.

When she approached the darkroom she discovered that her phone was ringing. The voice at the other end, so familiar, struck her as the last dart of harm she was able to withstand. She was glad to be alone. She sat down heavily on a plastic chair, and wondered if she might not be losing her mind. She covered the receiver so that Miles wouldn't hear her shocked intake of breath.

He told her that he had wanted to give her a call to wish her well on her father's wedding day; he had remembered the date. His voice was light, and he told her that he had missed her, and had called her just before he left last month, but that she had been out, so he had had to leave a message on her 'bloody answer-phone' – he had never liked to do that, at any time. He had taken a job in America, 'It was a last-minute thing.' His voice faltered as he went on, more tentative in this admission. 'Didn't work out, anyway, so I'm back, came in on the red-eye last night.' He paused. 'Did your old man mention I phoned?'

Katherine heard him clear his throat. He spoke quickly. 'Called from New York, had a wild idea just before I left that you might fancy a break. I was going to try to lure you out there after the wedding.' He laughed, as though to show her that even he saw how ridiculous a notion that was.

She could barely trust herself to speak. 'How long have you been away?'

'Only a few weeks.' He laughed again but sounded depressed: hadn't she even noticed he was gone? His manner implied that he had taken the job specifically with her in mind, but she couldn't believe that that was true. When they had been together he had insisted so fiercely on his independence that she had been glad to let him keep it.

'It's pitiful, I know,' he went on. 'I gave up my flat too, like an idiot. Sub-let it. Now I can't have it back. Couple of students with a baby. Never mind the contract, I wouldn't have the heart to chuck them out. I'm sleeping on floors until I find a place to rent. It isn't so bad, actually, feels quite liberating to have nowhere to go.' He didn't sound convinced. He fell silent. Was it true that he had been in America on the night of the fire?

She was conscious of someone moving about in the annexe, walking around on the other side of the thin plywood door. She clutched at his words, trying to read into them something she could believe. She found that she had missed his voice.

'You still there?' His tone was uncertain. 'Look, Katherine—'

If he was being honest with her, she had only to say the word, and she would no longer be alone. She wanted so much to trust him, but she could still see everything she had most feared. She had played the scenes so many times in her mind that they had built up to an image more plausible than any other. But perhaps she had been wrong. She had been wrong about so much else. She hesitated.

Before she could speak, she heard him clear his throat. 'When I was in New York,' his voice had become efficient, 'I got wind of a story about TriCo.'

She caught her breath and felt her skin go cold. Another second and she might have told him everything. She held the phone away from her as though it had burnt her. Until yesterday that name had meant nothing to her. But now she knew it was one of her father's subsidiaries. Her mind went dark and sluggish as though faced with an equation she struggled to fathom. He was trying to see how much she knew, but on whose behalf? A newspaper's, or her father's company's? Would it be better if he was acting alone?

Assuming she knew the name, he continued, 'I know this kind of thing's often in the air . . .' His voice faded, as though he had only at that moment questioned whether or not she knew about the bad press her father had received over the years. He went on, more tentative, '. . . but I wondered if that was the real reason you were in Gabon last month.'

She clenched her left hand and felt a vein of anger to rise up in her temples. She felt very cold, and suddenly almost calm.

'Was it the real reason?' he repeated.

He knew about TriCo's operations in Gabon. It might be public knowledge, or an insider tip-off, or he might have been instructed to ask her. Either way, he held the stronger cards; he knew more about her than she did about him. But what he didn't know about her was that she had been running alone now for so long that she had acquired a skill for secrecy he could not possibly suspect. Everyone else had kept secrets, been dishonest. So could she.

Now he was asking her if she'd lied when she said she was going out to Gabon to do some routine stock shots for a hotel brochure. No. She hadn't meant that to be a lie at all. It was the only reason she had gone to Libreville: a favour. She had not questioned it at the time, had not for a moment suspected that the favour came with a condition: do as you're told and keep quiet. She had gone there to take pictures, not to smooth the way for a cover-up. Sure enough, she had taken some shots off the record, but they meant nothing to her. Now the dishonesty of her position had been forced on to her. She hadn't asked for it, and could no longer sidestep it. The ice seemed to crack easily beneath her and she felt the coldness rush up over her head.

'Are you involved in some way, Kate?'

She could still hear someone moving about outside in the annexe: Mary and Alice, laughing at something she couldn't catch.

'I have to go.' She looked across to where she had hidden the nine remaining prints.

'Do you know anything?' He spoke quietly, as though with great effort.

Katherine was certain he could tell that she was concealing something. Well, if that was the game, she could play it. 'I'm amazed how little you trust me.'

'Kate?' His voice was imploring now. 'I only wanted to say I tried to throw them off the scent. I was too involved, couldn't be objective. That's partly why I'm back here in England — I couldn't hack it. But it's not true, is it?'

'I have no idea,' she tried to steady her voice, 'what the hell you're talking about. Is *what* true? You phone me up to try to trick me, to get me to dish the dirt on my own father, on his wedding day, what kind of—' She couldn't say anything else. She covered the receiver so that he would not hear her crying.

The phone went silent. When Miles spoke, it was only to say that he was sorry to have bothered her. She tried to listen for a note of duplicity but she couldn't find it. He had been acting neither alone nor on TriCo's behalf; he had just been doing his job, and thinking kindly of her. He had had nothing to do with the fire. And if he was ruled out, her worst fears were given licence: that favour had been to a family friend. She couldn't trust herself to say goodbye. He said it for her, and his voice was so remote that she was sure she would never hear from him again.

She set the phone down on the table and turned it off, burying her head in her hands. Her neck and back felt stiff, as though the secret history of her family, an impression formed in darkness over almost two centuries, was a weight too great for her to struggle against. She couldn't fight. She would protect her own, just as every Clements must have done for generations before her.

34

It was half past twelve, and the family had retreated to their rooms. But the house was far from silent. It appeared, in fact, to have been occupied by a company of strangers. Following in swift series after the arrival of Joanne's 'wedding manager' at eleven o'clock, representatives of numerous firms had drawn up in cars and vans, parallel parked as instructed, along the drive.

Joanne's manicure-pedicurist was among the first, to be followed an hour later by her masseuse, both from a small beauty parlour, which they preferred to call a 'holistic treatment centre', recently set up in Canterbury. The cathedral, according to the copy on their promotional brochure, provided 'powerful karmic forces for centring and balancing chakras', a description that had made Joanne howl with laughter when she related it to Peter. 'Just doing my bit for local business,' was how she described her weekly visits to be tweaked and varnished, although she once announced, confidentially, to Katherine, 'Without that tarts' parlour I'd be screwed.'

The florists had driven down from Chelsea. 'Posy Green' was

the girl's real name. At twenty-eight, she was, just, a millionaire. Her speciality: organic English wild flowers. She paid her brother, Tom, who lived in Shropshire, to grow them, and together they were nervously thrilled, and a little amazed, that no one had thought of it before. Today's theme revolved around wild berries: rosehip and hawthorn, the virginal clear red of early crab-apple.

The caterers, Blaines, were of older pedigree, having earned their Michelin stars in a restaurant in the late eighties. In a converted house near Seven Dials in London, the restaurant had lapsed from fashion, but they were regarded still as caterers of good standing. When everyone else was serving up ironic canapés of fish and chips, Blaines stuck to their guns: gravadlax on rye, caviar on pumpernickel, tiger prawns in filo pastry, seared tuna with lime and salsa. No surprises, but no disasters either. Blaines had been recommended to Joanne by the wife of one of Peter's business associates, an Upper East Side New Yorker resident in England since her schooldays, when she had been sent to Cheltenham Ladies College by her diplomatic corps father – 'And how much more on the money can a recommendation get?' as Joanne had put it.

Blaines had set up a temporary kitchen in the old stable block, running coolers and ice-makers from the mobile generator in their van. Twenty cases of champagne were on ice, along with several gallons of Chablis, a quantity of orange juice and mineral water. The order of the afternoon would be champagne and canapés at five, after the service, and a cold buffet served at six. 'We'll clear out when they do,' Mr Blaine junior had instructed his staff. He expected things would wind down around ten: few of the guests were local, and most would be driving back to town.

On the heels of the beauticians, florists and caterers, a small truckload of waiting staff arrived early, just after one o'clock. Taking advantage of the warm weather, though with a degree of reserve, they were lolling on the back lawn in the manner of a confident cast, idle before a well-worn cue. Some had scattered further afield and, not yet in costume, had rambled beyond the lower wall towards the lake. One pair in particular, adventurous by necessity, had strolled into the bottom meadow where, thinking they were unseen, they had stretched out on a torn-off jacket and begun to kiss.

Edie had spied them at it through her opera glasses: a brass pair 'borrowed' in her remote youth from La Fenice, before it was 'razed by lunatics', as she put it, as though in justification of her theft. That kind of activity was to be expected: she had seen it in the past. She averted her eyes, now as before, and went to lie down for a nap before the kick-off, which, according to Joanne's instructions, would be at three. That gave her an hour's snooze, an hour to get dressed – Mary would help her – and then . . . She thought of him, and slid further beneath the covers.

The annexe, meanwhile, had been taken over. The upper floor was out of bounds, but downstairs arrangements were in full swing. A whiteboard stood in one corner, and by midday Joanne's manager from Clapham, Helen Broad, had inscribed upon it a litany of instructions. 'No Chewing', emphasised by a pair of asterisks, appeared to be the most essential, followed a close second by 'Get them what they want'. Miss Broad frowned, dissatisfied, whenever she had cause to write down this command. It struck her as rather coarse, but how else could she put it? It would have to do.

The musicians would be the last to arrive. They were due at two, at which time they were under instruction to set up on the right-hand side of the lawn, beneath one of the pear trees. Should the weather turn bad, and when the light had gone, they would migrate to the marquee. In their repertoire: New Orleans jazz and thirties swing, Schubert sarabandes and Mozart gavottes. They took turns, that was their secret, and it 'kept them fresh', or so they maintained: a trombonist gave way to a viola-player from Purley; a young cellist could turn his hand with equal accomplishment to the drums; a girl good with the flute also sang, a talent she was at this moment displaying, in the back of a minibus on the M25, as her party made its way to Kent.

Inside the house, Edie had fallen into a light sleep. The twins were in the kitchen eating Heinz spaghetti with Mary and Alice. Joanne was stretched out on a warm mat in her bedroom, the curtains drawn, candles burning, as she was given an aromatherapy massage. Peter was in his study, filing correspondence, checking his watch: he expected a call.

By lunchtime, Katherine had run through her check-list so many times that she knew it by heart. She had gone about the house, seeing that everything was in place. Then she had retreated to the darkroom, and realised that she had no further reason to be there now. The boxes of film were ready in the fridge, the flashes charged, bulbs checked. She was going to use the Nikon for guest snaps, the Rolleiflex for the portraits. She had set up lights and reflector boards in the drawing room and secured the cables and extension leads with duct tape.

'It'll be plain sailing, kiddo, don't sweat it,' Joanne had said, appearing between pedicure and massage. 'And you're off the hook at six, remember?' That had been the agreement: Katherine would take pictures of the ceremony and formal portraits after-wards, remain on duty for an hour after that, to 'snap our first dance', as Joanne put it, '. . . and then *finito*, put the camera down, get sozzled, and thank your lucky stars you don't have to be on your best behaviour like I do.'

When she went through to the kitchen to find something to eat for lunch, the twins had just gone up to their rooms and Mary and Alice were alone. Katherine made a sandwich and took it upstairs. Had she lingered in the hallway, she might have caught Alice's remark, 'You think she heard?' followed by Mary's: 'Doesn't matter now.'

'I'll be glad when it's all over,' is what Mary had been saying. A few minutes earlier, she had settled herself heavily into a chair. She meant more than the wedding.

Alice glanced at her anxiously and moved to sit beside her. She took out a bottle of clear varnish from her bag and began to paint her mother's nails. 'You're going to be fine, though, aren't you?'

They had often discussed it: would she stay once Edie had died? Now it was less ambiguous: the Clementses were leaving Fareham, and Mary hadn't been asked to go with them to America.

'Should be.' Mary looked out of the kitchen window as though assessing her future. 'More than, perhaps.' She turned back to her daughter and smiled. She had capital.

In 1984, when Mary had left Fareham the first time, she didn't do so empty-handed. Julia Clements had 'wanted her to have something'. The two women had sat down at the kitchen table to discuss the matter. They had been alone together in the house. Peter was in London, Katherine was at school, and it was before Edie had come to live with them. Mary had listened to Julia's proposal, a kind of severance package with what she might have called 'a sweetener' or, in plainer terms, a bribe.

Mary had raised her hands in refusal when Julia outlined her plan. 'I don't want that.' She was astonished that Julia had suggested it. She hadn't seen herself, or what had happened, in quite those terms. Now she was to be paid off, her silence bought, although she had had no intention of ever speaking. Why should she? It was her child, not his.

She pitied Julia for not having had a better husband. But she blamed her too: she should have been able to control him or, if not that, at least have been prepared to fight for him. He had strayed too easily. She supposed that he had strayed before. There had been other nannies, or au pairs, as the earlier ones were called: Swiss, French, and a local Kentish girl. And then something occurred to her: the last thing she had suspected from a woman who, after all, she considered to be a good person. Perhaps Julia had thought it wouldn't happen with a black girl.

She had looked hard at Julia, watching her expression. The woman couldn't lie: she had horrified even herself with that idea worming its way inside her motives. Fear, pity, or just wanting never to have been involved – which was it that Julia was prepared to pay for? Mary shook her head. 'How much, Mrs Clements?' She uttered the words, lingering on the name.

Julia had stared down at her hands, held tight together on the table. Was she confessing, then, or calculating? It was impossible to say. Mary saw the transaction held momentarily clear of them both, and the sorrow of it hovering there – but only for a second, and what was left was only shame.

'I thought—' Julia's voice contained a great river of tears, and Mary heard the sound as a kind of triumph: yes, she knew. Mary waited for her to continue. She turned to stare out of the window, just as she would twenty-five years later, with a look of expectation, as though totting up a sound investment. She had been sorry for the woman, but not so sorry that she had been able to forget.

'I thought maybe I could see you set up in a house back in London.' Julia had cleared her throat. Mary said nothing, waiting for her to continue. 'I have my own money – I've been speaking to my financial adviser,' she went on, and at this Mary had breathed out sharply. How long had this been part of the plan?

'I can't buy the whole thing,' Julia had gone on hurriedly, 'but

I can give you a good deposit, and guarantee a small mortgage, and maybe we can find you somewhere where a lodger can live in the basement. That way their rent will help to cover it.'

Mary saw herself in this imaginary house built up in the mind of her employer. Could it be possible that she would thrive there? She stood up and went across to the sink. Unthinkingly, she ran the taps and washed her hands. She noticed that, outside, the sun was high over the trees and a brisk breeze skipped inside the branches. Without looking at Julia, she turned and left the room.

'Mum? Are you?' Alice nudged against her mother. Mary had been staring out of the window and had not properly answered her question. 'Are you going to be OK financially?'

Mary leant back in the chair and sighed, her chest shuddering as though she were setting down a long-held weight. Alice had paused in her nail-painting: she had never seen her mother's face appear so full of secrets.

'We're going to be just fine.' Mary pulled her daughter towards her as she spoke, hugging her, and not wanting her to see her eyes.

Financially, it was true: the house was in an elegant Victorian terrace in Vauxhall, a once-rough area now considered smart, the mortgage paid off, the value trebled during two housing booms. But in all other respects she felt she had been damned.

35

Just after three the first guests had parked along the drive beneath the poplars. Entering the house, they looked upwards, their eyes drawn by Joanne's concealed spotlights and by the newly painted cornices, which suggested the luminous height of a chancery or nave. The door was open to the garden, where a yellow-gold cordon marked the direction they should go and, on the terrace, Blaines were serving the first instalment of Veuve Clicquot.

'That's the daughter,' one guest whispered to her husband: Katherine stood just outside the front door in a pale green dress, a spare camera slung over one shoulder, the other taking pictures of the guests' arrival. Around a hundred and fifty were expected, mostly friends and business associates, with only a small number of family. Joanne's mother had felt she was too old to travel. She had sent her best wishes from South Beach, Florida, although not her other child, Joanne's elder brother, whom she 'needed' – Joanne had laughed derisively when she related this. Cousins, of oblique origin, would arrive from both sides of the family, but their distance from the proceedings was perfectly clear, and

Joanne would walk up the imaginary aisle with her two children, who were even now eyeing with suspicion the floral arrangements of berries and hawthorns – denuded, they hoped, of their spikes – which they were to bear before them.

One of the most striking impressions, stepping out from house to terrace, was the effect created by the arrangement of the five figures on the lawn: Edie, Peter and Joanne; and Mary and Alice, who had been on the point of moving away, when Joanne insisted, 'Help swell the ranks for a bit.' As the sun fell, their outlines were cast in stark relief – almost motionless, but as though held together by an unseen tension, for ever on the point of breaking away and acting out their separate parts. But no one moved, and the guests were obliged to brave the green expanse of lawn in order to be welcomed by their hosts. Most were empty-handed – presents had not been encouraged – which now made that journey seem the greater: the line of figures required some kind of offering to complete it; without a laying-down of gifts it appeared bereft.

Edie sat on a white basket-cane chair in the middle of this tableau, a tiny withered rosebud in ruffled violet silk against pale pink damask cushions. Peter stood on her right-hand side, lean and alert in an evening suit one size too small for him, according to Joanne. But he had had it since his university days; it had been made for him by his tailors in Savile Row, and he saw no reason to replace it. His bride-to-be stood beside him in full length duchesse satin: a strapless gown covered, for now, by a slender jacket trimmed at the neck and cuffs with marabou. She stood very slightly apart, as though wishing she could rush off and effervesce among the guests, rather than remain there in formal isolation. But it had been agreed — it had been her idea: appear for first drinks, disappear for retouching, reappear for grand entrance and ceremony. Now she had to live with it. On the other side of Edie stood Mary, in gold, and beside her Alice, an orchid corsage pinned to her mink-coloured cocktail dress.

The arrangement — Edie flanked by Peter and Mary — gave the unintentional impression that they were bride and groom, separated momentarily, and for the last time. With the sun falling low behind the line of figures, their silhouettes presented the suggestion of banishment, the sense of a burnt and broken stretch of fence left to stand in pointless demarcation of two bits of land. Some guests hesitated as they took in, then rejected this effect. But it lingered in their minds as they approached, and was another reason, aside from being presentless, for feeling briefly wrong-footed.

Guests arrived quickly, and in greater numbers. Mary and Alice moved away; Joanne whispered, 'Thanks for holding the fort', and the view of what by now most people — having heard of the move to America — thought of as the last guard at Fareham was obscured by a swell of hats and black-tie suits, tanned legs and brightly coloured dresses, the last exposure of a warmer season. The parked cars were crammed with woollen shawls, fur stoles, silk wraps and evening coats 'in case'.

On cue, at half past three, Joanne left Peter with a kiss and slipped back inside the house. Her jacket would come off for the ceremony, 'so that the dress can really make an impact', she had wriggled in satisfaction as she explained this earlier on to Katherine. Inside the house, Joanne would also be 'buffed up', as she gaily put it: the beautician and hair stylist had been employed for the whole day.

Joanne's exit was also the cue for Peter to be allowed to leave his position. Crossing the lawn, he was stopped by one of his friends, George Fitzgerald, the publisher of a national broadsheet, who took his host aside. Peter had expected a telephone call from George yesterday; it had not come. He himself had left a further message only that morning. They had spoken of such things before, and now George was confident that Peter would be similarly equable in the face of this latest bit of bad press. 'It'll break, I'm afraid, can't stop that.' Peter received this statement in silence. 'But I've seen it knocked from page two to the international pages. It's not going to be news. If we get a call from advertising – a late spot – it might even get spiked. I shouldn't worry.'

George laid his hand on Peter's shoulder. 'Not much of a wedding present, but it's the best I could do. The wife's bought a lovely bit of Tiffany crystal for Joanne. Presents not your line, I know.' He was eager to get away. Peter barely responded, but hung on his words, as though weighing each one in turn. Was the story more serious than Peter had implied? 'Damage limitation,' he had called it when he telephoned yesterday. But seeing his reaction, nervous and despondent, George wondered whether his old friend hadn't been trying to play him. It was the one thing he couldn't tolerate. He didn't mind helping out a good man from time to time. These things happened, in business especially. He knew that. It had been his bag, too, before the paper. But he refused to let himself be played, or ever taken for a fool.

'As much as I could do, I'm afraid.' George's voice was more clipped than he had meant it to sound as he turned on his heel and went to find his wife. He could just see the red plume of her hat over by the table where champagne was being served; she liked to drink, as did he, and he navigated his way towards her, leaving his host beneath the trees.

Watching this brief exchange, though from too great a distance to overhear what had been said, Lewis Briars remarked to himself that, after all, Peter had not changed. He had meant to intercept him on the lawn, but had been beaten to it by another man, whom he did not know but supposed was also involved in finance. Both he and Peter displayed the same habit when discussing money, in its various disguises: they smiled, even in the face of bad news. The hand on the shoulder spoke of its being bad, and it was a particular kind of smile that reached neither eyes nor any other part of the body beyond the lips and teeth. It was a smile that had been presented to Lewis on a number of occasions, and it had always been a method of exclusion: go away, you don't have sufficient funds – not that he had ever given a damn.

Lewis watched the two men and paused mid-stride, deciding

that, no, he had better not intervene in that particular conversation. He watched his host's face. He had never liked Peter. His prejudice against him had been instantaneous, and it had stuck.

The first time he had seen Peter was in the early nineteen fifties, in Smythson. He was quite sure that the man wouldn't remember the moment. To his mind, Peter was the most unobservant person he had ever met. It was a characteristic that Lewis had always deplored – he felt about it that violently because he couldn't see an excuse for it. In Peter's case, he supposed, it was probably the result of secure wealth. He had guarded that pot of money since his childhood, and it numbed him to every other influence. This had been one of the first impressions Lewis had had of Peter, who had been standing, passive as a blind boy, outside the shop, waiting for his mother to come out, while Bond Street roared and glittered all about him and he didn't even blink.

Lewis remembered that Peter had been sullen even then: the loneliness of an only child, perhaps it was that. His first instinct had been to see the boy as a burden he longed for Edie to be without. Now from the safety of the crowd he watched Peter standing momentarily forlorn beneath the trees. He glanced around to see if he could spot her.

It was how he had first met Edie: in a crowd. He had just finished at the Slade, and found himself talking to her parents at a Royal Academy Summer Exhibition. He didn't know them, but he had met his friend Hugh there, and he had introduced him. When they discovered that Lewis did portraits – he didn't, it had been a lie, but he needed the cash so volunteered the notion just in case – they had exclaimed that that was perfect, 'just the thing'. Hugh had wandered off, and Edie's father leant towards Lewis, lowering his voice: 'Been thinking of getting a portrait done of Edith. Go on, see if you can pick her out.' He had said this with a sly look. Lewis had already noticed a girl of around his age, her thick hair gleaming in the sun cast through the skylights. He prayed that it was her. Later, he wished that it was not: she was to be married to Hugh at the end of the summer, in just a few weeks' time. That portrait was a late engagement present.

He knew then that he should have refused, but she came to stand beside them in the high red gallery and he dared to hope. He did the commission. They were very young. She attuned him to a part of life that until then he had not known existed. He did not think ill of her for letting him seduce her: he had hidden inside a pretence of confidence, and so had she; it was where they met, inside that other world of heightened feeling. He had caught it in that picture. But that didn't mean the portrait was any good. It wasn't. He had not known when to stop.

He hadn't seen her, after that, for many years. Her wedding went ahead. He read the notice in *The Times*. He had not quite believed it was possible until he saw those few small lines of type, stating the facts. Later, when he saw the photograph of the portrait that her husband kept always in his wallet, he had felt the indignation of desiring another man's wife, and in that emotion read his age also: love belonged to youth, and he felt the anguish of time having passed. Lewis had watched the way Hugh pawed that photograph, and privately despised him for his weakness, for ever having married a woman of whom he was afraid. He felt quite sure that Hugh had never felt real passion for his wife. Another man's mark was on her and he had not even noticed: the monogram 'L. B.' half hidden in the folds of his wife's green satin dress.

The next time he saw Edie, that afternoon in Smythson, Hugh was dead, and his widow appeared to have canonised him in her mind. Even after a space of fifteen years, she had seemed to step out from that painting towards him and he had felt himself touched by grace. The love he felt for her then was far more dangerous than the rapture to which he had succumbed as a younger man. But it had been hard for him: he hated that abandonment now; the life lived in the dark.

He had stopped drawing 'properly' after the war, turned instead to commercial work, illustration and cartoons. He had done with all fine sentiment. He had seen Hugh's body blown apart. His secret. Even Edie did not know.

But there had been a moment when he had almost told her about it, later, learning of their families' tangled pasts. He had wanted to wound her, make her see the pain of keeping secrets. Of course he couldn't do it. And now his memory of the pride that had driven them apart was more painful than any of that: his pride, for which no price could sufficiently be exacted. It had ruined time. He knew she had not remarried, but he prayed she had been happy.

Now he wondered whether he would recognise her. He had few images of her in his mind. It surprised him that this should be so, and yet his sense of her was still more potent than any visual impression: her nearness; the warm cave of her body; her bones grazing his. It was private evidence, and not enough to go on, in public, and since then, there had been an entire life: a wife and family of his own. And would she recognise him?

When he had arrived, a few minutes earlier, he had stopped on the front drive and turned suddenly, setting his back to the house. He had leant, a little more heavily than was his habit, on his walking-cane. He took out his watch, looked for his handkerchief, blew his nose. A tall man, gaunt where before he had been lean, he was still strong, but he felt undermined, as though someone had kicked away his stick, by the sight of a young woman taking photographs at the front door. A surge of guests passed by, moving up to the house.

She did not, absolutely, look like Edie, but she had Edie's manner and lightness, wielding that camera with as little show as though she were merely gesturing in thin air to make a conversational point. Only when the guests had passed through the open double doors did they realise that they had been photographed. They entered the house startled, half turning as at the disbelieving suspicion of a pickpocket.

Alone now in the centre of the lawn, Lewis was at least a head above most of the people around him. He had been standing there for almost ten minutes. Apart from Edie and Peter, he didn't expect to know anyone. He glanced about through the forest of hats, and directly ahead of him, sitting alert as a bird on a frozen wire, was Edie. Her eyesight, perhaps, was bad. She looked in his direction, but evidently did not see him. He went towards her and her face, as he approached, emerged as from the shadow of a cloud, just as it had before, when she stepped out from photograph to painting to stand close and warm beside him. He bent down to kiss her. His back hurt to do it, and so, having no chair in which to sit, he lowered himself to one knee, speaking her name.

Both of them heard, but did not see, their picture being taken: Lewis was conscious only vaguely of it happening, out of the corner of his eye. He was less observant than he had supposed.

That picture of a tall, distinguished man, kneeling in familiar devotion beside an elegant, still-beautiful woman, their white heads bent together, would, in the future, seem easy to inter-pret: the portrait of two people who had spent their lives together.

From a distance Helen Broad, the wedding manager from Clapham, hissed sharply in the ear of one of the waiting staff, 'Get them what they want, I said. Poor old chap clearly wants a chair, so jump to it!'

36

'Go on,' the small blonde woman in navy blue nudged her friend. 'Guess how much. Have a bash.' Standing on the terrace, close to the open french windows, they had been discussing how much the wedding party might have cost.

'I'd heard he was on the skids.' Her friend, a fleshy redhead, gulped an inch of champagne, her eyes darting to a nearby tray of canapés. Although it was no longer warm, she was perspiring steadily into her beige Frank Usher suit. Beneath the jacket, the skirt cut a deep welt into her waistline. 'That's why they're off to wherever it is in the States.'

'No!' the first woman responded, her face losing its look of calculation and, for the first time, lighting up in delight. Her husband, until recently a manager in Peter Clements's company, had been passed over for promotion one too many times. Last month, he had taken a job elsewhere. 'No hard feelings, then' – he had been surprised to be invited to his one-time boss's wedding, and deeply flattered. He propped the engraved invitation on the mantelpiece of their house in Chiswick and wondered if he had been wrong to leave.

'Well,' the redhead continued, 'there's money in the move, or they wouldn't do it. Would you leave a place like this,' she cocked her head at the house behind them, 'unless you were in trouble, or after something better?'

The two women fell silent as they considered the wisdom of this diagnosis. The blonde frowned as she remembered something her husband had told her the previous week. She hadn't been paying much attention. She had been in the bath, he standing at the sink, shaving. They were going out that evening, to a dinner party in Docklands, and as he talked to her of bonds and percentages, the chaff of his day in the office – that was how she thought of it, and at one time it had annoyed her, as though after work he could offer her only the faint residue of himself – he had mentioned something about this very subject. Her frown deepened as she struggled to remember. She hadn't really been listening, but trying to establish the merits of her black velvet Nicole Farhi trousers over her grey Donna Karan shift dress.

She turned to her friend now as she remembered. 'It's the second thing, that's why they're off, Donald mentioned it to me the other evening. Oil.' She bit her lip as she saw her husband approach. 'I think.' She already wished she hadn't confessed, and now remembered the latter part of the conversation: a stray email, an overseen memo. Even Donald wasn't supposed to know about that oil. He'd be furious if he knew she had gossiped. She tried to retract her tone of conviction, but it was too late. 'Maybe it was something else. Perhaps they are on the skids, as you say.'

The redhead sucked in her cheeks and drank another inch of champagne, holding out her glass for more, her eyes narrowed. 'No, I'll bet you're right. They're going after more money, I'm quite sure. Did you know' – and this was her trump-card – 'that the family used to own slaves?' She smiled graciously at the waiter who filled her glass. Donald came to stand beside his wife, who had paled, and now looked around her hurriedly, as though she had just been informed of an imminent scandal. If that was true, she didn't want to hear it. That was one piece of gossip too far. She was shocked by her friend's indiscretion. But what else did she know?

'Must've cost a pretty penny.' Donald grinned, and his wife could see that he had been drinking. She wished he wouldn't. It gave his gestures a quality of femininity that she found chilling. She concentrated her attentions on a tray of gravadlax.

'We've just been discussing it.' The redhead beamed.

'It's not old money.' Donald leant towards his wife's friend, as though correcting her. 'This place is a front, really, built last century, on the cheap, *faux* everything. Used to be swamp.'

Both women had heard this before. Perhaps it had reassured them the first time: even the rich were flawed. But now it only reminded them they themselves were still not so wealthy as the Clementses: it was like drawing attention to a foul smell. Both women turned away.

The redhead was the first to recover. She was chronically short of cash. Her airy excuse of 'some reckless investments' was only half the story, as her husband had a string of mistresses. However, she liked to pull rank in terms of longevity: her family could be traced back to the Domesday Book.

'Donald is quite right, of course. Hardly surprising they're going to jump ship to America, go where the real money is, in oil.'

Donald, who had been smiling, froze. He tried to get his wife's attention by staring fixedly at her face: had she been blabbing again? But she refused to meet his eye.

The trio's conversation was closed by the sound of clapping: the master of ceremonies, calling for the guests to sit down. They moved away from the house across the lawn.

A little after four, hundreds of tiny lights were lit in the flower borders that edged the grass. Dusk had gathered beneath the trees. The temperature was dropping with the failing light, and already the gas heaters had been turned on inside the marquee.

The guests began to migrate towards their gilt and red plush seats. Seen from an upper window, the appearance was of a hungry crowd settling themselves in anticipation of an auction: the contents of an English country house to be dispersed and sold off to the highest bidder. The music had stopped and conversation diminished to a low buzz and chatter, broken only by the punctuation of a popping cork, a sudden laugh, a preparatory cough.

Just inside the french windows, which led out on to the back terrace, where she had been giving her appearance a final once-over in the Regency mirror, Joanne had been joined minutes earlier by Mary and Edie. The twins were already close to heel, perched on the edge of the sofa: they were under starter's orders with their bouquets, which matched the cherry red sashes of their clothes. Roy felt beneath the cushions to see that their secret project was still hidden there; on finding it, he grinned at his sister, and they waited for word from Joanne.

At Edie's request, Mary had come inside with her to offer their last well-wishes before the ceremony. They had been on the point of going back outside to sit down when they heard two women talking on the terrace, their voices lowered to the stage-whisper of discussing confidences. The subject of how much the party might have cost had just been broached, and the phrase, 'Go on, have a bash', had made all three women look up.

Joanne started to laugh, covering her mouth. 'Outrageous!'

Edie frowned. 'What terrible people.' She started to leave.

Joanne touched her arm. 'Let's see how close they get. I'll correct them later, or give them a prize if they get it right.'

They stood just behind the heavy curtains, listening in silence; they heard everything. The music stopped. The master of ceremonies announced that the guests should take their seats.

Edie put out a hand and leant against the piano, glancing at the children, who appeared oblivious to what had just occurred. Mary's eyes were fixed on Joanne, who stood very still, as though expecting more. But there was nothing, only the faint sound of muted conversation, the chink of glasses as they were drained and set down.

Joanne glanced at her hands and smoothed her dress, her head tilted to one side. She appeared to be waiting for a private sign that the way ahead was clear. For a second she stood very straight, then took a quick pace forwards, as though stepping away from everything she had just heard.

At the same moment Katherine came into the room, as planned, to take pictures of Joanne's progress down the aisle. When Joanne was ready, Katherine would give a signal to the musicians. She had not expected to find Edie and Mary still inside the house. She took their picture, and only then did she properly notice their expressions.

Joanne moved across to the mirror, touching her hair, the neckline of her dress, then turned back to face the room. Edie breathed out, a long exhalation as though on the point of speech. Joanne raised her hand, shaking her head to silence her.

Katherine lowered her camera. Her skin prickled. The three women were recoiling from something impossible to put into words. Only Joanne stood her ground. Mary, tight-lipped, had taken Edie's arm and seemed to be trying to drag her away, their weight off-centre. They all exchanged a look that excluded Katherine.

As though making a decision, emphatic and wholehearted, Joanne quickly crossed the room and smiled, her voice lowered to a whisper. 'Fuck them!' Then she laughed, throwing her head back, her eyes shining. 'This place!'

Mary moved a step towards her, taking her suddenly in her arms. 'Good luck.'

Edie kissed Joanne on both cheeks. 'You are superb, and quite right,' she said, shooting Katherine a look with the naughtiness of a child. 'Absolutely. Fuck them.' It was the first time that word had ever crossed Edie's lips.

Joanne roared with laughter. 'You'd better lead the way.' She motioned for Edie and Mary to walk ahead of her up the aisle. 'You'll give the cue?' she said to Katherine, who left the room with a sensation of sudden lightness: those women had the appearance of a family.

Edie hesitated. 'I'm not sure this is done,' she said, as the music began.

'I'm not sure I give a damn about what's done, do you?' Joanne nudged Edie and Mary ahead of her as she went out into the English afternoon to marry the man she loved. The guests fell silent as she made her entrance, preceded by Edie and Mary, followed by her two children.

'C'mon, kiddos, we're on!'

Afterwards, a redhead in an ill-fitting beige suit, accompanied by a small mousy woman in navy blue, hurried up to her to offer congratulations.

'You look sensational,' the redhead gushed.

'Beautiful,' her friend added, as though her friend's statement had needed that support. 'And such a wonderful party.' They moved on, the smaller woman stumbling as she left.

'Who were they?' Joanne whispered discreetly in her husband's ear.

He whispered back, with equal discretion and complete honesty, 'You know, I've no idea. Not my friends, I'm sure. I supposed they were yours.'

She shook her head and leant against him. It was true: she did not know who they were, but she would have recognised their voices anywhere.

37

At first the rain came only as a light mist. When guests stepped out from the marquee where the buffet was being served, they raised their faces and stretched out their arms, feeling the air's moisture simply as the residue of a long, warm day. But by the time the dancing had begun, shortly after eight, the rain was loud on canvas, running torrentially along the gullies at either side of the lawn, pummelling off the guttering of the house.

It had been a long time since Mary had caught sight of her daughter. She had noticed her earlier, slinking across the lawn in that slippery-looking dress towards the house, a dove-grey shadow beside the figure of a tall young man. That was before the bad weather had come, and Mary hadn't seen her since.

Now she had half an eye on the house, although only the lights were visible, shining yellow through the silver. Beside her, his back half turned to her, Peter was sitting out a dance, talking to Joanne, who had just sat down on his other side.

Katherine also had gone back up to the house and not returned: her duties were over for the night, and Mary supposed she was clearing away her things, private and efficient as her mother. It had rained this way the night Mary first left, when she knew she was going to have her daughter. She remembered very well the taxi at the front gate: the engine had stalled, and the driver blamed the weather, cursing as he went into the rain to lift the bonnet. She had waited, checking her watch, not caring that she had missed one train, and then another, looking back at the house with the windows shining golden in the warm wet night.

She had been in the bath when Edie had telephoned, years later. She had dripped until she was cold into the receiver. Mary had been adamant at first. No, she would not go back to work for the Clementses. She would prefer not to.

Edie had visited her the next day. She had arrived unannounced at tea-time, with a young girl on loan from a temporary nurses' agency. Mary watched the car pull up in astonishment, and was glad at least to have had the advantage of seeing Edie before Edie saw her: it gave her a chance to set her face, and not show the sadness she felt at seeing Edie white-haired, in a wheelchair, her chest oddly bowed as though she had been winded.

She went out to meet them on the step. Edie produced a box of biscuits. 'Dicky hip,' was how she explained the wheelchair as they went inside. 'Bad heart, too.' She added this casually, and then the nurse had explained. It had sounded as though Edie wouldn't live much longer. But still Mary had refused. She had not been close to Edie before, but she had been fond of her, and had always admired her directness. Mary thought of her, having lost her husband, her only daughter-in-law, living alone in the house with a son who, so Edie insisted, was 'never even there'. Mary noticed the expression on Edie's face as she supplied this bit of information: she wanted to emphasise something more than just her loneliness.

Eventually, Edie had fixed Mary with a look, and demanded to know why she refused to come back. 'Your daughter is grown-up now, already at college.' Mary had felt cornered. 'So why not come back to Kent?' There was only one reason, and Mary could not utter it.

A kind of madness had hung above their conversation. The two women and the young nurse sat around a low table in the sitting room, drinking Earl Grey. Radio 4 was on in the background, the afternoon play – something Gothic about a haunted house in Southwark – and they talked about the pros and cons of Mary returning to work at Fareham as though what had happened there was not real. And although Edie and Mary never spoke of the simple facts, that Peter was Alice's father, that the house was Julia's bribe for silence, Mary had felt certain that Edie was the one person alive who knew – and understood – everything.

By the time Edie left that day, Mary had agreed to return to Fareham to look after her. She was glad that Edie did not say anything like 'It's where you belong,' but it had felt like that, as though Edie was simply imploring her to do what, secretly, she should know was right. Saying yes had made her feel as though everything else had been a form of running away. It had been a cock-eyed, difficult route that she had been obliged to take, but Edie's request had made her see that she didn't want to run for ever. She went to bed that night with the odd, dulled excitement of having glimpsed a way back home.

She had been to the house only a couple of times in almost twenty years, just after Alice's first birthday. And although Julia had often visited Mary at home in Vauxhall, it was clear that Peter did not know she did this. On one of those occasions, she had arrived pale and fidgety, glancing at her watch, spilling tea, and at last she spoke: Peter had been wondering how Mary was getting along.

'He asked after you,' Julia was sitting opposite Mary on the sofa, 'so I told him you were doing very well, and that you had a baby girl.' Mary listened in silence. 'He hadn't realised we were still in touch. And he said why not have you and your daughter down to Kent, and bring your young man. I said I would put it to you when we next spoke.' Mary remembered the way Julia asked her if she would be prepared to do this — like inviting someone to walk on water. There were illusions wrapped so tightly round her request: show him the baby, and he will never believe for a moment that it is his, not with his own wife standing smilingly beside it.

She saw what was being asked of her, and understood the cruelty and forgiveness that were being meted out and offered. She went down to Fareham the following weekend.

'He couldn't come this time,' she said of her imaginary 'young man', and there were no expressions of surprise. A quick look of pity crossed Peter's face, and Mary glanced at Julia, imagining the conversation later: 'Has she married?'

'Actually, I don't think her boyfriend stuck around.'

Julia photographed her husband holding Alice in his arms. Mary was standing beside him, her breath suspended, longing for him to give her daughter back, as though if he held her much longer he might suspect the truth. But Peter did not enquire after the baby's age, though both women saw the question rise and descend to be buried in his eyes, never to be asked again.

She had stayed only a few hours, and on the train back to London she cried so hard, holding Alice tight against her, that a woman sitting opposite had stood up and left, embarrassed, pretending one of the small station stops was hers. Mary saw her do it, the eyes passing from baby to lone mother, then fixed on miles of streaming countryside as she calculated her suspicions. A stranger could tell, but not the father. Mary heard the doors open a little further along the carriage, and saw that woman again at Victoria station, her brown coat being swallowed by the crowd.

Even then, Mary remembered, she had had an intimation of the great tiredness she felt now – just the edge of it – the tiredness of too much lying for too long. It was as though she had held herself rigid, pitted against it, braced against the tension of a lie that wasn't worth the trouble. She had seen the way Julia turned from a lie with professional effort, simply averting her eye to look on something else, a different scene. And she had watched tonight the way Joanne jumped clear of lies – she weighed them against her love, cursed them for their unworthiness, and skipped forwards, as though her life were held clear of the mess, somewhere splendid in the future that she had merely to run to.

Mary had seen the way Edie looked at Joanne at that moment, as though only then accepting her into the family: both women had chosen to forget. It frightened Mary to see them do it.

She had watched Edie earlier, sitting beside that man – a stranger to her now, who had had a wife, children, an entire life without mention or note of Edie to be found anywhere within it. But all that time, it was perfectly clear, Edie had been haunting him, the figure in the background of the picture, turned the other way, the indecipherable shadow on the wall.

Edie had never told Mary her own story. She had not needed to. Over the years, and the nights Mary had spent sitting up with her when she was ill, certain images had slipped out. Mary had pieced things together, and in the last few days, with that portrait propped so Edie could see it from the bed, those images had rushed together into a clear picture, brought to life by the appearance of the man himself.

But Mary did not recognise the Lewis Briars to whom Edie had referred. The man who had appeared had a lifetime wrapped round him like a thick disguise. The sorrow was that Lewis and Edie recognised each other so perfectly: evidently he had been haunting her in equal measure. They sat together, very close, their arms touching, smiling sometimes at something the other said. Mary noticed Lewis move aside a strand of hair that had come loose from Edie's bun, slipping it back behind her ear. He had been in a kind of trance as he did it, and Mary noticed him look away quickly, his face hard. But then she saw him take Edie's hand and grip it very tightly, and Edie leant closer against him. Mary saw her shut her eyes for a second, and hold her breath. She had looked as though she was praying.

Mary had pitied them both. It was painful to her to see the waste of it. It only made her feel her own hidden years so much more keenly.

Now she looked up at the house through the rain, and loved it for being the place where she had conceived her only child, and hated it for being the place where so many years of lies had somehow thrived among all that beauty. It was as though the house itself had been the thing to break her heart. Soon it would perhaps be pulled down, and when both it and she were gone there would be nothing left to say that she had felt so much in one place and at one time.

She took a drink, and straightened her shoulders. She had just caught sight of Alice, rain giving her a halo in the candlelight, and beside her, their two dark heads at a similar height, Katherine. They had run through the rain from the house, and now were making their way, breathless, through the crowd towards her.

Joanne had just left Peter, who now sat back in his chair, and together they watched as Katherine and Alice came to stand in front of them. *Do you still not see?* Mary smiled up at the half-sisters, who were laughing together about the rain, and about a 'dreadful Lothario' – Alice raised her eyebrows – who had just 'tried it on' with her. 'The nerve of it,' she said, her voice rising in indignation. 'If Katherine hadn't saved me, he'd have had me cornered by now.'

'Where is he?' Peter stood up, his manner stern as an aggrieved father, scanning the marquee.

'Sent him packing.' Alice laughed, sipping a glass of champagne. 'He was wearing a wedding ring.'

38

Helen Broad, the wedding manager, her chestnut hair now springing free of its lacquered bun, her cheeks flushed with the nerves of exertion, and a little pride also — apart from the rain, the day had so far been a great success for her, and her pocket was stuffed with business cards (everyone, it seemed, had daughters) — had whispered in Katherine's ear, 'They're plain-clothes, so not to worry, haven't scared the horses. They arrived a while back.' She glanced at her watch and bit her lip. 'Over an hour ago, actually, but you were still on duty with the portraits and whatnot, and I explained you weren't to be disturbed. Said they were happy to wait. I put them in the drawing room.' She hesitated and studied Katherine's face. 'Is everything all right?'

Katherine blushed. 'Did they say what it was about?'

'Not a sniff, but I didn't see any handcuffs.' She smirked. 'Can't be serious.'

Katherine tried to smile but felt her heart race. She looked across the marquee, and saw her father standing half turned from Joanne, talking to someone Katherine could not see, at first. Then

Joanne reached for his arm, and as he moved towards her, Katherine saw Dennis James, who had telephoned her late that summer with a simple proposal: a trip to Gabon, a favour honoured. How had he put it? 'Now we'll be quits.' He was smiling broadly as he headed towards the drinks table. Katherine prayed he would not spot her. She turned to go, and Joanne glanced up in her direction and frowned, mouthing the question, 'You OK?' Katherine nodded, hoping that those policemen had come on her account alone. She felt sick at the alternative: what if the connection she most feared had led them here? Miles had got wind of a story. It was not unthinkable.

She placed her glass carefully on a table. The rain was still heavy. Golf umbrellas had been put at the entrance of the marquee; she took one and made her way back up to the house.

Stepping out from the rain, she almost bumped into Lewis Briars, standing just inside the doorway in an overcoat, smoking a cigarette. He smiled at her. 'I'm glad I've seen you before I left. Katherine, isn't it?'

She nodded, breathless from running up the lawn. She glanced into the hall. No sign of the police: she hoped that they were still happy to wait. She could hardly tell this man that she didn't have time to talk to him.

'Back home to Suffolk.' He gestured towards the door, as though that explained his going. She had been so relieved to see him arrive: she had worried he might change his mind at the last moment, or that if he came it would be for the wrong reason, and some of the old bitterness might resurface. She had feared what that might do to Edie. But she had seen them sitting next to one another, and she hoped he had left Edie with a note of kindness.

He finished his cigarette, looking sideways at her. 'Edie said I should say a word.' Katherine shook out the umbrella and handed it to one of the guests as they passed by outside.

'Of course.' She smiled. She was on the point of telling him how happy she was to have met him, when she felt his eyes studying her, as though he was trying to find out how much she knew. It was obvious she knew something: she had not even asked him his name. But he seemed to be waiting for a conclusive expression of surprise. She said nothing. She thought of everything Edie had told her about him, all that she had felt for him, and she was sorry that he had wanted her to profess no knowledge of their secret. She couldn't do it. It would be like snuffing out a last faint candle in a darkened room.

He cleared his throat, straightening his back, and Katherine saw the military image in his posture, a little stronger than the man himself.

'She always was a great romantic.' He spoke quietly, but there was fear in his voice: it sounded like the denial of all involvement. *I wasn't even there.*

His eyes were turned now to the garden and the falling rain. He cleared his throat again, and left the house. Katherine watched him go, his figure diminishing against the parked cars, the shade of trees.

A number of people were coming through from the garden.

She couldn't run the risk of having to explain the presence of the police to anyone. She quickly crossed the hall to the drawing room, shutting the door behind her. Two plain-clothes policemen, their names slipped from her, sat waiting. They rose as she entered; she offered them tea; they declined, and settled back on the sofa.

The twins' project now lay open on the low table in front of them.

'Very interesting.' The elder of the two men smiled. His thick grey hair was brushed forward over a low forehead, shoulders bunched thick as a boxer's, his short arms held close, as though ready for quick movement. His partner, pale-skinned and fleshy, apologised for having turned up on the day of the wedding. Katherine had already recognised his voice before he explained: 'We spoke on the phone the other day.'

He drew out a brown manila envelope from a briefcase that sat between them. 'Didn't expect we'd come down like this, but it won't take a minute and then we'll be off.' She tried not to appear too obviously relieved at what he said. If it was serious, or if it were to involve her father, they would have come straight out with it. At least, their manner would have been more formal. As it was, they seemed more at ease than she; almost as though they were local bobbies just dropped by to answer a neighbourly complaint. She smiled. She could do this. She hoped it wouldn't take long.

He riffled through a sheaf of papers and drew out two sheets of A4. 'Quick ID, that's all.'

The older man asked, 'Nice wedding, was it?'

'I've just come off duty.' She felt exhausted. 'I was doing the pictures.'

'You're a photographer.' He smiled at her, as though telling her something she didn't already know. 'We'll be off soon too, after this.'

'OK.' The younger man spread out the sheets of paper on the table in front of her. 'Not as good as photographs, but it's all we've got to go on.'

'Artist's impressions.' The older man pushed the pages towards her; the younger picked up the story.

'There were a couple of eye witnesses around on the afternoon before it happened. Didn't see the fire start, of course, but a lad working in the studio under your flat thought he noticed something a bit odd. Van pulled up, stayed in the street for hours, two men in it who didn't get out.

'Supposed they were taking an extra long tea break, he said. They were still there when he went home at six thirty, but after what happened he thought he'd better report it. He reckoned it was maybe a cable TV van, said it looked familiar, but couldn't say why.

'Another passer-by, temp dropping something off in an office down the block, said she saw a couple of men go into your building around eight o'clock. Noticed them because they were in overalls, even though it was after hours. Couldn't see much of their faces, too dark by then.'

The men were watching her closely as they spoke, their voices easy, relaxed as though discussing something inconsequential between themselves.

'Would've been more helpful if we had the plate number.' The older man raised his eyebrows. 'This is the best we've got to go on.'

Katherine picked up the drawings, and felt a surge of relief. They showed impressions of men she had honestly never seen before. If they were the ones in that silver van, they stirred no memories. She shook her head. The men exchanged a quick glance. She was being honest. She did not have to act. They appeared to believe her.

The older man leant forwards. 'And you're sure you haven't thought of anything that might've been sensitive, pictures likely to cause a scandal, anything at all?'

'I'm not that kind of photographer, I'm afraid,' Katherine said lightly. They had asked her this before.

Then the younger man sighed and, almost as though it was an afterthought, drew a third sheet of paper from the envelope and set it down in front of her on the table. She felt her heart miss a beat and the room around her grew very still, as though someone had just covered her ears with a thick cloth. It was not an exact likeness, but it was clear enough to her what it was meant to represent: the logo. She rubbed her eyes. 'I'm pretty tired. Long day.' Her mind drew a blank. What would be the natural thing to say? The men leant forwards, suddenly alert, all their casualness put aside; they had scented her fear.

She pretended to study the drawing, not looking up. 'What is it?'

They did not immediately reply, but when the younger man eventually spoke, his voice contained a taunt, almost as though he was daring her to confess that of course she recognised that logo: it was right next door in her father's study beneath the TriCo letterhead. She stared down at the sheet of paper, and tried to look as though she was merely puzzled, when in fact her legs felt numb with the sharp impulse, held in check by an effort of will, to run from the room, away from these two men who – with no proof, but with the absolute conviction of instinct – she knew, in that instant, were not policemen. She pushed her hair away from her face. Her hands were damp with nerves. She would not run away because she could not: she had nowhere to go.

The elder man spoke first. His voice was half musing, as though he had been sneaking along behind each of her thoughts, mocking her deliberations, knowing perfectly the conclusion she must by now have reached. 'This is the logo that was on that van we just mentioned.' He spoke as though wishing to remind her of its existence, and she felt her blood run cold with hatred. To these people it was just a game. She was terrified of them, just as they meant her to be, but she was almost more afraid of the violence of her anger towards them: she did not know what it would make her do. The younger man leant across the table towards her, and she had the impression that he had been about to nudge her arm, goad her to say something that would reveal just how much she knew. 'Do you recognise it?' His voice was almost sneering: he could see she did.

She drew back beyond his reach, and looked at them both, square in the eye. She had a sudden vision of the expression on Joanne's face earlier, just before the ceremony. That woman had been utterly fearless, in the face of what, precisely, Katherine did not know, but whatever it was it had seemed to crumble in the light of her expression. She could still hear her saying, 'Fuck them,' and secretly she said it to these two men right now. She would not bend. If this was a game, the stakes had been raised, that was all; they had not won yet, not by a long chalk.

She reached across the table, her hands perfectly steady now, and picked up the piece of paper. 'No, it doesn't mean a thing to me.' She handed it back to the younger man and looked at her watch. Her gesture was plain enough: get out.

She wondered what they had been hoping for. A kind of break-down under pressure, a sudden confession – yes, she recognised the men, the logo, but she wouldn't tell; a few more threats and she would get the message, same as she had when they burnt down her flat. It was their banality that she hated most: they had no idea her motives. They had presumed too much, coming here like a pair of thugs with menaces: how much does the stupid girl know? They were just messengers, acting on someone else's orders. The chain of command must be pretty poor – that fire had been a bad miscalculation on their part: what if she had been hurt? And what would happen if the police, the real police, discovered how it had started? She was sure her father would have a strong wall around him: the blame would never get that far. It would stop with men like this. The fact that they had dared to come here showed how little they understood, and was proof of how remote her father was from what had happened: they must have been dead certain they wouldn't be recognised. They probably didn't even know whose house it was: just an address in the dark. Just like her flat.

She sighed, deliberately, and stretched her neck. She had nothing more to say to them. They had feared for her loyalty, but they had no idea how strong it was, because they did not know to whom or what it had been given, or why. It was impossible to explain. It was everything that had happened in the last few days: her fear of death and desire to live; her love for her mother, and for Joanne, her passionate wish that both could find some peace; her sorrow at Edie's missed life; her grief over the loss of her childhood home; her discovery of Alice. It was the whole fragile thing, and their assumption that she might not care if it was destroyed only increased her desire to protect it: it would be malice in her to wish otherwise, whatever might have happened to her personally. She was mixed up in this because of who she was, born into a particular family, handed a favour by a family friend, but it didn't change the one thing that would keep her safe: she was her father's daughter. She looked at them with contempt. They couldn't touch her.

The younger man's eyes narrowed at her. 'You didn't see it parked there during the day?'

'What? The logo?' She hated them. She stood up to leave. 'I

wasn't around at all during the day.' It was true. She had been at the Langham Hilton all afternoon, spent an hour in a café, then went straight on to the party. 'I'm sorry you've come down here for nothing.'

The older man stood up. 'And you're quite sure about those impressions?' His manner was unmistakably hostile.

Katherine went to open the drawing-room door. 'If I think of anything at all.'

His partner nodded at Katherine in goodbye, his eyes fixed on hers, as though in a final interrogation. His arms flexed briefly at his sides. She stood her ground.

She remembered that when she had first entered the room, they had not properly shown her their identification. The older man had simply reached into the breast pocket of his jacket as he mumbled his name and had shown the edge of something that might easily have been a wallet. She hesitated as she opened the door. She was tempted to call their bluff and ask them for ID. She knew they would not be able to produce it. Music came in from outside; there were people in the hallway. Standing beside her, both men seemed suddenly very large: her nerve failed, her anger slipped from her as fast as it had risen, and as she opened the door she was conscious of trembling slightly as she backed away. If they were as remote from her father's command as she supposed, they might be capable of anything.

The younger man turned to her as he left. She tried to raise her chin but felt herself go cold. She almost expected him to draw a gun.

'Off to Chigwell.' His eyes were blank.

'Nice place here,' the older man added, glancing in resentment at the ceiling, which appeared to diminish him. He put his hands into his pockets as he left, stepping lightly past the guests, head down and silent in the wake of the younger man. She gulped in air and rubbed her chest: her heart seemed to have stopped.

She watched them disappear through the front door into the night, and was about to go back into the drawing room to look for a stiff drink, when she saw her father crossing the hallway towards her. He was agitated. 'That wasn't the doctor?' He glanced upstairs. While Katherine had been talking to the men, Edie had been taken ill.

39

'You'd better go up.' Peter's voice was lowered. 'I don't want Joanne worried, I'm sure it'll be nothing. I called the doctor out just as a precaution. I'll wait for him down here.' He turned from Katherine to speak to a couple putting on their coats at the front door.

The rain had stopped and, outside, the damp air was still. A couple of cars could be seen waiting at the far gate, their headlights reflecting off water gathered in the road. A group of people stood on the drive, and in the light from the house the white columns of their cigarette smoke could be seen rising unbroken into the evening. A car pulled up, its engine running, and a man, staggering, climbed into the passenger seat. 'Donald,' hissed a voice from inside.

Peter tried to see into the darkness, leaning forwards out of the light. But it was impossible. He thought he had just seen the two men to whom Katherine had said goodbye, walking towards a car left at the far end of the drive. He knew they were not guests, and was sure that he did not know them personally, but one had been faintly familiar. He supposed it was a trick of the light. But there was something in his square shape, the thickness of the back of his head – he put aside the thought. He was more concerned to see that the doctor arrived. Those cars at the gate looked as though they might be blocking the way, should anyone be trying to turn in from the road.

Peter cursed, drawing breath fast through his teeth, and glanced up to the head of the stairs where he just caught sight of Katherine's departing figure. He would be glad to leave this place, and for more than just those two weeks of honeymoon. Something felt wrong, but he couldn't place his finger precisely on the reason why. Perhaps it was the cumulative effect of its redecoration, brought to a head by being on this day so brightly lit, under-scored by spotlights and vivid licks of white paint, plants and flowers suddenly everywhere, as though the house itself had started to grow, the walls breathing, glistening with life.

Peter rubbed his forehead, waved at a departing couple on the drive, glanced back upstairs. Over the last few days, his daughter had only added to his disquiet. He had watched her at work. Even without a camera in her hands, her whole posture had been keen-eyed, attentive. She had seemed to notice everything, to be on the look-out for something in particular. He hated to admit that he might have anything to hide. Everyone did; he was no different. But whatever he had, he was quite sure that it was nothing she might be concerned with. Only this morning her attitude had appeared to falter and slip, and he sensed that she had suddenly decided to go no further with something. All day she had kept up that manner of her mother's: hidden behind a decision taken unreservedly, but in private. It had given her a kind of armour that he envied all the more for knowing that, at one time, he too had worn it.

He shook himself as he saw the doctor's Volvo approaching. The house seemed to shine about him now, as though at any moment it might turn its light towards him, and he would be exposed as no longer belonging within its walls. He stepped outside into the evening. He had had too much to drink. The clean air felt good in his lungs, the shadows kinder on his face. He loved his wife; he was keen to get away with her. Tomorrow couldn't come too soon. Thinking this, he prayed that his mother would be fine, and that this was a false alarm – there had been so many.

When Katherine entered the bedroom, Edie's eyes swung slowly towards her, and she smiled. Mary sat beside Edie on the bed, holding her right hand. Edie's skin was very pale on her bare arms, her throat and face. But at the high points of her cheek-bones a vivid flush had risen, as though she had just received a physical shock or jolt, a sharp pain that had proved exhausting.

'Stop trying to talk.' Mary spoke gently, although Edie had said nothing. 'She's been wanting to chatter, talking nonsense.' Mary glanced at Katherine, her eyes holding a warning: don't believe what she'll tell you.

Katherine went to the other side of the bed and sat down.

'I told you,' Edie's voice was no louder than a whisper. 'Hearing like a bat's.'

'See? She's talking nonsense.' Mary's finger was on her pulse, her eyes narrowed in estimation. 'Where's that doctor?'

Edie turned her head towards Katherine, her eyes milky and lightless. 'I hear everything in this house.' Her breath had shrunk to affect only her chest, the rest of her body still. She closed her eyes.

'What happened?' Katherine addressed Mary.

'She fell on the landing, at the top of the stairs – luckily at the top, not on the way down.'

Edie opened her eyes wide, her face still turned towards Katherine. 'Hearing like a bat. *"Always a great romantic."*' Her voice was faint but, as she uttered those words, it was not quite her own. She had heard what Lewis said. Edie looked back up at the ceiling.

Mary turned at the sound of footsteps coming rapidly up the stairs. 'Just a murmur, happened before,' she said, glancing at Katherine. 'You'll be right as rain, won't you?' Her eyes were worried. 'Hang on, that'll be him.' She went out on to the landing.

Edie seemed to be listening to the approaching footsteps with a kind of dread, her breath quickening. As soon as Mary was out of the room, she turned to Katherine, her voice high and thin. 'I've heard too much now.' Her head made little impression on the pillow, her figure shadowless beneath the covers. 'Don't you see yet?' She gripped tight to Katherine's hand. 'None of this was inevitable. It's all already over. They've all already gone. Your mother and I were just wives. It was never blood. The line stopped with Hugh, when I betrayed him with that portrait. Don't you see? Peter isn't a Clements, he's Lewis's son. You're not tainted by that – you're free.'

Suddenly Peter was at the door, followed closely by the doctor.

'A great romantic,' Edie whispered, shaking her head, squeezing Katherine's hand before she let it go.

'I'm not sure what she's saying,' Katherine lied. She stood up but her legs felt weak. She stared at her father who evidently read her shocked expression as concern for his mother, and went quickly to her side, putting his arm round her shoulders. 'She'll be OK, Katie.' He spoke in an undertone.

'*She*,' Edie began to smile, '*she*.'

Katherine and Mary exchanged a look: was it really only four days ago that Edie had said 'she' like that? Before, it had referred, disparagingly, to Joanne; now, only to herself.

As Katherine left the room, she noticed that Edie's portrait had been turned to face the wall.

By the time the doctor had left, most of the guests had also driven away, and the house was quiet. A cough, laughter, a shutting door, footsteps on tiles, the sounds of occupation became more rare, and the impression from upstairs was of only a few people moving in a restless blind search through the rooms for one another, never quite coinciding.

On the back lawn lights were still strung about beneath the trees, showing a pathway towards the marquee, but this was now in darkness. A few candles burned among the flower arrangements on the tables, and if you looked closely you could see the red gleam of cigarettes and cigars: a handful of guests still lingered, although all the staff had now gone, some to return to clear and pack up the following morning.

Joanne stood at Edie's window, looking out, her face close to the glass. 'What're they up to down there?' She wore a blue cardigan over her dress, and shivered as she turned back to the room. Katherine and Mary were sitting in chairs at either side of the bed. Peter had gone downstairs with Alice to make coffee for the family and remaining guests.

Earlier, the doctor had asked to be left alone with Edie, in the solemn manner of a priest. An elderly man past the age of retirement, Charles Finlay had been Edie's GP for many years. He was in notoriously immaculate health, and boasted of eight-mile runs before breakfast, his thin frame taut as a whippet's, his brown hair fine but still not grey. He had a quick-eyed habit of deflecting any hint of hypochondria. 'But you're perfectly well, nothing wrong with you,' had often been his diagnosis of Edie in the past, when her son had called him in, usually against his mother's wishes. 'Just a bit peaky, stop fussing,' she complained, triumphant when Dr Finlay agreed with her: 'Quite right, fit as a fiddle.' Privately, he would then confess his worries to Peter, but in front of Edie his policy had always been to 'treat her like a faker, best way. Soon as she thinks there's something up, that's it.'

Keeping Edie's heart condition as a publicly denied secret had worked. She knew the score, she took her medication, Mary fed her aspirins, and Peter relayed Finlay's favourable diagnoses, as instructed. Everyone knew what cards the other held.

Tonight, though, he had emerged from Edie's room frowning, and when he took Peter aside to discuss the situation, Peter had come away from the conversation pale, as though the doctor had just accused him of something he had been at great pains to deny. 'She's had a shock. She needs to rest. Keep her quiet, and then we'll see.' Dr Finlay had been uncharacteristically curt, and promised to return the next morning.

Now the lights in the bedroom had been dimmed, and around the bedside the three women's faces were indistinct. Edie had been drifting in and out of sleep, restless, refusing to let go absolutely. With Peter downstairs, she had revived slightly, as though she had been waiting for him to leave the room.

'Where is she?' When Edie spoke, Joanne crossed over to the bed, and perched on the arm of Mary's chair. 'I'm sorry,' Edie shook her head, 'she's gone now.' Joanne glanced at Katherine and, seeing this, Edie shook her head again, more violently, so that Joanne looked down at her, startled. 'I wanted to die,' Edie's voice was thin and drawn with remorse, 'so you could all go away. But she's gone now.'

There was the muted sound of the front door closing downstairs, and the figures in the room were held momentarily, alerted by that noise: who had just left? Joanne leant close towards Edie. 'Who has gone, Edie? Alice is the only one of us not here. Do you mean Alice? She's coming back in a second.'

Edie's voice lowered to a whisper. 'His first wife, not one of his daughters.'

There was a second's hesitation before Joanne stood up, and

the fact of that plural – daughters – was finally heard. Joanne turned to Mary, her hands loose at her sides, then crossed back to the window. 'There's no one left, by the looks of it.' Her voice was level. Edie's breathing, too, had steadied, her limbs occupying a tiny space beneath the tight-drawn covers.

A window on the attic floor above rattled in its frame, and a door closed softly downstairs inside the house. Two pairs of footsteps crossed the marble and started to climb the stairs: Peter and Alice. There was the tremble of cups on a tray.

'Julia—' Mary appeared to be addressing someone on the point of leaving the room, trying to call them back. Joanne turned to face her, and Katherine noticed that Edie's eyes widened, as though straining to see someone a little out of view. 'Julia did not want him to know.' Mary's voice faltered. She spoke quickly, but clearly. 'He doesn't know. Neither does Alice. Please.' She half rose, and Joanne went to stand beside her. 'We decided it was better to keep it secret, between ourselves.'

As Mary said this, she drew herself up, and although none of the women saw anything that they could name, they were certain that, at the sound of that 'we', Julia's presence could no longer be felt beside them in the room. It had been her, all along, and not her husband, who had been locked in suffering. And Edie had known.

When Peter re-entered the room with Alice, he was glad to see that Edie was calm. Colour had returned to her face, and although she was motionless, the life that had stepped a half-pace aside from her had now returned.

He set down the tray of coffee cups, speaking in a whisper: 'We should go downstairs, everyone's left.' Joanne was by the window, looking down into the garden. He went to stand beside her, taking her in his arms. All day he had longed to be alone with her. He had felt a strength in her today that even he had not suspected she possessed, and he wondered what had drawn it from her.

Joanne drew back very slightly from his arms, and spoke loudly enough for everyone to hear: 'I think we should stay here.'

'Don't want to wake her.' Peter's voice was lowered.

'No, I mean here at Fareham.'

Peter stood motionless, his arms still round Joanne's waist. Alice was the only one to speak, glancing at her mother: 'Oh, you should, I never saw how you could bear to go.'

'I think we should definitely stay here.' Joanne's voice was gentle, but the other women knew perfectly the challenge that lay within it. If Peter insisted now that they go to live in America, he would have to confess the reason why, confess to having carried out a survey of the land in Louisiana, admit to what he had found there, tell his wife that all this had been done in secret, before their marriage was announced. If he agreed to stay he would give up all that. Katherine held her breath: this would be the test; she prayed he would not fail.

'I'll sell the heap in River Road.' Joanne's eyes were fixed on Peter's face, her voice still soft. 'Actually spoke to a guy today who might be interested. It's not worth so much, needs money throwing at it.' Peter moved away from her, straightening the curtains. Joanne continued, 'This place feels more like home now, with all my family here.'

Peter glanced around the room. His eyes showed puzzlement, and realisation. Joanne took his hand. He looked anxiously at her. It couldn't be true. What had they been talking about while he was out of the room?

'Yes, then?' Joanne took his silence for assent. 'It's the right thing to do. You won't be sorry.' She embraced him. They left Edie alone, Joanne leading the way, flicking on the lights as they went downstairs.

40

Two days after the wedding, Katherine Clements packed the hired photographic equipment into her car outside the front door of Fareham. Charles Finlay had given Edie the all-clear, and Peter and Joanne, who had delayed their honeymoon by a day, had flown that morning to Italy: Venice first, then Amalfi, where they would remain for two weeks. Mary would look after the twins in their mother's absence. They were very happy about this: they had the run of the house, and had already elicited permission to set up a den in the attic.

Katherine had just received a phone call from Sergeant Holden, apologising for troubling her, but letting her know that there was some 'maybe good' news. She said that she was sorry not to have had anything to report sooner: they had had no leads to go on; no eye-witness reports; no evidence that it had been anything other than a burglary that had got out of hand. She made no reference to a visit by plain-clothes policemen. Katherine had not expected her to.

'The good news is that some of your stuff turned up in a skip a few streets from your flat. Thought you'd be pleased. Had your name on them — files of old pictures.' Katherine stood in the driveway, holding her phone very tight. Her private gallery.

'Hello?' The woman's voice crackled. 'Bad signal. You can hear me? We've brushed them for prints, but they're clean. Often happens. Must've been looking for something they didn't find. Chucked them after. Bit mucky, but we've got them for you at the station, just as soon as you want to collect them.'

As Katherine leant against the roof of her car and shut her eyes, she heard Mary crossing the hall to see her off. She had already said goodbye to Edie, and to the twins. She would be back in Kent the following weekend, maybe sooner, but first she had a great deal to sort out in London.

The story Peter Clements had feared had broken, but it had been bumped from a lead in the financial section of his friend George Fitzgerald's Sunday paper to a half-inch story that would appear at the bottom of the international page on Tuesday. He read it while he waited for his flight to be called at Heathrow. The focus was the cumbersome management structure of certain corporations; the need for reform of the Securities and Exchange Commission rules and the protocol of granting licences to foreign operations. It was hardly news, just a matter for the accountants and lawyers to pick over.

At no point had Peter been made aware of the exact methods employed in the outposts of his company's progress, in London or in Africa. But he had glimpsed what might occur there, and it had left him badly shaken. The destruction of evidence, anyone could tell you, was all wrong. He didn't want that kind of thing to happen, not on his watch. He wanted to be able to sleep at night, and not feel that his whole life could be jeopardised by a detail. There would be some redundancies when he got back from honeymoon. The company had become too unwieldy to be overseen from above. He had started to doubt the motives of certain employees: regional managers, in various parts of the world, taking ill-advised decisions for which he, in the end, might be accountable.

He thought of the slow stream of bad news coming out of Gabon. He had had his doubts about the place from the start: all those luxury hotels and airports built with foreign money. Even Peter's company had been obliged to enter into that racket. It was a form of barter, an expensive exchange of favours. They didn't think long-term, that was their trouble. No notion of building value. They were delighted with those multi-storey hotels and spanking new runways, but without a long-term plan those things just sprouted weeds and fell into disrepair, went back to forest, sooner or later. Now it had emerged that the extent of Gabon's oil reserves had been overstated. TriCo, gradually, would withdraw. But even leaving would prove costly. Still, he reassured himself, the company's stock was up, and in the long run it would thrive. He couldn't say the same for the country.

Of course, he might not suffer personally; he would survive, but he would pay for it. He saw the years opening up ahead of him, and tried to brace himself: there were so many things for which he should atone. He had not thought that Joanne might be so keen-eyed, or that she would be allowed so far into the heart of his life here – a place where he himself so rarely strayed. She seemed to want to help him, though, still, and for this he was more grateful than he would ever confess. When the news item appeared, there were no pictures. TriCo was barely implicated. The story would die there, Peter felt quite confident of that.

Katherine, of course, had had some idea of the story's significance. Over breakfast, the day after the wedding, Joanne had snapped her fingers as she chewed a muffin, 'Where was it you were off to last month?' She swallowed, took a gulp of coffee. 'Jesus, where have I been? Head in the clouds with my arrangements.'

Peter refilled Joanne's cup. 'Didn't realise you'd been anywhere.' He yawned, stretched.

It was late, around eleven. The marquee was being dismantled. Mary was leaning against the sink, watching it come down. 'Look at the lawn.' She turned back to the room, smiling at Joanne. 'Lucky you're away while it mends. That rain didn't help much, either.'

'So, where was it?' Joanne glanced at Katherine.

'Africa, Gabon,' Katherine said quietly. 'Place called Libreville.' She did not look at her father, but she felt him tense.

Joanne also noticed. 'Had enough?' She handed him the toast rack. He took a piece and put it on his plate. 'Confess I haven't heard of it.' Joanne sat back in her chair. 'Much going on there?'

'The mud!' Mary's voice rose, complaining. 'It's a swamp out there.'

'It was a favour, really, just work.' Katherine took her breakfast things to the sink.

'I'm off now,' Alice called, as she came through from the hallway. The conversation was closed. Everyone went through to see her leave.

'Your car's not stuck?' Mary fussed around her daughter.

'Maybe see you next week.' Katherine had suggested they meet up in London. Alice had smiled, hesitant, and Katherine felt that perhaps she had intruded; she wouldn't be persistent. She watched her drive away.

'That girl.' Mary turned back into the house. Joanne put her arm through hers. The trip to Gabon was not referred to again.

Later that day, just before she packed the car and left, Katherine went through to the darkroom and slipped the catch, locking herself in. She gathered together the nine remaining pictures taken in Africa and the reel of film from the night of the fire, and placed them in a metal tray.

She looked down at the top picture: a stretch of dusty road, a group of men in overalls leaning against an earth-mover, temporarily idle. The image might almost mean anything. Behind it lay a blank expanse to which no words had been supplied. A whitewash: nothing but fear and suggestion.

What else? She remembered the photograph found in that box of Julia's offcuts: the shot of the dining room, the child's leg, just moving, running, out of frame. Now the room no longer looked like that. It would be hard to say with any certainty that it had been taken at Fareham. It would be inscrutable to anyone else. She slipped it into her jeans pocket. She would keep it.

Then she took down the file of prints and negatives developed from her mother's film and put it on the table. She cut one of the negatives from the strip: her father, holding Alice in his arms. She heard Mary moving around in the annexe, and remembered her words: 'We decided it was better to keep it secret, between ourselves.' After a moment's hesitation, she placed the square of negative, with the print she had made of it, alongside the others in the tray.

She turned on the light-box and looked along the strip. There was nothing else. Just snaps. Her as a child with her parents and nanny. If a person didn't know what had taken place beyond those frames, the images would mean little. What did they reveal? Some skill; the light eloquent; the expression of love in the way the figures were arranged together; a kind of family, even to a stranger's eye. Katherine slipped the negatives she would keep back into their sleeves, and filed them safely.

Yesterday evening something had seemed to hover between the women in the room: a quick sylph of confession and forgiveness. The rise and fall of a shutter, a minute illumination, and it was over. It might have destroyed everything, and it was not clear, yet, what the effect might be over time. But the darkness had gone, and the house was no longer haunted.

She looked around for the box of matches brought for this

purpose from the kitchen. She turned on the fan so that the smoke would be drawn outside and, as she struck a match and held it to the images in the metal tray, she thought of the moment when she would leave Fareham: not, as she had feared, for the last time.

She struck another match, shuffled the smouldering prints in the tray. A photographer to her core? By no means. Her heart lay there, and all that had happened had only been leading her towards that secret further chamber. Turning away could take more courage than hiding: it meant that things had ended, and now she had found herself at the start of another journey.

When she left this house, she would have nowhere to go. She couldn't live in hotels for ever. She blew lightly on the flames.